GLADYS MITCHELL

# Watson's Choice

**VINTAGE BOOKS**
London

Published by Vintage 2011

4 6 8 10 9 7 5 3

First published in Great Britain in 1955 by
Michael Joseph

Vintage
Random House, 20 Vauxhall Bridge Road,
London SW1V 2SA

www.vintage-books.co.uk

Addresses for companies within The Random House Group Limited
can be found at: www.randomhouse.co.uk/offices.htm

The Random House Group Limited Reg. No. 954009

A CIP catalogue record for this book
is available from the British Library

ISBN 9781784708689

Penguin Random House is committed to a sustainable future for
our business, our readers and our planet. This book is made from
Forest Stewardship Council® certified paper.

Printed and bound in Great Britain by Clays Ltd, St Ives plc

TO
BEE BARFORD
IN LOVE AND
FRIENDSHIP

# CONTENTS

# CHAPTER 1

# AN INVITATION TO DINNER

'Sherlock Holmes and Father Brown have been summoned ... '
ALLAN MONKHOUSE – *The Grand Cham's Diamond*

\*

'So it is the Great Anniversary,' remarked Mrs Bradley one dingy autumn morning. 'And, in case we had forgotten to celebrate it in a fitting manner, here is an invitation from Sir Bohun Chantrey for us to attend a Sherlock Holmes dinner at his house on the twenty-fifth of November.'

'Us?' enquired her secretary, Laura Menzies.

'Certainly. You, myself, and Detective-Inspector Gavin, our dear Robert.'

'Why Gavin?' asked Laura, who habitually referred to her swain by his surname. 'You, of course; me as your amanuensis and general dogsbody, certainly. But why Gavin?'

'I gather that Sir Bohun wishes him to impersonate Inspector Lestrade of Scotland Yard. We are to go in fancy dress, it seems. Each one of us is to represent a personage in a Sherlock Holmes story.'

'Really? Bags I Irene Adler! Didn't she appear as "a slim youth in an ulster" towards the end of the affair?'

'Irene Adler is already provided for. Sir Bohun has sent a list showing those parts which are already filled. There seems to be a nursery governess who will represent "*The* Woman".'

'Too bad! Still, never mind – although there is scarcely much choice of women's parts in the Holmes stories. Apart from Irene Adler and possibly that nosey little governess in *The Copper Beeches*, there isn't a Holmes female I'd be seen dead as, unless – Oh, yes, I know! I'll go as that woman who had the black baby in the yellow mask. What was her name?'

'Mrs Grant Munro. An excellent idea. I myself shall impersonate Mrs Farintosh.'

'Don't remember a Mrs Farintosh. What a name! It sounds like three clans rolled into one!'

9

'Exactly. Farquharson, Innes, and MacIntosh. I have always been fond of the Scots, and it will be a compliment to you and to our dear Robert if I appear in Scottish costume at the dinner. What are the colours of the Farquharson tartan?'

'Green, blue, yellow, and red. It's a good design, too. I like it. And the only Farquharson I ever met I took to.'

'Beautiful! I will have the dress *au* Farquharson, then, and the mantle and bonnet in the ruddier weave of Clan Innes. Elastic-sided boots and a waterproof will help the company to identify one whose name, I feel, should become a by-word but not a hissing to the true disciples of the Master.'

'The Master sounds blasphemous, put like that. Anyway, who *was* Mrs Farintosh? I thought I knew my Sherlock Holmes pretty well. Are you pulling my leg?'

'She was the friend who recommended Miss Helen Stoner to appeal to Sherlock Holmes in the matter of *The Speckled Band.*'

'Oh, I see. But do you think she'll count? She doesn't actually come into the story, does she?'

'In a sense, no. Nevertheless, we must remember that, but for her, Miss Helen Stoner might not have heard of Mr Holmes, and, in that case, she would certainly never have been in a position to marry Percy Armitage, the second son of Mr Armitage of Crane Water, near Reading. You have not studied the text sufficiently, or you would not attempt to discredit her.'

'You know,' said Laura, putting her head on one side, and taking no notice of this criticism, 'I shall wear a bustle, I think. I'm sure a woman who married a darkie and produced a black baby and disguised it behind a mask "of the strangest livid tint" would have sported a bustle. Besides, it will give Gavin a jolt to see me with some extra *embonpoint*. He thinks I'm too fat already.'

'He will have to wear side-whiskers if he takes Inspector Lestrade upon him,' Mrs Bradley observed.

'Meaning that those will give *me* a jolt? Too right. I can't imagine anything more loathsome than Gavin in side-whiskers. But he's too tall and (although I say it) much too good-looking for Lestrade, who, as I recollect it, was a ferrety little man – how does it go? – lean, furtive, and sly-looking. Who else, besides the nursery governess, has been provided with a part? And why is a nursery governess bidden to the revels, anyway? I always thought they were the Cinderellas of this world. Oh, well, I suppose Cinderella *did* go to a ball. I take it that Sir Bohun isn't thinking of casting himself as Prince Charming – otherwise the King of Bohemia? He's only about forty-five, isn't he?'

'He is forty-seven, and personable. The point you raise had not occurred to me, but it is, perhaps, significant that he has given this Miss Linda Campbell the Irene Adler part. *The Woman!* An interesting speculation, that of yours, my dear Laura, although I cannot see how you jumped to such an idea. Your acquaintance with Sir Bohun is of the slightest, and Miss Campbell, so far as I am aware, is quite unknown to you.'

'One gets these bright thoughts,' said Laura, pleased with herself. 'But, look here, how comes it that a nursery governess has been imported into Sir Bohun's household? I thought he was a bachelor.'

'He explains in his letter that he has given a home to two orphans, his nephews, a brother's children. The nursery governess is to teach the younger boy, a child of six, and the older boy, aged ten, was to have had a tutor.'

'Wrong tense,' said Laura, looking over Mrs Bradley's shoulder at the list which Sir Bohun had sent with his letter. 'He's got him already! Don't you think Basil Grimston is the tutor? We know Tony Bell is the secretary. Who's Manoel Lupez, though?'

'I have no idea, but Sir Bohun, no doubt, has picked up acquaintances in various parts of the world. He is a man who seems to find it impossible to settle down.'

'I see. Well, do you want me to write back and say we can come? – or shall we see whether we can get the costumes before we commit ourselves?'

'Accept at once, child. Nothing will prevent me from playing Mrs Farintosh. I have immortal longings in me. When you have written the letter, please ring up our dear Robert and find out whether he will be able to join us.'

Laura obeyed, and returned from the telephone to say that Gavin thought the idea of a Sherlock Holmes dinner an admirable one, that he had already received a separate invitation which he had accepted, and that he had put in for a week's leave which had been granted.

'He says it's a sort of celebration,' Laura added morosely. 'He's going to be made a Chief Detective-Inspector. Fancy me a Chief

Inspector's wife! He wants us to be married in the spring. I've agreed.'

'And time, too,' said Mrs Bradley. 'You can have half this house if you like. You won't need to use the kitchen, as you can't cook, and I shall be nice company for you when Robert is away on a case. You can have half the Stone House at Wandles Parva, too, if you wish. It is really far too big for me.'

Laura, who had been dreading the thought of leaving her employer, walked rapidly out of the room. Mrs Bradley flicked open a scribbling pad and wrote: *Wedding present.* Then she went to the telephone, rang up Gavin, and congratulated him.

'I say,' said Gavin, 'thank you, and all that – I never thought she'd come to it, incidentally – but what about this Sherlock Holmes business? Why am I invited? I've never met Chantrey. Does he know I'm engaged to Laura?'

'I have no idea, child. He told me some months ago that he thought his life was in danger, but whether that has any connexion with his inviting you to dinner I find it impossible to decide.'

'I see. Has he told the local police?'

'I don't know. He was a patient of mine during the war. That is how I come to be acquainted with him.'

'Went off his onion, you mean?'

'He was seriously affected by the air-raids. He was living in London at the time.'

'You cured him?'

'Possibly. Possibly not. He ceased to walk the streets armed with a hammer with which to hit Germans on the head. More I cannot say.'

'Good Lord! And you think he might still be a bit crazy?'

'I do *not* think so, no.'

'Well, then, do you think he was serious when he said his life might be in danger?'

'He was serious enough, yes. It does not mean that he was right, of course. The persecution mania may still persist, although I do not think it does.'

'But if it did, would he be dangerous? This hammer business, I mean.'

'Yes, he would be dangerous if he weren't cured.'

'A pleasant thought. Anyway, I have accepted the invitation. I say, could you and Laura dine with me to-night at Pesquero's?'

'Laura can. I can't.'

'Good. I mean I'm sorry you can't. D'you know, I do hope nobody bumps Sir Bohun off while I'm actually in his house – or that he doesn't do ditto to one of his guests. Bad publicity for the Yard. I'll pick up Laura at your house at seven, then, if that's all right. Good-bye.'

Mrs Bradley rang off, and, seating herself in an armchair, unrolled a length of repulsive-looking knitting. When Laura returned she told her of Gavin's invitation and sent her up to dress. When Laura, looking extremely handsome, had gone off with Gavin in a taxi, Mrs Bradley put away her knitting and rang up Sir George Sirrell.

'Come and eat your dinner with me,' she said, 'if you've nothing else to do.'

Sir George was a specialist in nervous diseases, and knew Sir Bohun Chantrey, for it was Sir George who had passed the blood-thirsty baronet on to Mrs Bradley in the first place. He was delighted to accept the invitation to dinner, for his wife was away and he disliked equally the thought of dining alone and that of dining at a restaurant.

'Chantrey?' he said, when Mrs Bradley's maid had cleared the table and brought in the coffee. 'What's he like in these days?'

'I have not seen him for some months,' Mrs Bradley replied, 'but he thinks his life is in danger, and he is giving a dinner in honour of Sherlock Holmes.'

'Dear, dear! Bad as that again, is he?'

'I don't know. I have accepted an invitation to the dinner as the surest way of finding out exactly how bad (or the reverse) he is. It is quite on the cards that his life *is* in danger. He has travelled extensively and can be, on occasion, boorish, dishonest, and a satyr.'

'Can he, by Jove! Yes, any or all of that might easily lead foreigners to think the worst of him. What about the idea of this Sherlock Holmes dinner?'

'That's probably reasonable enough. He was always interested in the Conan Doyle stories, and the Master-Mind is being toasted everywhere this year. It is probably a good excuse for him to give a party.'

'Well, I hope he won't want to take a hammer to his guests! Are there going to be Germans among them?'

'No, but there seems to be a Spaniard, a man named Manoel Lupez.'

'Lupez? Lupez? No, the name means nothing to me. Who else is going?'

Mrs Bradley produced Sir Bohun's list. Sir George pursed his lips over it, but handed it back without comment, except to say, 'It seems to be a fancy-dress affair. I see he has cast himself for a rôle, too. Professor Moriarty, of all things! And now, Beatrice why did you ask me to come here?'

'To eat the dinner Laura didn't need.'

'Not ill, is she?'

'No. She has gone out with dear Robert Gavin.'

'The policeman fellow? Is *he* going to this Sherlock Holmes affair?'

'Yes, he is. I think Sir Bohun wants him to act as bodyguard.'

'It sounds like a case of obsession, doesn't it? – unless, as you suggested, by his conduct at some time or another he has been given cause to fear violence.'

'He is obsessed, certainly, with fear for his life. I shall be interested to observe him again. What did you think of the report about B.X. in Middlemarsh's last book?'

'I thought he was wrong in his conclusions. It seems to me that the patient showed all Lewis's basic symptoms –'

'Schizophrenia, in fact. The complete forgetfulness, followed by the resumed monologue being based upon an entirely different and totally unrelated subject does seem to indicate the thought-blocking symptom of schizophrenia, certainly, but didn't you think the reactive repressions were interesting?'

'Yes, and his neologisms, too. He seems as obscure as a Gertrude Stein, although really some of his mind-coinings were remarkably clever, I thought.'

They were in deep discussion of the book when Laura returned at midnight.

'Were you talking about Sir Bohun?' she enquired when the guest had gone. 'It sounded a bit baboonish.'

'Why should you think of Sir Bohun – oh, I see.'

'A clear case of the infantile reproduction of sounds to which the infant apparently attaches no meaning,' said Laura in Sir George's precise and scholarly tones. 'Seriously, I wish you'd tell me what you really think Sir B. is like. I know his age, and

14

you appeared to indicate that he isn't bad-looking, but –'

'You will know what he is like when you meet him. Go to bed, child.'

'Why wouldn't either the tutor or the nursery governess have done for both children?'

'I have no idea.'

'What about the man who is to be Sherlock Holmes? I seem to have heard his name somewhere. Mildren? . . . Mildren?'

'I have never met him. He is a professional actor, I believe.'

Laura poured herself out a glass of beer, produced a packet of potato crisps, sat down at the dining-room table and proceeded to make good those inroads upon her natural energy which had occurred between her dinner and her return to the house. Mrs Bradley watched benignly.

'I shall be glad to see Sir Bohun again,' she remarked.

'You mean you think he may still be barmy?' Laura enquired with eager interest. 'A barmy baronet is quite Wilkie Collins, I'd say. Do you know anything about the other people who are coming to the dinner? It isn't such a *very* big party.'

'I know that a certain Mrs Dance, whose name appears on the list Sir Bohun sent us, is a swordswoman.'

'A what?'

'Foil, épée, sabre. Fencing in general, in fact.'

'Good, is she?'

'I am told that she is. However, as she has never taken part in a recognized competition, it is difficult to assess her proficiency.'

'Oh, well, she *sounds* all right,' said Laura. 'I'm rather partial to people who can *do* something.'

'Her husband is to be at the dinner, too. They were ticked off on the list as people who had accepted the invitation. They are – at least, *he* is – vaguely connected with Sir Bohun through a business partnership. I am surprised they have both accepted. I understand there are grounds for a divorce.'

'Wonder whether Gavin and I will ever cut the Gordian knot? No, better leave that unsaid. We haven't even tied it yet. It's much more fun *not* to be married, I feel. Oh, dear! I've finished these crisps.'

She inspected the greasy bag, drained her glass and went moodily out of the room. Mrs Bradley took out Sir Bohun's list of invited guests and studied it thoughtfully. The two names at the top were

15

those of Charles and Ethel Mildren, and, as it happened, this devoted but indigent couple of troupers were about to settle down to a cooked supper after a very long rehearsal of a provincial pantomime.

'Fifty guineas each, and a jolly good dinner,' said Charles Mildren. 'It's a certain amount of hay, my dear, don't you think?'

'I think it's lovely, Charlie,' replied Ethel Mildren, turning the sausages in the frying-pan. 'Who is this Sir Bo?'

'Boon, it's pronounced. He's rich. Diamond mines, or something. Financed *Chance Is Your Uncle* in '49. Hardly anyone knew who the angel was, but it ran – well, you know how it ran. There was only one snag in it for me. I should have had the juvenile lead, but he insisted on giving it to a pal of his, a chap named Dombrell. I've never had the same chance again.'

'You shouldn't have took to the bottle, Charlie. That's been your undoing.'

'I'll have to get hold of a script,' said Mildren, scowling at this home-thrust but otherwise ignoring it. 'I hate Sir Bohun's guts, but I need the money and he's even prepared to pay for the hire of the costumes.'

'What is this Mrs Hudson I've got to play, Charlie?'

'My landlady. I remember that much. Don't you worry. The costume will carry you through. I'm the one that's got the headaches! I suppose it's his idea of doing me a bit of good to ask me to play Sherlock Holmes!'

'I always did say you had the look of Basil Rathbone about you, Charlie,' said Ethel Mildren, pacifically, aware of tension in the air. 'Strain the potatoes, dear, and put some marge in the saucepan and a little milk. Is this Sir Boon good for the money all right? That's all *I* want to know. You say he's a rich man, but fifty guineas each for one performance, with dinner and the costumes thrown in, seems rather a lot. I suppose there's nothing fishy about it, is there? Why haven't you ever told me before that you knew the angel of *Chance Is Your Uncle?*'

'Too bloomin' sore with him,' said Mildren shortly. 'It was *my* chance, and he took it away.'

He pounded the potatoes until bits flew all over the kitchen. Ethel drew in her breath and bit her tongue. It would not do to tell Charlie off when he was in this sort of mood. Mildren put the saucepan down and continued to unburden himself.

'It ran for three hundred and fifty-eight performances, and if I'd had the part – ' he said bitterly.

Ethel dished up the meal. The food improved Mildren's temper.

'I wonder what his *idea* is, about this Sherlock Holmes dinner?' he said. 'It says, "Guests must be prepared to join in games and competitions designed to test their knowledge of the *Adventures* and the *Memoirs*. There will also be dancing." We shall certainly have to study the book of words, old girl. I read all the Sherlock Holmes stories I could lay hands on when I was a kid, but I'm a bit hazy now as to details. Still, our money and the dinner seem to be in the bag all right, and if it's going to be a proper sort of old-fashioned party with guessing games, I ought to be well in the swim. I was a devil at Postman's Knock when I was ten!'

Several hours before the veterans of the legitimate (mostly repertory-company) stage were eating sausages and mashed potatoes and drinking draught beer from 'round the corner', Mrs Dance, a dark-haired, pretty woman with a wilful nose, innocent eyes and a mouth both provocative and tender, was telephoning a friend.

'It's sickening, Joey, but I shan't be here. No, I can't very well get out of it. It means a lot to Toby to keep in with this wretched baronet person . . . business, you know, and perhaps a wee bit in his will. Yes, well, all right, I can tell you're annoyed. You don't have to say so. I'm not very pleased myself. But, hang it, it isn't as though I *hate* Toby, or want to do him dirt. It's just that I like you better. No, I do *not* love you! I don't love anybody. It only makes a muddle . . . Now, be good, and listen: I'm going to this dinner and I dare say we shall be asked to stay on for a bit, *but* – are you going to listen or *are* you going to keep on with these rude interruptions? – I repeat . . . *but* I promise to spend Easter doing exactly what you like. Yes, I can come to Paris. Toby is going over to Ireland to see his mother. *All* right, then. Be good. So long and cheery-bye, and do *not* write to me until I say you can. If you're naughty or silly, I shall explore the possibilities of Manoel Lupez . . . No, you've never met him. It's all right, silly, neither have I! He's Sir Bohun's bastard, I think. *Not* a dago, dear. An Anglo-Spaniard, or Mexican, or something. His mother is a bull-fighter's daughter, and Manoel is coming to this Sherlock Holmes thing, and that's all I know, so keep calm. Have a nice trip to Montreal, and look out for icebergs on the way. 'Bye!'

17

Disregarding a blasphemous prayer for patience from the other end of the line, she gave a delicate little cat-smile and rang off. Then she went to the table and picked up the book which had accompanied Sir Bohun's invitation.

'Royal command,' she soliloquized, carrying the book to a deep armchair beside the electric fire. She curled her sleek body and wriggled until she had achieved the maximum of comfort and then she glanced down the index page of the complete collection of the Sherlock Holmes short stories. 'You will take the part of Miss Mary Sutherland in *A Case of Identity*,' she remarked, quoting from Sir Bohun's peremptory letter. 'Shall I, dear Bobo? Let's see.'

She turned to the story and read it. As she did so, a little frown, half angry, half ruefully amused, appeared between her dark brows. She looked up as the door opened.

'Hullo, Brenda,' said a voice uncertain of a welcome.

'Oh, Joey! You darling!' exclaimed the siren, patting the arm of her chair. 'Come and sit down and listen to this! Did you ever in all your life!'

'I thought you'd be annoyed with me for coming,' said the tall cavalier who had entered. 'You sounded undeniably terse over the phone just now.'

'That was to get you flying round here. I meant what I said, though. But, first of all, just listen to this! This is to be me at this Sherlock Holmes party. I could massacre Sir Bohun, the ill-natured old miser!'

'Is he old?'

'He's nearly fifty. I suppose that isn't old for a man.'

'If he's a miser he won't cough up for Toby or you or anybody, so don't you count on it.'

'He's my godfather.'

'Nonsense! You're thirty-one!'

'All right, don't shout. Listen to this, and tell me whether it's intended to be funny or insulting.'

'Get up, then, and let me sit down.'

Mrs Dance obliged, and, when he was sprawled in the chair, she draped herself comfortably over him, stuck an elbow in his chest so as to be able to support her book more easily, and read, in an agreeable voice, Doctor Watson's description of the self-deceived, myopic heroine of *A Case of Identity*.

' "Well, she had a slate-coloured, broad-brimmed straw hat, with a feather of a brickish red. Her jacket was black, with black beads sewn upon it, and a fringe of little black jet ornaments. Her dress was brown, rather darker than coffee-colour, with a little purple plush at the neck and sleeves. Her gloves were greyish, and were worn through at the right forefinger. Her boots I didn't observe. She had small, round, hanging, gold ear-rings, and a general air of being fairly well to do, in a vulgar, comfortable, easy-going way." '

'He's determined to teach you where you get off,' commented Mr de Philippe unkindly. 'Serve you right for creeping and crawling to miserly, rich old men when you might be week-ending in a civilized fashion with me.'

'How do I come by such an outfit, do you suppose? – Oh, he *might* have let me be Irene Adler, the mean old moke!'

'You'll have to have a lot made, and a pretty penny it'll cost you, and a dead loss it will be, for it won't even do for a fancy-dress dance on board ship if we go to the West Indies next spring. Ha! ha!'

'Ha, ha, to you, and see how you like it! And if you want another good laugh, here it is: I have to be prepared to join in competitions to show my knowledge of the Sherlock Holmes stories! Come and read one to me while I have my bath. Sir Bohun is the type who might give a prize of a thousand pounds. He's perfectly stinkingly wealthy.'

'Prizes of that sort give rise to wangles,' said the experienced Mr de Philippe. 'The thousand will stay in the family. "Kissing goes by favour" isn't a proverb; it's a truism.'

'There isn't any family, except Manoel and two little nephews and a sort of niece or something, and the niece's mother, a kind of cousin. I suppose they'll be coming.' She consulted Sir Bohun's letter, which was inside the dust-jacket of the book. 'Yes, they are. Celia Godley – that's the niece – will represent Mrs Watson. Mrs Watson? Oh, yes, Doctor Watson got married, didn't he? That will make Celia poor old Toby's opposite number. He *will* be pleased! She's only just left school or college or whatever it is, and is training to be a secretary.'

'Less of the "poor old Toby". I don't like it.'

'Nonsense! I shall call him what I want to call him. And he *is* poor old Toby, look at it how you will.'

Mr de Philippe, who thought that the divorce was a certainty, emptied her out of his lap, stood up, held her at arms' length, then kissed her.

'So he is. Poor old Toby,' he said. 'And I wish him joy of little Celia.'

Little Celia, at that moment, was mixing herself a gin and French in her bedroom, and was thinking about Manoel Lupez. She had not met him, but she had seen him; seen him, moreover, under such fascinating and exciting circumstances that she felt she could scarcely wait for the date of her uncle's (or, more accurately, her second cousin's) dinner-party before actually being introduced and so putting herself in the position of being able to say charmingly but slightly offhandedly: 'Oh, yes? . . . Señor Lupez? Didn't I see you at the *corrida* in Seville last year? I thought your Half Veronica was very pretty, but perhaps your opening gambit could have been – well, I mustn't say a little more dignified, but could we say that it might have been, with advantage, a little more like Manolete's, do you think?'

This would serve the double purpose of proving that she was a true *aficionada* of the bull-ring, and of putting him in his place if he needed this treatment. Yet – Manolete? After all, she had never *seen* Manolete. She had only read about him and looked at photographs. It might be better to leave Manolete, that statuesque and noble figure, out of it. She doubted whether she could sustain a conversation about him. One had to be *rather sure* about things like bull-fighting and the ballet and Sartre and – who was that other foreign author? One didn't really feel *too* sure about the Ravenna mosaics, either, although one had seen them three times. But that, of course, was by the way.

Celia banished Manolete and decided to concentrate upon Manoel Lupez himself and to bring the conversation round to Mexican bull-fighters and Aztec art. He would hardly be likely to know much about Aztec art. She should be on pretty safe territory there. It would be a good idea to marry Manoel if he did not prove to be too much of a savage. Uncle (cousin?) Bohun's money would have to go somewhere when he died, and Manoel, the natural son, and herself (for Mummy would have died by that time) the nearest other relative, if one didn't count those two delicate children, could save a lot of trouble and legal expenses if they were man and wife.

She finished her gin and French and daringly poured herself another. She gazed at herself in the dressing-table mirror and raised her glass.

'Manoel! Manoel!' she murmured.

It was on the following day that Manoel Lupez pressed his flat black *montera* well down on his head and bowed to the President's box. Then, one of half a dozen young men who paraded in the October sunshine, he slipped aside to his left through a gap in the fence which protected the spectators from the bulls, collected his *capote de brega* from his sword-boy's leather case, slung his magnificent gala cape to a friend in the front row of the bull-ring, and waited for the flick of the umpire's handkerchief – the signal for the bugle to sound.

It was the end of the bull-fighting season, and it marked Manoel's last public appearance until the following March. In the interim he would visit his natural father in England, and this time he would go not as a penniless, proud boy, but as a bull-fighter of Spain who had made a name for himself, yes, and money for himself, too. He would demand recognition. He would have his rights. No cap in hand for him! The Englishman had had what he wanted of Manoel's mother. Take what you want, says God, and pay for it. The Englishman had taken what he wanted. Now, thought Manoel, glancing down at his gold-embroidered trousers, he should pay.

# CHAPTER 2

# THE SHERLOCK HOLMES PARTY

'Everyone to his taste, as the old woman said when she kissed her cow.'
ANONYMOUS – *Old Proverb*

\*

THE Sherlock Holmes dinner, given by Sir Bohun Chantrey at
the third house he had bought since his accession (so to speak)
to the throne of his cousin's fortune, was destined to be, in some
respects at least, a success beyond even his own secret wishes.
Apart from all other considerations, the weather was most
obliging. He had fixed upon a date towards the ènd of November
in the hope that a descent of twentieth-century fog would provide
the illusion of a true, vintage, Baker Street pea-souper, and his
reward was to have his house-party arrive on the day before the
revels in welcome if wintry sunshine, and his less-favoured guests –
those who had merely been invited to dinner and to take part in
the competitions – drive up to his door on the evening of the
festivities when what had been a wet but yellowing mist all the
afternoon was beginning to clamp down an impenetrable blanket
of the dark upon all that part of England and most of the London
area.

Owing to shortage of dancing space and a dining-room which,
although spacious in the manner of the late seventeenth century,
could not be expected to make itself any bigger, nine people were
the most which he had felt able to invite. These, with himself, his
secretary, his elder nephew's tutor, his younger nephew's nursery
governess and the two children themselves were to have mãde up
the numbers to fifteen, but, as the finishing touches were being
added to his list, he had received a communication from his natural
son Manoel Lupez, proposing to visit him and stay a week or so,
and Manoel he could scarcely refuse. At any rate, that was his own
feeling in the matter.

'We must see that he has a part,' said Sir Bohun to his secretary,

22

a violently red-haired young man whose appearance had cast him for the part of Duncan Ross of the *Red-Headed League* in the forthcoming revels. 'I had intended to take Dr Watson upon myself, but I am wondering whether the part of Moriarty will not give me more scope. As Manoel is coming, I shall give him the part of young Arthur Holder, the misjudged and heroic son in the story of *The Beryl Coronet*. It is an easy part, and, if he will wear the clothes of the period, he can scarcely go wrong, for all else he need do is to put on the lofty expression which seems to come naturally to him, and there it is!'

The secretary, who disliked the unfortunate Manoel intensely, and suspected the Spaniard of looking down his nose at him, replied briefly, 'Very good, Sir Bohun. I will write him to that effect.'

'Brenda Dance – a divorce is pending, but nothing has been done about it yet, I am happy to say – will play Miss Mary Sutherland, and serve her right. She has no business to make herself happy with a paramour. Miss Campbell seems highly pleased with the part of Irene Adler, and Grimston, of course, with his good looks and his rather astonishing poise, is to represent Lord Robert St Simon, the *Noble Bachelor*. There is nobody else who could do it. Now I wonder whether I am right to take on Moriarty and not Watson? I don't *see* Toby Dance as Watson, and yet – is it quite the part for me? Too phlegmatic, perhaps?'

'Grimston is not too happy about that character part, Sir Bohun. He would prefer – ' began the secretary.

'Whatever can he find to dislike in it?' demanded Sir Bohun annoyed at having his self-analysis interrupted by an underling. 'Hang the fellow, he will have the most becoming costume of us all, and if he does not like the part he will have to lump it! I don't pay him to dictate his likes and dislikes. He will do as he's told. There is only one person who will not.'

'Mrs Lestrange Bradley,' said the secretary unemotionally.

'How did you know?'

'I file all your correspondence, Sir Bohun.'

'Of course. She wishes to have the part of Mrs Farintosh, and, you know, Bell, I was flummoxed, completely flummoxed, for the moment. I could call to mind no such person as Mrs Farintosh in the *saga*. I had to look her up! And when I did, I realized that the thing is in the nature of a jest. Ah, well, as we have had previous reason to know, Mrs Bradley has her own peculiar sense of fun. I wonder how she will interpret the part? It will be interesting to see how she does, for there is nothing in the chronicles to guide her.'

Bell permitted himself a restrained chuckle. Like most young people, he was attracted by the extraordinary old lady.

'It will be very interesting, Sir Bohun,' he agreed, 'but Señor Lupez' costume may cause some difficulty. He may say he'll be too cold, dressed only in his shirt and trousers, and, of course, he is used to a hot country, and it is, after all, mid-winter, almost, over here.'

'Nonsense!' exclaimed Manoel's natural father vigorously. 'He mustn't be namby-pamby. He is to hold the Beryl Coronet in his hands. His figure will look well enough in shirt and trousers, and the coronet is an excellent prop. Everybody will recognize him. What more can he possibly desire?'

'Grimston would willingly change parts with him, Sir Bohun. It might suit both of them, I think, if that could be arranged.'

'No, no, no! I will *not* have my plans upset! Manoel would look *ridiculous* as Lord Robert St Simon. It needs the English touch. And, talking of that, I am not best pleased that Mrs Bradley's secretary-girl wants to come as Mrs Grant Munro, mother of a piccaninny. However, if that's her idea – Who else have we got? Oh, yes, there is my niece Celia as Mrs Watson – a lot of nonsense, incidentally, for Mrs Watson is quite a redundant character. She is only brought in to redeem the good doctor from the taint of celibacy. And for Holmes himself –'

'And for Holmes, himself, Sir Bohun,' put in the secretary quickly, 'have you decided finally – ?'

'Oh, Mildren. I know I've changed my mind several times about him, but I think he will carry The Sage as adequately as we can expect. My good Cousin Amelia Godley will do as Mrs Barclay in *The Crooked Man*. She is a singularly unimaginative woman, and we shall just have to *tell* people who she is, for they'll never guess. Now, about the competitions I have planned –'

The baronet and his secretary went into a huddle, and came out of it over an hour and a half later, when Sir Bohun, smiling delightedly, smacked his secretary on the back and said:

'Charming, charming, my boy! Oh, very, very good! Very good indeed! If anybody guesses them all, he'll deserve half a dozen prizes! Now don't drop the faintest hint, for that would ruin the fun.'

'I certainly won't hint, sir,' promised Bell with a cynical smile. His employer's childishness was sometimes irritating. 'By the way, if it *should* turn foggy, as you hope, the orchestra may be late and so may some of the guests.'

Sir Bohun waved this aside.

'Late-comers can be coped with, and, in any case, there will be a running buffet in the long parlour. There is no occasion to worry. It would be a pity about the band, but you and Grimston could take turns at operating the radio-gramophone, which will probably keep better time than a "live" orchestra,' he said.

'Then there is the question of the little boys,' said Bell. 'Mrs Call tells me they confidently expect to be present at the dinner-party and have, in fact, received a promise from you, Sir Bohun, to that effect.'

'Yes, yes, they have,' admitted the boys' guardian, speaking hastily. 'Won't hurt them to stay up for once. They needn't take the whole dinner. Soup, and a slice of breast will be about their mark, and then some ice-cream and fruit.'

'Mrs Call seemed perturbed,' began the secretary, 'to think that their normal bedtime – '

'Nanny Call has a bee in her bonnet about bedtimes,' snapped Sir Bohun. 'I *must* have the small chaps at the party. Philip is to be little Master Rucastle, and he is to be provided with a slipper to kill cockroaches. A pity he is not a more villainous-looking child, but that can't be helped. He is being got up Fauntleroy style. Very amusing. Timothy – yes, why not? I hadn't really thought of a part for *him*, but he's not more than a baby, really, and will make up nicely into a little girl, and since that wrong-headed secretary of Mrs Bradley's is determined to be Mrs Grant Munro, we'll just black-up little Timothy and put a frock on him, and he can be her merry little piccaninny. He need only wear the yellow mask for a few minutes at the beginning of the evening. Now, then, how many stories are being represented, counting the competition items, I wonder?'

Bell recited the list from memory and without hesitation.

'I wonder why?' said Laura, half to herself, hoping for some reaction by the teak-faced, taciturn young Spaniard who had been introduced as Manoel Lupez. She was studying the titles of books in a small, handsome, mahogany, glass-fronted bookcase in Sir Bohun Chantrey's library.

'It is a guilty conscience,' said Manoel. He moved over to the bookcase and crouched down to scrutinize the titles. '*The Memoirs, The Case-Book, The Return, His Last Bow, The Sign of Four* – yes, it is the sign of a guilty conscience. Do you believe, Miss Menzies, in the theory that conscience doth make cowards of us all? I think the poet Shakespeare has said so. Is that your experience' – his sophisticated Latin eyes summed her up (whether rightly or wrongly was immaterial to Laura) and he hesitated for the fraction of a second – 'or are you, perhaps, too young to be aware of experience?'

'Oh, I've had a fair amount of experience, one way and another,' said Laura airily, 'especially in nipping in the bud.'

'Nipping in the bud? I am afraid – '

'It's an English metaphor,' explained Laura, waving a large but very shapely palm. 'No doubt in Spain you have a word for it. But never mind that now. What's all this about Sir B. and his guilty conscience? He hasn't robbed a bank or anything, has he?'

Manoel smiled.

'His money is his own,' he said. 'I think you would like some tea. I have been acquainted with English ladies from time to time, and all of them wish the same thing – "Oh, Señor, that I shall have some tea!"'

'I suppose you drink nothing but sherry?' commented Laura. Manoel, who had risen from his crouching position by the bookcase, raised himself on his toes, pirouetted suddenly and with extreme grace on the point of one supple, highly-polished shoe, and then replied, 'I drink no wine except in the winter, and then not much; otherwise the *tauros* – the bulls, you know – would – how say you? – catch me bending.'

'You're a toreador?'

'*Si, señorita*. One day, if you permit, I will show you my sword and my cape, but I have not them here. My father has an *espada*, however, from Mexico. I show you its use.'

'Did Sir Bohun ever do any bull-fighting?'

'He? No. He bought souvenirs. After the war, you know, when there are many bull-fighters dead, and the sport drifts for little money, no doubt there are mothers and widows and sisters with many fine things to sell.'

'I suppose, sir,' said Nanny Call, 'the young gentlemen will have their own little table?' She surveyed Sir Bohun's careful arrangements disparagingly. 'They will hardly eat with your guests.'

'Would they prefer their own table, Mrs Call?' Sir Bohun cast a proud eye round the dining-room and altered the position of a spray of copper-beech leaves which he had been especially treasuring for some weeks. 'It would simplify matters, certainly, if it did not disappoint them to be put on their own.'

'It would be best, in the circumstances, sir. They would not then notice missing out most of the courses, as, of course, you would hardly expect them to eat through the whole of the dinner.'

'Oh, there is that, yes. All right, then. How do they respond to the idea of dressing-up, and Timmy having his face blacked, eh?'

'They have changed parts, sir. I thought it best.'

'Changed parts?'

'Yes, Sir Bohun.' Nannie Call looked her employer so firmly in the eye as she imparted these tidings that he coughed apologetically and said:

'Really? Really?' in a feeble and conciliatory tone.

'I could not have Master Timothy's face blacked-out,' pursued the faithful dragon. 'It would have frightened him terrible. And Master Philip took umbrage at the black velvet tunic and little straight knickers and the deep lace collar you ordered. He said he wasn't the princes in the Tower, and made himself very awkward, so I've shortened them up for Master Tim.'

'I see. I see. All right. Just as they prefer it. Quite settled now, is it? No more bother, I mean?'

'No, sir. Thank you, if that is all.'

This, to Sir Bohun's angry astonishment, although the first, was not the only indication that his writ did not necessarily run. Mrs Bradley and Laura, invited, as were the Dance pair, for the day before the party and to stay on for a few days after it, turned up at tea-time on the twenty-fourth of November, and were formally introduced to Brenda and Toby. When tea was over, Brenda Dance collared Laura and went upstairs with her. Laura, who had given unwinking attention to the siren, to her soft, dark, beautiful 'little-girl' hair, to her candid eyes and her fighter's forearms, and had decided that she liked what she saw, invited Mrs Dance into her room and displayed the outfit of Mrs Grant Munro.

'Not really my kettle of fish,' Laura mournfully observed. 'Wish

27

now I hadn't taken it on. I've been re-reading the script, and it seems to me that something in the line of Miss Mary Sutherland would suit me ever so much better. I'm big enough, goodness knows, and I'd adore to wear a boa and a picture hat, and look good-hearted and common. Besides, I can type, and I always get ink on my fingers and wear holes in my gloves.'

'Mrs Grant Munro?' said the enraptured Mrs Dance, eyeing Laura's preparations. 'Married to an African, and a black baby thrown in for good measure? My *dear*, this is where we change parts! It may take us all night and all to-morrow morning to make over the clothes, but who cares? And dear Bobo will be frantic at having his arrangements upset, and I do love him when he's frantic!'

'Here, I'm not a bit of good in the dressmaking line,' said Laura hastily, alarmed by the suggestion that needlework would be involved in the changeover.

'No need. I have a certain genius that way. Basically, you see, we need do very little to the costumes except to let down my hems for you, and take yours up for me, and adjust the other measurements a bit,' Mrs Dance blithely explained.

So, to Sir Bohun's inarticulate fury, Mrs Dance, mischievous and pretty, appeared as the adventurous, experimental Mrs Grant Munro, and Laura scored a major success as the inhibited, faithful, cruelly misled bride-left-at-the-altar, Miss Mary Sutherland, boa, picture-hat, and all.

This shock to the host came at a bad time. No sooner had Mrs Dance first broken the news to Sir Bohun that she and Laura had changed costumes than she added that she refused to dine wearing her bustle. Then Manoel expressed the view that his Young Holder shirt and trousers were *ignominioso* and caused him to feel *vergonzante* – the latter an adjective which, in his case, Mrs Bradley thought singularly inept, as he was quite the least bashful or shamefaced young man she had ever encountered. In the end it had been decided that the whole party should dine in ordinary evening dress, and then go up and change.

When dinner was over and the party came down again in late nineteenth-century dress, it was seen that Manoel had changed parts with Dance. The stocky, serious, not unlikeable husband of the delicious Brenda was in the Holder undress shirt and trousers, whilst Manoel had taken on the outfit of Doctor Watson.

'But I shan't know who *anybody* is, once we begin the competitions!' screamed Sir Bohun.

'Why should he *want* to know who anybody is?' muttered Laura to Mrs Bradley. Her employer did not reply, and Mrs Dance came up at that moment and said to Laura:

'Any clues to what happens next?'

'There is some talk of Terpsichore,' Laura replied. 'Personally, my get-up makes me think that that particular Muse is one with whose company I can readily dispense this evening.'

'Oh, I don't know,' said Mrs Dance, with a coquettish hitch of her bustle (for she had accepted Laura's view that this appendage constituted the major attraction of the costume of Mrs Grant Munro) 'it's preferable to the frightful games which Bobo is wishing on us when those kids have gone to bed.'

As though to clinch the argument, Sir Bohun chose this moment to lead Mrs Bradley out for an old-fashioned waltz. He twirled the eccentric draperies of Mrs Farintosh with so much energy that he ended up out of breath, but his partner, not one black hair out of place, seemed as cool as when they had begun, and congratulated him upon his prowess.

She escaped after that, however, by taking charge of the two little boys and telling them a Bowdlerized version of *The Yellow Face* and *Copper Beeches*, for the black girl in the yellow mask had intrigued them, and nobody, it seemed, had troubled to explain what their dressing-up indicated. The character of young Master Rucastle came in for no criticism. The slaughter of cockroaches with a slipper did not occasion anything but common-sense approval from Philip.

'It's hurting things that matters; not killing them if they're pests,' he declared. He yawned. Timothy observed: 'I wish the big dog had *eaten* Mr Rucastle!' Mrs Dance came up as the radiogram ended another waltz.

'They ought to be in bed,' she said. 'I know where they sleep. Come on, lads.' With a swift kindness which might well have been unexpected in her, she scooped up Timothy and bore him off. Mrs Bradley followed, accompanying Philip, but he turned at the door and said, 'There's a whole book about another big dog. I've read it once, and I wanted to read it again, but it's disappeared.'

Sir Bohun had noted the departure of the boys, for, as Mrs

Bradley turned at the door to come back into the room, he came up to her and said genially:

'Nuisance about the band. Dare say they've given up trying to locate us. Fog's thicker than ever, Bell says. He's just been outside on to the terrace to see if he could get a glimpse of them, but couldn't see an inch beyond the balustrading, and only that far because of the arc lamps I've had installed out there in readiness for to-night to help people find their way. We are most lucky to get this pea-souper. Well, now, talking of pea-soupers, I want to begin the real business of the evening – the Sherlock Holmes competitions.'

He went to the middle of the large room and addressed his guests, informing them of pencils and paper to be found in the library and of lists to be compiled, the longest correct list to win a prize. Mrs Dance returned in time to groan into Laura's ear, at the mention of pencils and paper:

'How I do *loathe* having to write things down at parties! What do we write, anyway?'

Sir Bohun and his secretary's next remarks explained this.

'On view, not hidden, but put in (possibly) unexpected places and sometimes slightly disguised,' he began, 'are, altogether – how many did we say, Bell?'

'Ten, Sir Bohun.'

'Oh, yes! Well, go on. You tell them.'

'There are ten items, all of which are mentioned as being of great importance in the problems which Sherlock Holmes so brilliantly solved,' said Bell. 'I repeat that these objects are all of first-rate importance such as would be known to, and recognized by, any person even moderately well-read in the classic collections of stories entitled, respectively, the *Adventures* and the *Memoirs* of Sherlock Holmes. It is understood that no competitor removes or alters the appearance or position of any object, and Sir Bohun trusts that there will be no collusion. Each competitor is requested very earnestly to work alone. There is a time-limit of one hour, to begin with, from when Sir Bohun gives the word to begin searching. The objects are in various parts of the house, and every room – the nursery quarters and the servants' rooms, for example – which is out-of-bounds is clearly marked with a notice on the door.'

'When you say there is a time-limit of one hour *to begin with* –' observed Laura.

'Ah, yes,' said Sir Bohun. 'If, at the end of an hour, the majority, that is, more than half of you, want an extension, you can have it. The objects are not hidden away exactly, but there's no reason why you should not open cupboards and drawers and so forth. However, you need not ransack the rooms. The idea isn't to have a treasure hunt. The objects can all be found very easily; it's the identification of them which is the test, for you will find on your competition papers two columns. One is for the name of the object; the other is for the title of the story in which it is mentioned.'

Mrs Dance groaned aloud this time, and one or two others, notably Mrs Godley, her daughter Celia, and Mrs Mildren, looked alarmed. Manoel laughed heartily and Mrs Bradley grinned mirthlessly.

'I shall excuse myself, on the score of my advanced years, from taking part,' she announced. Sir Bohun nodded.

'Thought you'd contract out of it,' he said. 'You can sit and talk to me in my den, from which I shall do the time-keeping. Nobody else is excused.'

Mrs Godley began to protest, but was waved to silence. Sir Bohun looked at his watch and gave the word for the participants to go to the library. As soon as they had picked up a competition paper and a pencil, they were to set to work without loss of time.

'And how many of your ten objects do you anticipate that the successful competitor will identify?' Mrs Bradley enquired, when he and her host had retired to the small snuggery which openeds out of the library, and the secretary, Bell, the only other non-competitor, had taken himself off to enact as discreetly as possible the rôle of umpire.

'Shouldn't wonder if Grimston doesn't manage to get the whole lot. Clever fellow, although mad as a hatter,' Sir Bohun replied.

'Really?' said Mrs Bradley, referring to the cleverness, and not to the madness. Sir Bohun misunderstood her.

'Yes. You remember I mentioned my life is in danger? Well, Grimston's the chap. Always lock my door at nights and keep Bell dancing attendance during the day. Bell doesn't know what I think about Grimston, of course. Libellous to tell him. But while you're here, Beatrice, you might just keep him under observation – Grimston, I mean. He can bear watching. Very peculiar fellow. Jealous, you know. Suspicious. Bee in his bonnet and, as I say, bats in the belfry. Interesting study for you. You'll enjoy it.'

Mrs Bradley, whose private opinion of these disclosures would not have flattered Sir Bohun had he been permitted to know it, said courteously that she was certain she would find it interesting to observe Mr Grimston.

'But what makes you think him dangerous?' she enquired.

'Ah, that,' said Sir Bohun, 'would be telling! I may hint that his attitude is not unconnected with Linda Campbell, but possibly I mentioned that before. Let us change the subject. He will be safe enough and happy enough to-night, poor fellow, pitting his wits against those of Bell and myself. Bell, I must say, has been invaluable in arranging all this.'

Bell came in at this moment to report that the ladies felt at a decided disadvantage compared with the gentlemen because their costumes were a nuisance, even a danger, on the stairs. Mrs Dance, reported Bell, was particularly concerned about her bustle.

'Nobody asked her to wear a bustle,' snapped Sir Bohun. 'No bustle is mentioned in the text, so far as I am aware, as being part of any lady's costume. Nobody but Brenda Dance would have thought of wearing such a tasteless and frivolous appendage.'

'I regret to inform you that my secretary, Miss Menzies, thought of it,' remarked Mrs Bradley. 'Her sense of humour is occasionally elementary, I am afraid.'

'May the ladies change into more convenient costumes, Sir Bohun?' pursued Bell.

'I suppose so, but they won't be allowed extra time. What about Young Holder? Is he warm enough in his shirt and trousers?'

'He has assumed a dressing-gown, Sir Bohun.'

'Oh, well, that's reasonable, I suppose. All right. Pop back, there's a good fellow. You know what cheats these people are if you take your eyes off them!' Having disposed of the probity of his invited guests and his trusted employees thus, he sighed with relief as the door closed behind Bell, and added, 'What do you think of Manoel? He is a wealthy man now. He has gone into the bull-fighting racket and cleans up to the tune of a thousand pounds an afternoon, or so he tells me. Shouldn't have thought there was that much money in the game. I'm a bit – he's rather a problem at the moment. His mother's still alive, you know, and it's only a question of time before somebody lets the cat out of the bag and tells him I may be thinking of marrying – and *not* his mother.'

'Not his mother? Is he fond of her?'

'He's haughty, like lots of 'em out there, and he doesn't like being a bastard.'

'Who would? I should think, from what I have seen of him, that he might be a more implacable enemy than Mr Grimston, to whom you referred a moment ago,' said Mrs Bradley reasonably.

'Oh, well, let's talk about something else,' said Sir Bohun uneasily. 'What are you reading just now?'

## CHAPTER 3

# UNSCRIPTED APPEARANCE
# OF AN EXTRA

'... I crave but four days' respite: for the which you are
to do me both a present and a dangerous courtesy.
    Pray, sir, in what?
    In the delaying death.'

WILLIAM SHAKESPEARE – *Measure for Measure*

\*

IT did not take Laura long to change into a suit and some comfortable shoes. She was prepared to enter the competition with
zest, not for the sake of the prize, which, in the face of what she
supposed would be the concentrated opposition of the tutor
Grimston and the dark-horse nature of the rest of the field, she
hardly expected to gain, but because it was a unique opportunity
to explore most of the house.

Exploring old houses was a hobby of hers, and Sir Bohun's
home, although not the exciting affair it might have been, in her
eyes, if it had been built a hundred and fifty years earlier, nevertheless offered, in the way of staircases, fireplaces, carved overmantels,
and cupboard doors, much that was both interesting and delightful. It belonged to the late seventeenth century, a period of which
she knew a considerable amount so far as its domestic architecture
was concerned.

The spectacle of a large stuffed goose, a white one with a barred
tail, recalled her to the contemplation of the paper and pencil
in her hand. This happened as soon as she came out of her room,
for the bird, looking extremely disagreeable, was perched in a
glass case on a tall-boy on the landing. She rested her paper on the
seat of a chair which stood near the tall-boy, and wrote trium-
phantly:

*Either the right or the wrong goose. The Blue Carbuncle.*

She glanced at the next flight of stairs with its stout posts and
spiralled banisters, and decided to ascend. The flight was short,

and soon turned to disclose another which led up to the landing, so that, by the time she heard the footsteps of people below her, she was hidden from these people and they from her.

She hoped that they would not mount behind her. She preferred to explore on her own. Very soon it was clear that they did not propose to join her, for a man's voice said:

'All right. Let's park in here. We can stick down some rot or other on our papers. There are only a limited number of things to choose from. I'll tell you what they are, and then we can cook our papers so that they don't look quite the same. I want you to get quite clear the fact that – '

'I don't see any point in going over it all again. It won't work, and, anyway – ' was the last that Laura heard. She had no instinctive desire to loiter for the sake of overhearing other people's conversation, and she certainly shrank from overhearing this one. The man's voice was that of Toby Dance and the other was that of his wife.

'Talking about the divorce,' thought Laura glumly. She liked the couple. She went into the first room she came to, and discovered that it was full of lumber and old clothes. It looked, she thought, a happy hunting ground, for she could not believe that most of the Sherlock Holmes objects would be placed in as obvious a position as the goose from *The Blue Carbuncle*.

As she was ferreting about, two more of the seekers came in, the stage couple, Ethel and Charles Mildren. Laura greeted them cheerfully and asked whether they had had any luck. Charles thought he had managed to identify two of the objects, but Ethel shook her head and said she had not a clue, had forgotten everything about the stories except the racehorse one and the one with the governess in it, and proposed to stick to Charlie for a bit and then to find a quiet spot somewhere and put her feet up and wait until the gong sounded.

'Sir Bohun won't like it,' said Charles Mildren. He had retained his Sherlock Holmes costume and, for Laura's benefit, put on a waggish act with his magnifying glass. He did not seem too steady on his feet, and Laura wondered whether his wife's faithful attendance on him was occasioned less by *ennui* on her own account than by a certain amount of anxiety on his.

Laura grinned politely at his antics, but was not sorry when his wife, remarking that it would take all night to go through *that* junk, took him away. She heard the sound of a stumble on the stairs, followed by a cheery but slightly thick, 'Whoa, there! Git up them stairs!' The running buffet had been patronized by several people during the dancing, but Mildren, she thought, must be unaccustomed to drink or very tired or a remarkably quick performer to have reached, so early in the proceedings, a stage where his wife felt it imperative to keep an eye on him.

Suddenly Laura realized that she was staring straight at a pair of Victorian stove-pipe trousers. They were untenanted, and were slung over a coat-hanger dependent from a cupboard door. Laura examined them, and then wrote on her list:

*The knees of Vincent Spaulding's trousers. The Red-Headed League.*

She thought for a moment and then said aloud:

'Well, I know what *I* should have done if the job had been left to *me!*'

Feeling like an adult and extraordinarily intelligent Alice, she opened the cupboard door and looked inside. On the shelf facing her was a glass jar containing an object which was interesting, but, to the ordinary eye, without charm. Laura wrote:

*Victor Hatherley's Thumb. The Engineer's Thumb.*

She felt extremely pleased with herself. Most people, she thought, would have been so delighted at having identified the trousers that it would not have occurred to them to open the cupboard. Conversely, many others, having opened the cupboard and identified the thumb, would not have thought of examining the trousers.

'There ought to be a stuffed snake somewhere,' she decided, 'and possibly a hank of red hair.'

She found the snake in a discarded and broken meat-safe (the receptacle, she thought, was a clue, in a sense, although it was the wrong kind of safe). She wrote, with rising satisfaction:

*Doctor Roylott's Swamp Adder. The Speckled Band.*

It began to seem too easy, but after that her hunch failed, for there seemed to be nothing else in the room which had any connexion with the competition. She was leaving to pursue the search elsewhere, when she almost collided with her betrothed.

'Good evening,' said the handsome young man. 'Any luck so far? – or doesn't genius burn to-night, Jo March?'

36

'Getting on,' replied Laura, very pleased with herself. 'How's the arrogant C.I.D. doing?'

'I've got six. It seems pretty simple,' Gavin replied. 'But I perceive that you're feeling smug, so, if you don't mind, I'm going to have a good look round in here. Vincent Spaulding's trousers . . . um . . . bound to be hiding something behind that cupboard door, I should imagine.' He opened the cupboard. 'I spy, with my little eye, the engineer's thumb, do I not?'

Complacently he noted it down, and then went straight over to the meat-safe.

'Blow you, Gavin!' said Laura jealously. 'That makes you nine out of the ten!'

'I shall fall down on the tenth, I expect,' said Gavin generously. 'I have a hunch it's in here, too. Do you mind if I continue to look around? Don't let me detain you. I believe you were about to depart.'

Laura hit him and departed. She was puzzled and perturbed. She respected Gavin's emotions and understood them, except where she herself was concerned, and she knew that his dismissal of her meant that he was feeling worried about something.

'Oh, bother the competition!' she suddenly thought. 'What on earth does this Chantrey man matter? He's a selfish old pig, except that he's good to those kids. I don't see why we should all play silly games just to please him!' But then she reflected further that, after all, she need not have accepted the invitation, that she had enjoyed her dinner, and, up to this encounter with Gavin, the competition. She went back to the lumber-room which Gavin was still patiently and methodically searching.

'What's the matter?' she asked abruptly. He was squatting on his heels beside an open suitcase, but, at the sound of her voice, he stood up, looking even taller than usual in the police uniform of the previous century. He hunched his shoulders, spread his palms, and said:

'Don't know yet myself, Dog. Something wrong with the set-up here. I'm supposed to be holding a watching-brief on behalf of our host, but it's not the cagey Sir B. that's on my mind.'

'What, then? Spit it out to Auntie Laura.'

Gavin walked to the door and closed it.

'Here it is, then, for what it's worth . . . and, spoken aloud, it comes to nothing. Charles Mildren, who's been telling me his life-story, particularly the bit when Sir B. did him out of a fat part back in 1949, is half-seas over, and that worries me because I'm sure it's out of alignment. Ethel Mildren is worried stiff, and not *only* because Charles is blotto. Then, at least half the competitors are not walking round the house at all. Where they are, and what they're doing, I don't know, but I do know that two of the rooms which were not originally out of bounds are out of bounds now. It's no business of mine if people have chosen to take themselves out of the competition, but it seems a bit odd of them to seal off a couple of rooms when they've all got their own bedrooms. After all, none of the bedrooms has been used. All have been marked as being out of bounds. Then – nothing to do with this evening particularly – but why a tutor *and* a nursery governess for those two little chaps? Sir B. thinks money's no object, but he said openly to me that education *has* no object; that Linda Campbell is moronic and that Grimston is a madman and a freak. Then, where does he get off in the little matter of Manoel Lupez? The gallant bull-fighter obviously hates his guts, and Sir B. is manifestly afraid of him. Why have him here, then? Last, and, possibly, quite least (since each may not have known that the other was to be invited), why both Dances in the same house? I know each item separately sounds nothing, and perhaps the whole lot together sound nothing, either, but that's what's on my mind. Now tell me it's all a lot of rot, as well you may, and I'd love to believe you.'

'I don't know *what* to tell you. I can answer the various bits, but that's not the same as answering the whole lot of bits when they're put together. Two more rooms being put out of bounds probably means that people don't want to be bothered with the competition but do want to get together (probably complete with eats and drinks) and be sociable. There are a tutor and a governess because the governess is Sir Bohun's mistress and he has to give her some sort of standing in the house because of the guests and the servants. Manoel may hate him, but he may feel he has a duty to Manoel. Besides, a bull-fighter has to have rather more self-control than most people, I would say, and therefore is an unlikely person to be a murderer – meaning that I don't think he'd do Sir Bohun any harm, no matter how much he hates him.'

'Yes, I see. Sometimes you're a comfortable person to talk to, Dog.'

'As for the Dance couple,' went on Laura, 'I think you've hit the nail on the head there. I don't think each knew the other had been asked here, and, personally, I think they're both putting a pretty good face on it. But I do agree with you. One or two of these little points – yes. Explanation probable and doubtless correct. But there are too many little points. So where do we go from here?'

'Personally,' said Gavin, looking at his watch, 'I'm going down, with my nine correct answers, to mix myself a drink. How about you?'

'Something to do first. I *must* catch you up,' replied Laura. 'So far I've managed to get four answers, three of which came out of this room. Would you mind if I carried on for a bit?'

'By no means. Good luck. Don't forget to listen for the gong.'

They parted (definitely, this time), Gavin to go to the ground floor, Laura to carry out a plan she had formed directly she had heard what he had to say. But first she was determined to inspect the suitcase with which he had been engaged when she had returned to the lumber-room.

She was rewarded. Already handled by Gavin was a wooden box. That he had opened it she felt certain. That he had failed to appreciate its significance she was equally sure. The fact that the lid slid back instead of opening on hinges was the first indication that here was something which gave a clue to the probable contents.

'*The Musgrave Ritual*,' muttered Laura, and she quoted, under her breath, 'a crumpled piece of paper, an old-fashioned brass key, a peg of wood with a ball of string attached to it, and three rusty old discs of metal.'

They were all there. Excitedly, this time, she wrote the tally on her list. Then she went down to the first floor of the house and opened the bottom drawer of the tall-boy. Within was another find. She wrote:

*Alice Rucastle's (or Violet Hunter's) Hair. The Copper Beeches.*

Then, what that timid Macbeth Gavin had not dared to do, his lady was determined to accomplish. Laura had the kind of imagination which had been the terror of her pastors and masters when she was at school and college. It had been fired by her fiancé's report of two rooms which, having been left in the game at the beginning, had been taken out of it during the course of the competition.

These rooms she was determined to reopen. Her plan was simple and bold. She was certain she knew which of the rooms had been placed out of bounds originally, and the other two she was prepared to march into and inspect, making neither apology nor excuse if they proved to be occupied. Of course there might have been a change of mind in the baronet himself, and over him Laura wrinkled her brow. She did not like Sir Bohun. He was an oddity, and Laura, although she did not know it, disliked and distrusted any deviation from the normal, at any rate so far as men were concerned.

Before she inspected the two extra out-of-bounds rooms, she decided to enter an open room which, so far, she had not searched. She collected, almost immediately, a prize. It was lying on a walnut table and a paperweight kept it in place. It was a bill. Laura inspected it and said aloud:

'*Oct. 4th, rooms eight shillings, breakfast two and sixpence, cocktail one shilling* – (cocktail? Didn't think they were invented before 1920) – *lunch two and sixpence, glass sherry eightpence.* Golly! Wonder whether I've got a scoop? This is Francis H. Moulton's hotel bill.'

She wrote this down on her list, and added: *The Noble Bachelor*. Then she continued upon her rounds, and, finding nothing to arouse her suspicions, she mounted to the first floor again, cast a grateful eye upon the white goose with the barred tail, and then began to go from door to door.

She had not far to go before she found what she had been looking for. It was a bathroom – the one, in fact, which she herself had used that evening. She remembered quite well that when she had passed it on her way down to dinner it had borne no label. But now it bore a notice similar to those on the bedroom doors.

'Now, why?' muttered Laura. She tried the handle. 'If anybody decided to take a bath he'd only to lock the door. Why the phoney notice?' The handle turned and the door opened. There was nobody within. On the window-ledge stood a bottle of laudanum. 'Well!' thought Laura wrathfully. 'What a dirty little trick! Somebody spotted the laudanum and put the label on so that nobody else should get it! Wonder which of them would do a thing like that!'

She wrote on her paper:

*Isa Whitney's Laudanum. The Man with the Twisted Lip.*

Then she took the notice off the door and left the door wide open so that the phial was in full view of anybody who cared to look in. As she was cramming the notice into the pocket of her suit there was a gasping sound, and she looked up to see the tutor Grimston, white-faced and horror-stricken.

'Hullo,' she said. 'This door had one of the notices on it. It shouldn't have, should it?'

'I've – I've no idea,' Grimston stammered. 'I – I shouldn't think so.'

'Pretty feeble of somebody,' said Laura, severely. She went off to find Gavin and to tell him, casually, that she had removed one of the new notices. She found him helping Ethel Mildren to get Mildren to his room, and waited while, between them, they dumped him on the bed and took off his boots, his collar, and his tie. When Gavin emerged she told him about the bathroom, but, keeping to the rules of the competition, she did not mention the laudanum.

'Funny ideas some people have,' said Gavin. 'Have you identified the other room which was sealed off?'

'Oh, yes, but I haven't been into it yet. Well, I'll be seeing you. I've still to find two or three more items.'

She found the first of these in the room which held the buffet supper. Poked in among a dish of oranges was an envelope.

'Eureka!' said Laura, extracting the five dried orange pips which it contained. She put them back again, replaced the envelope, and added the item to her list. 'Only one more to find.' She glanced round the rest of the room so that she did not miss anything, and was very glad she had lingered. Among a collection of cutlery – for the buffet supper was a substantial one – was a small knife which had never been intended for use at table. Laura picked it up, put it down hastily as someone else entered the room, and wrote:

*John Straker's surgical knife. Silver Blaze.*

'Score – ten!' she thought. Then an uneasy touch of suspicion crossed her mind, for among the food with which the table was so generously laden was a partly-consumed plate of curry. 'Oh, Lord!' she said aloud. 'I was wrong! It isn't the laudanum bottle. This is the thing.' She crossed out the reference to the laudanum, and added at the bottom of her list:

*Stable-lad Hunter's opium-drugged curry. Silver Blaze.*

'And yet, I don't know,' she thought. 'It would be better not to have two items from the same story. And yet, again, isn't it a rather subtle idea, in a way? People would be so bucked about identifying Straker's scalpel that they wouldn't think of another *Silver Blaze* clue.'

At this moment the room was filled with the sound of the gong which Sir Bohun himself was beating just outside the door. Laura went out immediately, and from various parts of the house came the guests and employees, Charles Mildren the only absentee. Sir Bohun took them all into the ballroom and collected their lists. These he handed over to Bell, who disappeared with them.

'Gone to do his homework,' said Toby Dance, who, although by no means as drunken as Mildren, appeared to have helped himself fairly freely to the whisky. 'Let's have a dance while he does it. Where's the band? Thought there was going to be a band. What's happened to it?'

'Lost in the fog,' replied Sir Bohun. He stared hard at his inebriated guest. 'Sorry, Toby. The ladies don't want any more dancing. Sit down, everybody. I've got a surprise for you all later on, but we'll have it after the prizes have been awarded. While Bell checks the lists we'll vote for the two most effective costumes – can be two men or two women, or one of each; doesn't matter. I've got a bet on about this, but I shan't hint. Now, then, people, what about paper to vote on, eh? Bell should have left some somewhere. And pencils? Everybody got a pencil?'

Brenda Dance went to a window-seat, picked up some slips of paper and began to distribute them. As she crossed the room she turned her head, and then she walked towards the wide door which opened on to the terrace.

'What the deuce is Brenda up to?' demanded Sir Bohun.

'Please, sir,' said Laura, in the classic schoolboy phrase, 'she thought she heard a noise. And I did, too,' she added, *sotto voce*.

'Oh, that will be the orchestra, then,' said Sir Bohun. 'It seems a bit late, but I suppose we'd better have 'em in. Open the door, Grimston, and tell 'em to come straight in here. They'll see you framed in the doorway against the light.'

But as Grimston joined Brenda and fumbled with the fastenings – for, during the absence of all the household from the ballroom, the servants had thought it wise to bolt the door top and bottom and put the chain on – the usual precautions at night – the electricity failed, and, except for such light as was given by a large and blazing fire, the ballroom was in darkness.

The door to the terrace swung open. Grimston gave a shout of surprise and stumbled backwards. Framed in the phosphorescent light which gilded its enormous body was a creature neither human nor nameless.

'Good lord! *The Hound of the Baskervilles!*' shouted a voice. There was a general stampede, and the sounds of the slamming of doors gave evidence of the reaction of those present to the phenomenon. Alone of all the invited guests, Mrs Bradley and Laura were left together in the ballroom, and at that moment the lights came on again.

'Come, boy,' said Mrs Bradley, holding out her hand to the dog.

'Poor old chap! He's hungry. Wonder what's left of the buffet supper?' said Laura. The great hound wandered in. His friendly, unintelligent, square head was lifted to Mrs Bradley's caress. The luminous spottings on his coat were rendered invisible under the strong electric light of the ballroom. Mrs Bradley talked to him quietly and confidentially while Laura foraged. He was fed.

'And now, friend,' said Mrs Bradley, 'outside for you.' The dog sighed and did her bidding. Laura closed the heavy door and looked enquiringly at her employer. Mrs Bradley laughed, and then looked thoughtful.

'I wonder why?' she said. 'We had better let the others know that the dog did not tear us in pieces.'

'They don't deserve to know it, the silly haddocks,' said Laura. 'Let them trickle back when they think the coast might be clear. Talk about Bottom with the ass's head on him! They ought to be impersonating Quince and Co. But isn't it just a bit odd?'

'What is?' Mrs Bradley enquired.

'Why, that Sir Bohun ran away, too. After all, I suppose he was responsible.'

'For what, child?'

'Beth-Gelert, or whatever the hound is called.'

Mrs Bradley shook her head.

'I don't think Sir Bohun knew anything about the dog,' she said, 'for if he had known about it he would not have run away with the rest of the party, but would have remained here with us to enjoy the success of his surprise item.'

She went to the door which opened into the hall and pushed at it. A sheepish collection of individuals followed their host into the room.

'Well, well! Well, well, well!' said Sir Bohun, rubbing his hands together. 'Where has that fine fellow gone? Your idea, Beatrice, I take it? Vastly entertaining, I *must* say. Wish I'd thought of it myself! Oh, very good! But how did you get him here? You didn't bring him from Kensington?'

'I didn't bring him at all,' Mrs Bradley composedly replied. 'I know no more about him than you do.'

'I shouldn't be surprised,' interposed Brenda Dance, 'if it means the band has turned up, Boo, darling. I expect the dog is their mascot, and they painted him up to help out the Sherlock Holmes party. They'll probably expect a thumping tip.'

'Might have frightened some of you ladies into a fit,' remarked Sir Bohun, ignoring his own ignominious flight from the *Hound of the Baskervilles*, 'and that's what I shall say to them. Go out, Bell, and tell Cummins to send them in. They've delayed us long enough already. We'll just give them time to warm up, and, meanwhile, we'd better cast our votes.'

Bell went out, but returned shortly to inform his employer that there was still no sign of the orchestra.

'So the dog wasn't theirs,' remarked Laura. 'We turned him out again on to the terrace. I'd better go out and make certain he doesn't eat the band if they *do* turn out.'

'No, no, Miss Laura. I'll go,' said Toby Dance chivalrously. 'It's damned foggy and cold out there.' He did not wait for Laura to answer, but went out of the room, flinging back the end of the sentence as he shut the door behind him.

'I hope he's got a torch,' said Bell. 'Hullo! What's happened to Miss Campbell? She hasn't come back into the room.'

Linda came in at that moment, escorted by Dance.

'There you are, you see. It's quite all right,' he was saying as he led her up to the fire and put her into a chair.

'Hullo, m'dear,' said Sir Bohun, looking gravely concerned. 'Gave you a bit of a turn? I'm sorry about that. But no fault of mine, as you'll realize.'

Linda Campbell tried to smile, but her face was stiff with fright.

'Basil, go and get her some brandy. She's had a shock,' said Brenda Dance, at once. Grimston, looking thunderous, went out for the restorative, and when he came back he announced that the orchestra had appeared and were thawing out in the servants' hall.

'They can't waste time there,' said Sir Bohun. 'Grimston, you and Bell collect the voting papers. Now, Linda, how do you feel?'

'Better,' the pallid girl replied. 'I'm sorry, but I'm terrified of dogs, and that was such a big one, and it looked – it looked so very horrible!'

Sir Bohun nodded, went out of the room and brought in the orchestra, who were certainly cold and damp and seemed delighted to get into the brilliantly-lighted, centrally-heated ballroom.

'They've been delayed by the fog, as I expected, and I suppose they brought that great brute with them,' he said, calmly appropriating the theory advanced by Brenda Dance. The orchestra leader, however, disclaimed all knowledge of the dog. He had not even *seen* a dog, he declared. He and his men tuned up and began to play.

Manoel again came over to where Mrs Bradley was sitting. He was a teak-faced, black-haired young man, grave and stern, with square, practical hands and a stocky yet sinuous body. He looked enquiringly at her. Mrs Bradley grinned, but this horrid sight appeared to encourage the boy. He showed white teeth in a foreign, attractive smile.

'You offer psychological advice, yes?' he said, giving a stiff little bow before seating himself beside her.

'Certainly, if and when it is required of me.'

'Good. I am in a difficulty. It is not easy to commit murder which is not found out, I believe?'

'Not in England, at any rate.'

'Not in any country. What would be the best way?'

'To commit murder, or to avoid being found out?'

'Of course, both. I ask for information so that in my thoughts I can think somebody not dear to me is murdered. An academic murder, I think I would call it.'

'I see. Wouldn't it be sufficient to imagine that this person had died naturally?'

'Sufficient to me, no. I was born naturally. That is enough that is natural. I would like to think of his agony.'

'We are referring to . . . ?'

'To my natural father. But I see that you do not find the subject interesting. Tell me, therefore, of something else. In English law, if he should die . . . when his time comes from God, you understand . . . shall I become his heir? There would be nobody with a higher claim, I think.'

'He would have to acknowledge paternity, or else he would have to make the necessary testamentary depositions.'

'I see. I must ask him to do one or the other, then. You admit that I could have the right to do that?'

'I see nothing against it.'

'Did *you* produce the big dog? I saw that you and Miss Menzies were the only ones not afraid.'

'No, it was nothing to do with us. Laura likes dogs.'

'And you? Are you an English dog-lover?'

'Not particularly. But I saw that the dog was harmless.'

'No, I do not believe you did. I think you have too much human dignity to run from an animal.'

'Nonsense. If I met a really savage creature I should be out of sight in a moment.'

'So you say. Will you give me once more of your help?'

'Say on, as my secretary would remark.'

'Suppose that my father should marry again, and have children, would my claim to the inheritance be gone?'

'It would not be such a good claim, but, again, your share of the property would depend upon his last will and testament.'

'Yet I should still be his eldest son,' said Manoel, quietly. 'Nothing can ever alter that. You know, when we *toreadores* come to the point at which the bull must die, we call it "the moment of truth". One day I think my father must come to that moment. What, then, will he think of me?' He looked thoughtful, and then added, 'If I kill my father, what will *you* think of me?'

'The same as I do at present,' Mrs Bradley replied.

'Comes a lady who wishes her luggage to be carried to her hotel,' said Manoel. 'She attempts to engage a mendicant who has asked her for alms. But, because he is a Spaniard, he replies that he is a beggar, not a station porter. And I am a bull-fighter, not an assassin, I think. You understand?'

Mrs Bradley nodded. She partly understood, even at that time. Later, she fully understood.

# CHAPTER 4

# AFTER THE BALL WAS OVER

'Many the heart that's aching,
If you could read them all –
Many the hope that has vanished
– After the ball.'

*Victorian Song*

\*

MANOEL left Mrs Bradley's side and went over to speak to Toby
Dance whom alcohol had rendered somewhat gloomy. Scarcely
had he dropped into a chair beside Dance when Bell returned
from marking the competition papers. He was followed by the
butler bearing a salver on which reposed a book, a very large
envelope, a small gold-coloured box and a silver tankard, pint
size. Bell walked up to the orchestra and stopped the music. The
two couples – Brenda Dance and Gavin, Celia Godley and
Grimston, who were the only dancers, retired to the side of the
room, and Sir Bohun took the floor, with his secretary a half-step
behind him and the butler a little more aloof.

'Well, my dears,' said Sir Bohun, 'we have the competition
results. Would you care to be seated?'

Laura, who had achieved ten correct answers, received the
envelope. It contained, not the rumoured cheque for a thousand
pounds, which she would have refused, but an autographed letter
of Edgar Allan Poe.

'Oh, I can't take *that!*' she cried delightedly. Sir Bohun wagged a
kindly if consequential head.

'Couldn't offer a Highlander *dross*,' he replied. Mrs Bradley,
for Mrs Farintosh's costume, received a ruby pendant embodying
the five orange pips wrought in gold – 'Blood, you see, blood,'
remarked Sir Bohun, indicating the rubies, which were many and
tiny. Gavin, as runner-up to Laura, was presented with the tankard
– 'most unoriginal, my dear Chief-Inspector, but had not expected
such a close finish' – and the book, which proved to have a hand-
tooled leather cover and to be a copy on hand-made paper of
Keats' *Endymion*, was presented, amid applause, to Mrs Godley,

47

Celia's mother, with the gallant remark from its donor: 'Here you are, Katie, my dear. You've borne with all the nonsense very patiently for a woman who doesn't know *Silver Blaze* from the Great Fire of London!'

The presentation ceremony being over, the company tended to drift towards the room in which the drinks were still to be found. Laura gravitated towards Mrs Bradley, and they admired one another's awards. Then Mrs Bradley asked:

'Well? And what's the matter?'

'I don't know, exactly,' Laura replied. 'Nothing. But Gavin doesn't like it, either. He thinks there's something cooking in this house, and so do I.'

'An emanation from Sir Bohun, who goes in fear of his life?'

'I shouldn't think so. It's a collection of tiny bits . . . ' Under cover of the music which the orchestra still deemed its duty to disseminate, although nobody was dancing, she recounted the events of the evening so far as they had affected her, and so far as she had exchanged opinions with Gavin.

Mrs Bradley nodded, but made no contribution regarding her own experiences that evening; neither did she put forward any suggestions to account for Laura's feeling of unease beyond the one she had already offered. Herself aware of tension in the air, she felt it centred around Linda Campbell. She did not say this to Laura, but stated, instead, that she felt she had had enough of the Sherlock Holmes party and would now say good night.

She was on her way upstairs when she became aware of voices in altercation on the landing. She coughed, with the intention of indicating her presence, but had heard the following fragment of conversation before the voices ceased and a sound of scuffling, and then of light, running footsteps, indicated that the speakers had made off.

'I can't help it. I didn't ask you to fall in love with me, so mind your own business!'

'But, look here, Linda, he's old enough to be your father! And you've let me think all this time, damn you – '

'I never intended to marry a poor man. We Jane Eyres have need to look out for ourselves and to seize our chance when it comes. I admit I *did* like you at first, but you're never going to be anything better than an usher – '

'Oh, shut up, Linda! There's no need – ' At this point Mrs

Bradley coughed again and the voice broke off. When she gained the landing, the doors leading to the servants' staircase were still swinging, although neither of the wranglers slept in the servants' wing. She had recognized the voices.

Although she had retired from the ballroom, she had no intention of going to bed; but she was glad to get out of her heavy costume and to take off her boots and her bonnet. She put on a dragon-strewn dressing-gown and fur-lined slippers, inspected the books on her bedside shelf, chose poetry, and settled down in an armchair beside a comfortable fire.

In at the slightly-open window swirled the fog, not even the heavy curtains serving to keep it out. The smell of it was ghostly, and Mrs Bradley, unimaginative where the supernatural was concerned, found herself speculating, with detached, analytical mind, upon the theories that ghosts materialize more easily in fog than in clear weather, and that the most dreadful apparitions are not those that wait upon the chimes of midnight, but those that emerge, sudden and silent, at noonday.

Upon these thoughts intruded another – that somewhere downstairs she had heard a door slam. It was an outside door, she felt certain, but there seemed no reason to believe that, in the thick fog, even supposing she went to the window and drew aside the curtain, she would be able to see who had gone out. It was somebody leaving early; that was what it would be.

Instinct, however – too strong for reason – caused her to cross to the window, draw aside the curtain and peer out. The terrace was so brilliantly illuminated that, in spite of the fog, she caught a glimpse of the person below, but all that she could distinguish for certain was that the midnight stroller was a woman who might have been the governess, but might equally well have been Brenda Dance. In any case, in an instant the woman had stepped into the fog and was lost to sight. Mrs Bradley, realizing that, although her curiosity was aroused, the incident was none of her business, settled down again to Dylan Thomas, and at half past one went to bed and to sleep – this in spite of the orchestra, which had come to play dance music whether anybody danced or not.

Breakfast was served to her in her room next morning and she did not get downstairs until a quarter to eleven. The fog had not entirely disappeared, but it had lost its impenetrability. From the morning-room windows she could see the vague outlines of trees and above them a faint blue sky. She decided to go for a walk, and to do so before anyone could find the opportunity to suggest accompanying her.

She slipped out of the morning-room, therefore, hoping that she would not encounter any other of the house-party. Nobody seemed to be about. She supposed that the party had ended not before four o'clock, and that those who had seen it out to the end were spending the morning in bed. These probably included her secretary, she thought.

As she came downstairs again with her hat and coat on, she came face to face with the tutor and the delicate-looking child, Philip.

'Oh, I say, Mr Grimston, couldn't *we* go for a walk?' exclaimed the boy, at the sight of Mrs Bradley in her outdoor clothes.

'No, Philip,' replied the young man. 'We're late for work already. You've a lot to catch up, you know, if you're going to be ready for school in Switzerland in the spring.'

He nodded to Mrs Bradley, and took the boy off to the library. He was not the *Noble Bachelor* of last night's ball, Mrs Bradley remembered, but the owner of one of the two quarrelling voices on the landing, and she wondered again whether the woman who had left the house at midnight was the person with whom he had been quarrelling. She could not help wondering, also, at what time the governess had returned to the house, if it had been indeed she who had gone out. It was rather unlikely, though, that she had risked encountering the mysterious dog on the terrace, for there was no doubt that her terror of the animal had been genuine. Mrs Bradley was not the person to be deceived when the primitive instincts were involved. Grimston, she thought, looked strained and over-tired, but that might be due to the late hour at which the ball had ended. No doubt he had not liked to leave early as he was an employee in the house. He had gone back to the ball-room, probably after the quarrel with Linda Campbell, and had remained there until the party was over.

The library door had scarcely shut behind him and his charge when another door opened and the grey-haired Nanny Call appeared with the younger boy.

'I beg your pardon, madam,' said the woman in respectful tones, 'but could you tell me anything about Miss Campbell? She should have come for Master Timothy an hour ago, but I haven't set eyes on her yet, and she's not in her room.'

'I have not seen her either, Mrs Call,' said Mrs Bradley, who had been personally responsible for introducing Nanny Call when Sir Bohun had demanded a nurse for little Timothy. 'I wonder whether Philip's tutor would know anything about it? He has just gone into the library.'

'I'd better ask him, madam, though I don't suppose he'll thank me if he's begun work with Master Philip. He's a very conscientious young gentleman.' Her tone indicated that he was also rather a disagreeable one, and Mrs Bradley, recollecting the conversation she had overheard on the previous evening, thought that there might be some reason why he should be.

As soon as the nurse and the small child had turned towards the library door, she picked up an ash-plant from the collection of walking-sticks and umbrellas in the hall and stepped briskly on to the terrace. The sun was making a gallant attempt to disperse the thinning fog, but there was almost no wind, and it seemed likely that as soon as the sun went in the fog would return to its former density.

Preferring the mud to the crunching gravelled surface of the drive, she crossed the park by means of a slippery path which led to a gate in a high wall, and followed the main road until she reached a large and hideous pub. It occurred to her that a glass of sherry would be pleasant, so she pushed open the door of the lounge bar and went in. It was a place which did most of its business in the evening, and there were not more than a dozen people in the bar. One of these she recognized. With some surprise she observed that the nursery governess was seated at a table in an alcove. She was talking to a moody-looking young man who spent most of the time staring into his half-empty glass and occasionally nodding his head.

It was no concern of a guest at Sir Bohun's house what one of his employees did with her time, but Mrs Bradley could not help wondering whether the girl was absent from her duties with or without permission. The latter seemed the more likely, as the nurse, Mrs Call, had expected to find her in the house and had not been told that she would be absent.

Mrs Bradley sipped sherry and studied her. She saw, as before, a good-looking, fair-haired, generously-built young woman with a face too hard and arrogant for her years. She felt that Sir Bohun might have made a happier choice of a nursery governess if appearance was anything to go by. On the other hand, the girl might be feeling tired after the party, and her apparently hard expression might be due merely to fatigue. She could not help remembering, however, something which she had noted only absently at the time, and that was the look of fury on Linda Campbell's face when the copy of *Endymion* had been presented to Mrs Godley. So it had been intended for Linda, Mrs Bradley suddenly realized, and one of Sir Bohun's fits of freakish and rather cruel humour had caused him to change his mind about the recipient – probably at the very last moment, if Mrs Bradley knew anything of his mentality.

'He probably *does* intend to marry the girl,' she thought, sipping her sherry and glancing idly round the room, 'and that was one of his ideas for bringing her to heel before he actually commits himself, I suppose. He ought to know by this time that it is well beyond his scope to bring *anybody* to heel, let alone a hard-faced little minx of this type!'

Mrs Bradley finished her sherry and glanced at her watch. She would be late for lunch if she did not leave at once. She was nearer the door than were the girl and her companion, and she did not think they had noticed her, for their conversation appeared to absorb every scrap of their attention, although, from their attitude, it did not appear to be based upon any very pleasant topic, for neither the man nor the girl did anything but frown in concentration over it.

The road-house – it could not be called anything else – adjoined the heath. Mrs Bradley slipped out and took a narrow path which led on to the heath and continued across it to a village. At first the path bordered fairly closely upon crowded, ancient bushes, mostly of hawthorn, beside which it wound a meandering, muddy way, but beyond the bushes there was open country whose rough grass and coarser weeds covered deep beds of gravel except where these had been laid bare by excavation, an excess of which had inundated the landscape with unlovely stretches of water. The village to which the path led possessed a Norman church, an Elizabethan manor house, and some beautiful eighteenth-century houses. Mrs Bradley had been told about it, and a sudden fancy took her to visit it that very day.

She had not gone far across the heath, so she returned to the road-house, found a public telephone in the vestibule, rang up Sir Bohun's house to say that she would not be in before tea-time, and went into the road-house restaurant for lunch.

She ordered steak and kidney pie and a half-bottle of Burgundy, finished with biscuits and cheese, and, after a thoroughly enjoyable meal, picked up her ash-plant and on her way out peeped in at the door of the lounge bar. She saw that the nursery governess and her acquaintance had gone; they had not come into the restaurant.

By this time the sun had almost dispersed the fog, but what remained, dense over the gravel-ponds and thicker about the bushes than on the open heath, contrived to give an unreal, dream-like effect which she enjoyed. The air was mild, and she did not feel in the mood to hurry, particularly so soon after lunch, so that it was past two o'clock by the time she came to the first of the gravel pits and to the mechanical aids with which the gravel was exca-vated, cleaned, and separated into its components of various-sized pebbles and rough sand.

In parts of Cornwall the china-clay hills, and, in the north of England, the slag heaps, contrive to make the landscape almost intolerably hideous. On the heath the long mounds of waste material from the gravel beds, although less striking, were equally ugly and unnatural. The desolate appearance of the sheets of placid water which bordered the excavations was not particularly interesting, either, and Mrs Bradley was not at all sorry to get away from the gravel pits and to see before her the squat tower of the village church. As she approached it she passed a plump elderly woman who was exercising what Mrs Bradley felt certain was the Hound of the Sherlock Holmes party. She registered the fact with interest but without apprehension.

The little church possessed no features out of the ordinary. True, it held a pre-Norman font and a *rebus* in the form of a skeleton, this last in memory of a certain Septimus Boddy, vicar of the parish in the early seventeenth century, but Mrs Bradley was unable to admire either of these furnishings, or to seek and find evidence of the existence of a rood staircase, identify a squint, admire an eighteenth-century sounding board (still in a complete state of preservation and looking rather like a small-scale model of King Arthur's Round Table) or pause beside an unusually-shaped holy-water stoup by the south door. In other words, she found the church locked! She was not in the least surprised, and, shrugging philosophically, she stepped out briskly for home.

By the time she reached the road-house, the fog and the darkness, between them, had made the use of her electric torch imperative, and it was with pleasure but not with surprise that she found her own car, its orange fog-light on, awaiting her at the road-house. Her chauffeur had parked it beneath the tremendous arc-lights which, advertising the place, were powerful enough to defeat the fog and the darkness, so that she saw the car at once. The man opened the door and had her inside, with the rug over her knees, in a matter of seconds. He had been in her employment for a quarter of a century and had learned when, and when not, to expect her. When her telephone message had been communicated to him by Sir Bohun's butler, he had allowed her a couple of hours, had driven to the road-house, and, having enquired for her there, had settled down with his usual patience to await her return from her walk.

Mrs Bradley reached Sir Bohun's house to find her host in a fine mixture of apprehension and indignation – fretting and fuming, in fact, and, it appeared, with some reason.

'She hasn't been here all day,' he said. 'It's extremely unsatis-factory. And now that fellow has gone chasing after her, and with-out leave! If he weren't so reliable and good as a tutor to Philip, who is twice the lad he was since Grimston came along, I'd sack him out of hand. Besides, he's in love with the girl, and that doesn't do when they're both under the same roof all the time.'

'I saw Timothy's governess this morning at the *Queen of the Circus* road-house,' Mrs Bradley remarked.

'Did you? What the heck was she doing at a place like that?' Sir Bohun sounded interested, not indignant.

'She was drinking beer and talking – possibly quarrelling – with a handsome – possibly disillusioned – young man.'

'Good heavens! In *my* time and on wages *I* pay! And even if she *was* at the *Queen* this morning, where is she now? It's nearly dinner-time, and the fog is thicker than ever. Do you suppose she's got lost?'

'It would be easy enough. I have an excellent bump of locality, but, even with the aid of an electric torch, I found it needed con-centration to find my way back across the heath in the late after-noon. The fog is much thicker there than here.'

'Well, she'll have to find *some* reasonable excuse when she *does* get back,' said Sir Bohun. 'Hang the girl! I never *could* manage women! Thank God my adopted brats are boys! My brother had *that* much sense! But what makes you mention the heath? She wouldn't be going over there. No, she's off on a toot up to Town, and, what's more, that fellow Grimston's gone with her, although I must admit that *he* had the grace to ask for the afternoon off! Hang it all! I pay the girl to teach young Timothy, not to mess about in public houses! You say they were quarrelling, she and this whoever-it-was?'

'Well, at any rate, they appeared to be arguing some grave matter. It did not strike me that they were having a lovers' quarrel. It seemed something deeper, more impersonal, than that.'

'I should hope so, indeed. You know, Beatrice, I've looked at the girl once or twice myself. I haven't a son, except Manoel, and I don't want a bastard for my heir.'

'Bastards are conceived before they are born,' said Mrs Bradley pointedly. 'As for Miss Campbell, I advise you to leave well alone.'

'Why? Don't you like the girl, Beatrice?'

'My liking has nothing to do with it. It is your own which would need to be consulted.'

'Oh, *I* don't like her at all. But we should not need to see very much of one another. I have my own interests, and naturally she would have hers. And I should not be mean about money.'

'No. She relies upon that.'

'What on earth do you mean?'

'Nothing, except that she has refused to consider marrying Mr Grimston because he is poor and not likely to become rich. It seems to be her only reason.'

'I knew Grimston was after her, poor young devil! No, he'll never get far. It doesn't take a genius to see that. The girl's got sense if she's turned him down. I'll try to get him another job, though, when I've finished with him for Philip. Fair's fair, after all. What do you think of Philip, Beatrice? Anglo-Indian children often get off to a bad start. The boy is a nice little chap, intelligent, bright – but delicate, very delicate. Hoping he'll grow out of it. Nothing like decent English air to build up a delicate boy.'

'Then why are you sending him to school in Switzerland?'

'Oh, that's Baynes' idea. Doctor's orders, if you please! Can't go against them, though, can I? 'Tisn't done to know better than the doctor.'

'Is little Timothy going with him?'

'Haven't decided yet. Seems a bit young at present. See at the end of July. He'll be turned seven by then.'

Sir Bohun glanced at the clock, and then took out his watch and compared the two. As he did so, the dressing-bell sounded. Sir Bohun looked contrite.

'Oh, Lord, Beatrice! You haven't had any tea! I'll get some sent up to your room. You can have it while you dress. Don't bother about much war-paint. We shall be a family party to-night.'

Mrs Bradley went to her room and found her secretary installed in an armchair beside a small table. Laura got up as Mrs Bradley came in.

'I'm parked here because I want to talk to you rather particularly,' Laura announced.

'It is always a pleasure to see you,' her employer politely replied. Then she added, 'It is about Miss Campbell, I imagine.'

'Uncanny,' said Laura. 'That's what it is – uncanny. Tell you what, though: it's serious, too. The bird Grimston came skulking up to me in the shrubbery – to be exact, the conservatory, where, again to be exact, I was stalling off the amorous advances of that bull-fighting Manoel boy – between ourselves, no Valentino! – and confided that he happened to know that the Campbell was almost certainly dead and that her body was to be found over against the gravel ponds on the heath. I asked him how he knew, and how he had been able to see it in the fog. At that, he merely wagged his head in a daft kind of way, and, giving Manoel a dirty look – my open palm had found a ready mark on that swarthy cheek – he toddled off. I thought you had better know as soon as possible. Personally, I think Grimston's cuckoo.'

Mrs Bradley clicked her tongue.

'It is true that Miss Campbell is still missing from this house,' she said. 'I will speak to Mr Grimston, and then, if his story remains constant and bears any evidence of being true, well, we have a policeman among us.'

'Gavin? Yes. What does he mean by risking my maiden virtue with the Manoels of this wicked world?'

'He is not in the house?'

'Of course he's in the house. He's teaching Philip to play billiards. He's taken a fancy to the child. Thinks well of his intelligence, I gather.'

'And the boy thinks well of Robert's handsome manly appearance, I make no doubt. Robert is good with children. I have marked it before.'

'Oh, people always fall for Gavin,' said Laura offhandedly. 'I don't know why I don't fall harder for him myself. I doubt whether I am cut out for wifehood. I think, after all, I will wait until I'm forty. I shall know my own mind by then. Hullo! Here's tea. I haven't had any yet. Too busy. May I join you? There seems plenty for two.'

'You will spoil your dinner,' said Mrs Bradley, watching, with fascinated gaze, Laura's ruthless dealing with buttered muffins and cherry jam.

'Impossible,' replied Laura, 'as well you know. Another cup of the Suchong? Refreshing stuff, and they make it rather well. I say, there couldn't *really* be anything in Grimston's yarn, could there, do you suppose? An elaborate and somewhat tasteless leg-pull, should you think?'

Mrs Bradley shrugged her shoulders. Laura looked at her, a startled expression in her eyes.

'The last I saw of Miss Campbell,' Mrs Bradley said, 'was at the *Queen of the Circus* road-house on the heath. She was with a bitter-looking, thoughtful young man, and by the time I had finished my lunch the two had gone.'

'Were they having a row?'

'Not at all, so far as I could tell. Their talk was serious, concentrated, grave, but not, it appeared, acrimonious.'

'He's murdered her,' said Laura, 'mark my words. And Grimston knows!'

'What a thing it is to have an imagination nourished at its inception among the dark hills of the firm, true, and tender north,' said Mrs Bradley. 'But I also have something to disclose. I have met the Hound of the Baskervilles.'

'Again?'

'Yes, again.'

'I say, where?'

'On the heath, where it skirts the village of Common Row. It was in the company of a retired chorus girl.'

'But that doesn't make sense!'

'Yes, it does, if the dog was hired for the occasion. Still, no matter.'

Laura looked at her with great interest.

'My thumbs prick,' she observed with lugubrious relish. 'We haven't heard the last of that dog!'

# CHAPTER 5

# A TUTOR'S DREAM

'So wonder on, till Truth make all things plain.'
SHAKESPEARE – *A Midsummer Night's Dream*

\*

As soon as a maid had taken away the tea-tray, Mrs Bradley rang up Sir Bohun on the house telephone. Sir Bohun was in the bath, and took the call from there.

'Grimston says she's dead? Out on the heath? Oh, nonsense! He must be mad! I shall have to call the police if she doesn't come back to-night, though. I wish Bell hadn't had that sudden call from his father. He'd know what I ought to do. What the deuce has come over the girl? She seemed such a sane little party! Thank heaven I didn't commit myself to anything! By the way, is Manoel behaving himself as he should? He came to me with a complaint that your Miss Menzies slapped his face, and wants me to order her out of the house. If he doesn't behave with the women guests, he can go – and so I've told him!'

'Laura can take care of herself. Do you think you should speak to Mr Grimston?'

'Yes, I do, and I'd like you to be present, and that policeman chap, too. I'm not well pleased with Grimston for telling that sort of tale. There can't be anything in it, but it's not the kind of joke I like very much.'

'You don't think he can be serious?'

'Hardly. What do you think yourself?'

'I do not commit myself to an opinion. When shall we talk with Mr Grimston?'

'Immediately after dinner. There will be no time for anything before that. If she *is* out there on the heath, we'd never find her in this. It's thicker than ever. I'm going to ring off. This dashed water's getting cold.'

Mrs Bradley knew better than to suppose that Sir Bohun would be able to refrain from questioning Grimston until after dinner.

As soon as the soup-cups had been removed, in fact, Sir Bohun demanded bluntly of the so-far silent tutor:

'What's all this about Miss Campbell?'

'It looks as though my dream is coming true, Sir Bohun,' Grimston coolly replied.

'Dream? What dream? What are you blethering about now?'

'I dreamt about Miss Campbell last night. I dreamt that she left the house before the conclusion of your party, and that I followed her on to the heath, just where the path goes down by the side of that new road-house – I forget what it's called.'

'You couldn't have followed her! Fog was as thick as a stew!'

'Not in my dream, Sir Bohun. In my dream there was no more than a moonlight mist. As I was saying, I followed Miss Campbell over the heath, taking that winding path which leads to Common Row village. In front of us loomed a structure which, at first sight, I took to be the turrets and bridge of a battleship. . . . '

'Nonsense, man! Just the machinery they use to excavate gravel!'

'Yes, sir, but you will remember that I am describing what took place in my dream.'

'Moonshine! Do you mean to tell me that you attach importance to a *dream?*'

'Many psychologists to-day believe that dreams may foretell the future as well as illuminate the past, sir.' Grimston glanced at Mrs Bradley as though challenging her to refute this statement, but her brilliant black eyes gave away none of her opinions. 'Moreover,' continued the tutor, 'Miss Campbell's unexplained absence from this house has been causing me much anxiety, and therefore, at risk of incurring your scorn and contempt, Sir Bohun, I felt I would be wise to relate my dream in case anything could be done, although, as you point out, in *this . . . !*' He waved a firm hand towards the window. Sir Bohun looked at him without scorn or contempt, but in simple wonderment. Manoel, who was seated between his father and Mrs Bradley in obvious avoidance of sitting next to Laura, suddenly laughed aloud, a harsh sound which caused his father to turn to him and say:

'So that's what *you* think of it!'

'*Dreams!*' said Manoel. 'If Antonio were here he would know all about these dreams!'

'But in that sleep of death, what dreams may come . . . ' Mrs

Bradley quoted solemnly. 'Pray continue your reminiscences, Mr Grimston.' Grimston shrugged helplessly.

'Yes, go on, Mr Grimston,' said Laura. 'My Highland imagination is all on fire to hear the rest of the story. You don't mind, Sir Bohun, do you? I'm not going to miss the bloodiest part, if I can help it.'

'There wasn't any blood,' said Grimston quickly. 'She was simply lying there, by the water. I knew exactly where to find her. She was lying there by the water, and I knew she was dead. And then I knew I had killed her. You know how it is in dreams. There's often no real sequence . . . anyhow, none that one can remember afterwards. I had been following her, and then my attention was distracted by this ship-looking erection . . . really the gravel-digging machinery, of course, as Sir Bohun points out . . . and then I came upon her dead body, and I knew I'd killed her. And I'm worried. There's *something* wrong, even if she isn't dead. If everything's all right with her, where is she now?'

'A moot point,' said Mrs Bradley, noting with interest that the conversation had continued, unchecked by the entrances and disappearances of servants changing plates and bringing in dishes. 'We must investigate.'

When dinner was over, and the others were retiring to the drawing-room, Sir Bohun waylaid Mrs Bradley at the door.

'What do you think of that mad fellow's story, Beatrice?' he demanded.

'I think we should inform the police if Miss Campbell is still missing by eleven o'clock to-night. Even supposing that nothing untoward has befallen her, the fact remains that she was not in the house last night. If I had not happened to come upon her in that road-house, you would have informed the police, before this, of her disappearance, I take it?'

'I suppose so, yes.' Before he could say more, Gavin came back to the room.

'I don't want to butt in,' he said, 'but how would it be, Sir Bohun, if I had a semi-official word, so to speak, with the local police? I could, perhaps, tip them the wink that there may be something fishy about Miss Campbell's disappearance, and give them Mrs Bradley's description of the fellow she was with at the pub.'

'I'd be very much relieved if you would,' said Sir Bohun, his relief evident in his voice. 'It isn't a bit like what I know of the girl for her to have made off like this. I don't know what to think about it, and, as her employer, I feel responsible for her safety.'

'I'll get on to them right away,' said Gavin, 'if I may use your telephone. I'll ring them to say I'm coming, and then go and see them personally.'

'The fog's beastly thick, and part of the road is alongside the river. Take care, you know. Very easy to drive over the edge of the bank if you don't know your way.'

Gavin left the house and did not get back until eleven. He asked immediately whether Miss Campbell had returned. She had not done so.

'Proof enough that we've done the right thing in telling the police,' said Sir Bohun. 'What was their attitude, Chief-Inspector?'

'What one might have expected. They don't recognize the description of the fellow she was with at the pub, but they're prepared to take up the chase if she isn't back by to-morrow. Even if they were prepared to search the heath on the strength of Grimston's dream, it just isn't possible to-night. The darkness and the fog together have put paid to any such idea.'

'Well, I'm extremely grateful to you,' said Sir Bohun. 'I was worried about the girl. This is a tremendous weight off my mind. Where has Grimston gone, by the way?'

'He went to bed, Sir Bohun,' said the butler, who had come in with the whisky.

'Went to bed, did he? Hm! Doesn't say much for his feelings,' remarked the host, when the butler had gone. 'I thought he was sweet on the girl!'

Mrs Bradley also went to bed, but she felt wide-awake, and, at two in the morning, she got up, wrapped herself in her dressing-gown and chose a book. The fire was not out, so she poked and replenished it, and settled down in comfort to read. An hour passed. Somewhere a clock struck three. The handle of her door began to turn. Mrs Bradley's ears were keen. She looked up, and watched the revolution of the handle. She had no sensation of fear, but felt considerable curiosity. This was satisfied when her visitor proved to be Grimston. She betrayed no surprise at his entrance.

'Well,' she said, looking up, 'and what can I do for *you*, my poor child?'

Grimston stood still, and put his back against the door which he had closed very softly behind him.

'I was going to ask you – ' he said.

'Yes?'

'I was going to ask you what you thought about Linda Campbell. Her disappearance, you know. Isn't it rather odd?'

'Very odd indeed, I should think. And isn't this rather an odd time to canvass my opinion?'

'I really sneaked in to have a look at your diary.'

'I see. What makes you think I keep a diary?'

'Don't you? I've seen you writing in a small book that you keep in the deep pocket of your skirt.'

'Ah, yes. That is not a diary. It is my professional notebook, and would mean very little to you if you saw it. Indeed, you are quite welcome to see it, if you wish. There it is, on the dressing-table.'

Grimston strolled over, his hands in the pockets of the dinner-jacket he was still wearing. He picked up the book and glanced through it, but Mrs Bradley's self-invented shorthand and illegible, neat writing defeated him, as she had known they would. He laid down the book, and turned and faced her.

'What did you think of my dream?' he demanded. She had put down her own book, but had not risen from her armchair. She looked up at him and shook her head.

'Realistic and invented,' she replied.

He nodded.

'Exactly what I should have expected you to say. Look here will you come with me to the heath in the morning? After all, Linda *hasn't* come back. I went to her room before I came here, to make sure. And she's – I mean, there are several people who've got it in for her. She's told me bits, and I've guessed a lot more than she's told me. It isn't difficult to put two and two together with anyone as transparent as Linda.'

'You're in love with her, aren't you?' said Mrs Bradley. It was more of a statement than a question. Grimston looked surprised, and said:

'In love with her? Oh, no, she is not my type at all. In fact, rather the reverse. She's hard, you know . . . a bit of a gold-digger, too.'

'And you?'

He gave a short laugh. The abrupt query was a criticism, and he knew it.

'Me? Oh, I don't know. One can't judge oneself. Pretty soft, I expect. Bit of an idealist, I'm afraid. No money, and no particular prospects. A dead-end kid, in a way; and, in a way, not. I've contemplated suicide at times. I'm not interested in living to a ripe old age, neither have I any intention of growing a paunch in my middle years and padding about in the back garden of a suburban villa, still less of exhausting my mental powers trying to teach louts how to read and write English. *Will* you come with me to the heath in the morning?'

'That remains to be seen. You had better go to bed now, and allow me to do the same.'

'Yes, very well. I'm sorry to have disturbed you, but I saw the light through your keyhole, so I guessed that you were still up, and wouldn't mind if I came in.'

He went out, closing the door without a sound. Mrs Bradley turned the key in the lock. She was not afraid of Grimston, but she did not approve of being called upon in the early hours of the morning by young men who babbled of dreams and murder. Grimston's mental state, it did not take much intelligence to infer, was in anything but a healthy condition. Very thoughtful indeed, she sought her bed. She was wondering why he had lied about being in love with Linda Campbell. On the other hand, suicides, she reminded herself, rarely confess beforehand to suicidal impulses. They prefer to leave letters to be read after their deaths.

The next morning she rose as soon as it was light, went downstairs, and found Gavin gazing out of the morning-room french window at the woolly mist which allowed little of the grounds to be seen beyond the terrace parapet. He wore riding breeches and a waterproof.

'Don't believe I want to ride in this,' he said, indicating the thick haze. 'Think it will lift after breakfast?'

'I have no idea. The countryside is low-lying, and there is a great deal of water near here, so probably it will not. If it does, I want you to come out with Mr Grimston and me.'

'Willingly. May I ask where, and, if it isn't ungallant, why?'

'Certainly. We are going to find out whether dreams come true.'

'Good Lord! You didn't take him seriously, did you?'

'Considering that he entered my room at three a.m. to urge upon me the necessity of investigating the disappearance of Linda Campbell . . .'

'At three this morning? The fellow must be crazy! Is he?'

'He is undoubtedly unbalanced. I suspect suicidal tendencies. In fact – ' Gavin waited, and then said:

'And you think we ought to prove to him that he needn't dream about murders that don't happen?'

'It is quite possible that this one *has* happened, child. That is why I want you to accompany us.'

'Right! At your service, as always!'

The proposed expedition was abandoned, however, for Linda Campbell appeared at breakfast, having returned to the house at six that morning, to the disguised astonishment and disapproval of the butler and the undisguised annoyance of Sir Bohun. She had a story of kidnapping to tell, the details of which she gave at an interview in the library directly breakfast was over.

Sir Bohun emerged from this impressive lair looking puzzled and worried, and went in search of Mrs Bradley, whom he found in the gun-room reading *The Times* aloud and stroking a handsome tortoiseshell cat. The reason for the first activity seemed to be the presence of his son Manoel, who was cleaning a twelve-bore gun as he listened to the declamation of the leading article. The second did not appear to depend upon logic.

'*Buenos dias, padre mio*,' said Manoel, scowling as though in disclaimer of the politeness of this filial greeting. Sir Bohun grunted, and turned to Mrs Bradley.

'I say, Beatrice, come along to the library, if you don't mind. I want you to vet this girl's story. I can't make head or tail of it. She *must* be lying!'

Mrs Bradley was anxious to obtain first-hand details of Linda's real or imaginary adventures, so she leered at Manoel, put down the paper, and accompanied her host to the library.

Linda, flushed and looking defiant – an expression which hardened her face and yet gave her a childish appearance of defencelessness – was seated in a leather-covered armchair beside the fire, while the chair opposite still bore the imprint of Sir Bohun's heavy and muscular hams.

'Sit down, Beatrice,' commanded the master of the house, indicating a third armchair and giving it a hospitable shove towards the fire. 'Now, then, Miss Campbell, I shall be obliged if you will repeat to Mrs Bradley the tale you've just told me.'

'It isn't a tale; it's the truth. I can't help it if you don't believe me,' returned Linda, tilting her chin.

'I didn't say I didn't believe you. I *don't* . . . but I haven't said so. Now be a sensible gal, and let Mrs Bradley have the dope.'

Mrs Bradley smiled – a grimace only – and nodded.

'I saw you at the *Queen of the Circus* road-house,' she said, 'so you may begin from there.'

Linda's expression changed. She glanced appealingly at her employer.

'I know it was wrong,' she said. 'It was on account of that letter. I had a letter,' she went on, turning towards Mrs Bradley, 'asking me to meet Stephen Cutts at the *Queen of the Circus* because he had something very important to tell me. I've known Stephen for years. He's a private enquiry agent, and I'd asked him to try to trace my father, who left my mother when I was seven. I scarcely remember him, but when my mother died three years ago, and I was left completely alone, I thought I'd like to get in touch with my father again, especially as, since I've been grown-up, I've always thought the separation was quite as much my mother's fault as his. She was a nagger, and men won't stand being nagged.'

'Quite right,' agreed Sir Bohun, looking haughty. 'Mind you remember it, my dear!'

'Well, when the letter came, I didn't know what to do,' went on Linda, continuing to address Mrs Bradley's beaky mouth. 'The time and place were very definitely fixed, and I wasn't at all sure that Sir Bohun would give me leave of absence in the middle of the morning like that, because of little Timothy. So I'm afraid I just took French leave, hoping nobody would tell Sir Bohun that I was not in the house.'

'Hark at her!' growled Sir Bohun. 'Anybody would think I was an ogre to hear her talk!'

'I was afraid you wouldn't believe my story of a business meeting, especially as I'd burnt the letter and so couldn't show it you, Sir Bohun,' explained Linda, simpering a little.

'All right, all right. Go on.'

'When I got to the *Queen of the Circus* a strange man . . . quite young and not bad-looking . . . came up and asked me whether I'd come to meet Stephen Cutts, as he was his partner. He said that Stephen had had to take on another assignment at short notice, so had sent him to interview me. He said that news of my father was now in their possession. They had traced a man who, they were practically certain, was he, but who was calling himself Porterhouse. Did I think I could remember my father sufficiently well to be able to identify him? Well, I've a portrait of him, and I said I thought I could, unless he had changed a great deal in sixteen years, so when the man put me into his car, I just felt I couldn't get along quickly enough, I was so excited.'

'Put you into his car!' growled Sir Bohun.

'After that, everything happened. I was driven to a house in Bloomsbury, taken up three flights of stairs, shown into a room which wasn't very well furnished but which was neat and clean and had a good fire and plenty of coal in the scuttle, and there I waited for just on an hour. Then I went to the door with the intention of saying that I couldn't wait any longer because I had to get back to my job, but the door was locked. I was terrified. I banged and shouted, but nobody came. I went to the window, but the houses opposite had been blitzed, and there wasn't a soul to be seen.

'It began to get dark, and I was hungry. I made up the fire once or twice, and then, in desperation, I opened a cupboard. It was well stocked with food. There were cut ham, slices of tongue, plenty of bread, some butter, a knife and fork, and a couple of quarts of beer. They didn't mean me to starve. Well, there I've been ever since. I tried the door again, and it opened, but only to admit me to a bathroom and so forth. There was a staircase door. and that remained locked all the time, so I was still a prisoner, Then, late last night, I was released.'

'Strange,' observed Mrs Bradley. 'Did you find out why they let you go? Or, in fact, why they had imprisoned you at all?'

'No, I did not. The same man came for me. He told me that he was taking me home, and said I need not begin making a fuss. I made no fuss. I was thoroughly cowed. He drove me back here, pushed me out of the car, and, before I had reached the gate, he had gone. I still don't know who he was or why he kidnapped me. And I still don't know where my father is, or why Stephen Cutts didn't contact me. I shall write to Stephen at once.'

'Well?' demanded Sir Bohun when he had sent Linda off to look after Timothy. 'Truth or lies? I confess I should like to know.'

'Why don't *you* employ a private detective?' Mrs Bradley asked.

'Me? Why should I think of anything like that?'

'Because you still intend to marry the girl,' Mrs Bradley replied in deliberate tones. 'That being so, you had better satisfy yourself as to where she went and what she did. You need to set your mind at rest. Curiosity killed the cat, you know.'

'Yes, yes, I must get to the bottom of it somehow. I feel sure she's lying. Would you recognize the fellow she was with if you saw him again?'

'Certainly I should, unless he has a twin brother.'

A week later, when they had returned to their house in Kensington, Laura showed Mrs Bradley the newspaper announcement of Sir Bohun's engagement to Linda Campbell.

'Queer?' she asked. Mrs Bradley did not reply. Laura glanced at her, waited a moment or two, and then said tentatively, 'What did you really make of that story she told about being kidnapped and held in that house in Bloomsbury?'

'I thought about a book by Lilian de la Torre, a brilliant reconstruction and explanation of an eighteenth-century mystery,' said Mrs Bradley.

'*Elizabeth Is Missing*,' said Laura. 'You know, I have a feeling that Manoel knows a thing or two. You noted the reference to Antonio?'

'Good gracious me, child! I should never have given it a thought!'

Laura wagged her head solemnly.

'Young blood! Young blood!' she murmured. 'What's sauce for the goose is sauce for the gander, but, there! I may be wrong.'

## CHAPTER 6

# CAVILLING CRITICS

' . . . and heard great argument
About it and about, but evermore
Came out by that same door wherein I went.'

*The Rubaiyat of Omar Khayyam* in the
English version of EDWARD FITZGERALD

\*

MRS BRADLEY was so much intrigued by the announcement of Sir Bohun's engagement to Linda Campbell, especially in view of the story of her kidnapping, that when Christmas was over she decided to call on him and congratulate him in person instead of by letter.

'Nobody else likes it,' he said gloomily. This statement was borne out, if not in its sweeping entirety, at least to an extent which he must have found embarrassing and infuriating, by the attitude of several more or less interested persons.

Mrs Bradley, prevailed upon to stay a day or two, as she could easily be reached if anything urgent cropped up with regard either to her work or her domestic affairs, received what best can be described as clandestine visits from these persons. It seemed to be the general impression that she could be used as a clearing-house for grievances, and, in view of what happened afterwards, it was interesting that this should be so.

She had unpacked, with the unnecessary assistance of a house-maid, the bag she had telephoned for, and was about to descend for tea when there came the sort of tap at the door which, in her experience (and it was a long one, where matters confidential were concerned), heralded a caller with secrets to disclose. It turned out to be Mrs Dance, who seated herself on the bed and asked whether she might have a word in private.

'Do you mind?' she enquired, obviously taking it for granted that Mrs Bradley did not. 'I just thought I'd like to come and talk to you.'

'Of course,' Mrs Bradley agreed. 'You came to talk about this ridiculous business of Sir Bohun Chantrey and the governess.'

'So *you* see it like that, too,' Mrs Dance smiled and looked, at the same time, impressed. 'Somehow, I didn't think you would. I formed the impression that you would probably be a socialist.'

'In what sense? I thought we were all socialists since the National Health Scheme came in. I do not see how we can avoid being part of the social conscience nowadays. You remember your Rupert Brooke, of course?'

'Rupert Brooke?'

'Certainly. I am thinking of "one pulse in the Eternal Mind – " and also, perhaps, "there shall be no more land, say fish." Not to mention – '

> *'There's an end, I think, of kissing*
> *When our mouths are one with Mouth,'*

quoted Mrs Dance surprisingly. She laughed. 'I have good reason to dislike the young person,' she went on. 'She will make Boo-Boo look ridiculous. Think of the difference in their ages! She's only twenty-three or twenty-four, and he can put twenty years on to that. I can't think why he wants to make such a fool of himself.'

'Have you known him long?' Mrs Bradley enquired.

'Long enough to know that the girl won't suit him. She's what used to be called a designing minx. I wouldn't be a bit surprised to learn that she has blackmailed him into this engagement. He's very hasty and sometimes rather silly, and I dare say he committed himself with her in a way she can prove, and so got him into her clutches. I wouldn't trust her an inch, and I do *not* think she can be a good influence for that little boy. However, that is no concern of mine.'

She got off the bed and went towards the door.

'I think young children are everybody's concern,' Mrs Bradley remarked, slipping the gold bracelet of her wrist-watch over a yellow claw.

'Yes, of course they are, and I'm rather fond of them, especially of Tim. He's sweet.' She brooded a moment or two. 'Why don't you use your influence with Boo-Boo and make him break it off?' she suddenly demanded. 'He's sensitive to your opinion, and he'd listen to *you* where he *wouldn't* to any of *us*.' She returned to the bed and sat down again.

'I see no point whatever in interfering,' said Mrs Bradley, her brilliant black eyes meeting the innocent orbs of her visitor. 'If he really *has* been blackmailed (as you call it, and you may very well be right, for he is a selfish, impulsive, reckless, undisciplined man), he would not feel able to follow my advice; and if he really is fond of the girl, or is attracted physically by her, then it would be both wrong and unkind to object to the marriage.'

Mrs Dance shrugged. Then she caught Mrs Bradley's eye again, and her *gamine* face curved into sudden laughter.

'All the same, that big bad wolf story of hers was all hooey,' she remarked, 'and I don't believe for an instant that Boo-Boo fell for it. No, there's something *behind* this engagement, and blackmail is by far the most likely thing. If it is, she ought not to be allowed to get away with it, and I *still* think you ought to ferret out the truth and save the silly mug from himself.'

'From himself – or for you?' Mrs Bradley wondered; but, as this was not a question it was possible to ask, she was silent for a while. When she spoke, it was upon another subject.

'What did you make of the *Hound of the Baskervilles* at the Sherlock Holmes party?' she enquired.

'Manoel, I think. I've turned the thing over in my mind, and he is the only person who would have thought of it – unless your Laura has a talent for practical joking.'

'Manoel?'

'Well, he's used to bulls, so I shouldn't think he'd be afraid of a dog.'

'Laura?'

'Well, I shouldn't think she's afraid of anything.'

'She is afraid of my displeasure,' said Mrs Bradley solemnly, 'and she would know that I should be very much displeased if she introduced a large and savage dog into the middle of a small and civilized gathering, Sherlock Holmes and the Hound notwithstanding.'

'I see. *Was* the dog savage?'

'No. On the contrary, it was an obedient, intelligent, extremely docile animal.'

'There you are, then. Manoel. He would like to make his father look a fool, and Boo *did* look a fool – you can't deny it.'

'It interests me,' said Mrs Bradley, 'to note that the fact that Manoel is Sir Bohun's illegitimate son appears to be known to everybody.'

'Oh, well, Boo's proud of it, you know. He tells no end of a good tale about it all – so gallant, so romantic, and, I am perfectly certain, all lies. Anyway, Manoel undoubtedly exists, and undoubtedly he is Boo's son. What is more, he hates Boo with an old-fashioned Mexican hatred that would give me nightmares if I were in Boo's shoes. Boo's shoes,' she repeated thoughtfully. 'It sounds like one of those novels where they make up half the words. Boo's shoes, shoes boo the crowd, boos through Boo, shoos away coos – I mean cows – oh, dear! How silly!'

She grimaced, grinned, slid to the ground and was gone, closing the door behind her with scarcely a sound. Mrs Bradley looked thoughtful. There was no doubt that Mrs Dance was both shrewd and forthright. She had sensed the feeling that Manoel had for his father; she had summed up Linda Campbell; and she had no illusions whatever about Sir Bohun.

Mrs Bradley went down to tea and found her host alone with his fiancée. Linda looked at her smugly, and then slid her hand into Sir Bohun's. He looked surprised, stared down at it and cast it off.

'Nice of you, Beatrice,' he said. 'Thankful we've got *one* friend and well-wisher, anyway!'

'One?' Mrs Bradley enquired, seating herself by the fire and opposite the engaged couple.

'The others – even Bell – and what business it is of his I *don't* know – are dead against this set-up.' Sir Bohun indicated the tea-pouring Linda with a jerk of his head. 'I can understand young Grimston, of course. I've cut him out. But why on earth anybody else should object, I don't follow at all.'

'Spongers!' interpolated Linda. 'And that Bell boy is afraid he'll lose his job when we're married. And so he will, if *I* have any say in the matter. He's far too big for his boots, and he knows far more of your business, Boo, than is good for him or for you. When we're married *I* can do his job.'

'Not in addition to your own, my dear.'

'Of course I can! Running a staff of servants doesn't take all day.'

'I was thinking of little Tim.'

'Tim? Oh, but I shan't be teaching Tim after we're married, Boo! You'll have to get rid of those boys. We can't have *adopted* children in the house. They'll be horribly in the way.'

71

'I beg your pardon, Linda!' said Sir Bohun with the utmost sharpness. 'No nonsense of *that* kind, *please!* Whether you continue to teach Timothy or not is at your own discretion, of course! I thought you were fond of the kiddie, that's all, and would like to push him along at his lessons until he's ready for school. But if you don't choose to do it, he'll have to have another governess, that's all, for Grimston, of course, will have to go. I can't have him mooning about when we're married.'

'Then *I'll* choose her,' said Linda, laughing, but with a suggestion of malice in her mirth. 'I'm not going to brook any rivalry!'

'Really, Linda!' said Sir Bohun, obviously shocked. 'Don't be a common little chit!'

Mrs Bradley thought it high time to put an end to these embarrassing exchanges.

'Did you ever find out where the *Hound of the Baskervilles* came from that night?' she enquired, putting down her cup and helping herself to a sandwich. Sir Bohun shook his head.

'Never set eyes on him again, and everybody denied all knowledge of him,' he replied. 'Somebody's lying, of course, but I can't find out who it is, or where he went when you and Miss Menzies got rid of him out of the house.'

'Horrible great brute!' said Linda Campbell. 'I'm terrified of big dogs. I shall always believe you did it yourself just to frighten me.'

'Why the devil should I want to frighten you?' Sir Bohun testily demanded. 'Something better to think about than frightening damn' silly women with damned great dogs! What *I* still want to know – apart from who painted the dog, the thoughtless fools! – is who dared put two more rooms out of bounds than were agreed on between Bell and myself!'

'You had better ask Brenda Dance,' said Linda Campbell, with so much malice in her tone that Mrs Bradley was immediately, although not obviously, interested. 'You should have arranged a few sitting-out places, my poor Boo, if you didn't want your precious little-boy plans upset by a dirty little – '

'Linda!' shouted Sir Bohun, endeavouring to drown the last word.

'Well, so she is,' retorted his *inamorata* cattishly. 'You know it as well as I do. And, what's more, if I hadn't grabbed you out of her clutches you'd be a co-respondent in the divorce court by this time, and, with *your* high-falutin' ideas, you'd have had to marry her as soon as she'd got rid of Toby. And how would you have liked that?'

'Quite as much as I like this, I dare say,' replied Sir Bohun. 'Stop talking nonsense and pour out more tea. There's a scold's bridle hanging up in the attic, and don't you forget it, my girl! As for high-falutin' ideas, I didn't marry Manoel's mother, did I?'

'Is it true that Manoel comes from Mexico, not Spain?' Mrs Bradley enquired, with the object of putting an end to the embarrassing exchanges.

'He's lived in both countries. Why do you want to know?' demanded Sir Bohun.

'Only that I would rather make an enemy of a Spaniard than of a Mexican,' said Mrs Bradley calmly.

'Who says I've made an enemy of Manoel? Have you been pumping the boy?'

'No. But he wants to kill you. Didn't you know?'

Sir Bohun began to swell and turn purple. Linda Campbell laughed aloud. Sir Bohun raised his hand as though to strike her across the face, caught Mrs Bradley's basilisk eye, and, with a choking sound, went out of the room.

'Poor Boo!' said Linda lightly. 'I shall have to cure him of that naughty temper when we're married.'

'He has had it rather a long time,' said Mrs Bradley, eyeing her benignly. The drawing-room, when Mrs Bradley went down for dinner that night, was inhabited by Dance, who seemed to be at a loose end.

'Ah,' he said, when she came into the room, 'splendid! Now I can ring for cocktails. I was getting desperate. Well, and how are you? Have you recovered from Christmas?'

'Oh, yes. I always keep it in Oxfordshire.'

'Why Oxfordshire?'

'My favourite nephew and his wife live there, and, as a family, we all tend to gravitate to them when there is more work than usual, as at Christmastide, to be done. Shopping, catering and fitting guests into appropriate spaces seems to be water off a duck's back where they are concerned, and one always takes advantage of that sort of hospitality. One cherishes the illusion in such households that one is no trouble.'

'It's the same here. This is a very well-run house. The housekeeper is completely efficient and completely unobtrusive. I always enjoy staying with Chantrey. I wonder what it will be like with Linda at the helm?'

'There will probably be less efficiency for a time, but Sir Bohun, I hope, will prefer it. Of course, Miss Campbell may elect to keep the housekeeper in her present position of authority.'

'I shouldn't be surprised. I fancy Linda is a lazy little baggage. Why on earth Chantrey wants to get tied up to her I can't for the life of me imagine. They don't hit it off a bit. She's always nagging the man. If it's like that now, I simply can't think what it will be like when they're married.'

Mrs Bradley could not, either. She took a glass of sherry from the tray that was held out to her, sipped it appreciatively, and then remarked:

'I did not see you at tea.'

'I had it in the billiard-room with Lupez. Can't stick listening to Chantrey and the Campbell bickering. (You can't call it anything else.) It gives me the willies to hear her bullying the poor chap all the time. She's going to do this; she's not going to have that; she's going to sack Grimston . . . that bird's getting pretty well browned-off, I can tell you. One of these days he's going to beat her up and walk out of this house. He's one of those slow-combustion maniacs, and he's sweet on the nasty little shrew. Did he but know it, he's had a lucky escape, but he hasn't got around to that yet. Mind if I have a cigarette? Would you care for one, too?'

The next *confidante* was Nanny Call, and after her came Manoel.

'There's going to be trouble, madam,' said the pleasant-faced, elderly woman when Mrs Bradley asked her, when she met her on one of the landings after dinner, how the children were getting on.

'How do you mean, Mrs Call?' Mrs Bradley enquired. She did not gossip with servants unless she was engaged upon detective work, but she knew that Nanny Call was sensible and discreet, a decent, staunch old body.

'She's going to make him turn those little children out, madam. What's more, she must have told Master Philip so. He came to me in real distress the other day. "Nanny," he says to me – as white as a sheet he was, and his eyes like saucers – "Nanny," he says, "if she turns us out, where shall we go? I don't want to go to an orphanage," he says, "and that's the only thing I can see for it if she won't let us stay here." Did you *ever*, madam! Wicked and cruel, I call it, and when I get my notice I'm going to tell her so! But what can you expect of a jumped-up, common little thing like that!'

'It is extraordinary that people will torture children,' said Mrs Bradley, who did, indeed, find this the most extraordinary of all human aberrations. 'It satisfies some feeling of egoism, I suppose. It makes one wonder whether cruelty is not one of the natural instincts. So many people are cruel that it seems cruelty must be part of our nature, doesn't it?'

'Master Philip is such a sensitive boy,' said Mrs Call, not attempting to answer Mrs Bradley's question. 'But the trouble is, madam, that if she's made up her mind to have him and little Master Timothy – who's really no more than a baby – turned out of this house, turned out they'll be, even if it was only to sleep under a hedge and starve to death tramping the roads.'

Mrs Bradley admired this forceful imagery in silence for a moment, then she said:

'Sir Bohun will have a voice in the matter, you know. As he volunteered to take the children in, I can scarcely imagine his agreeing to turn them out.'

Nanny Call shook her head.

'You don't know her as we're beginning to know her, madam. I would have said that the master was a strong-minded man.' Mrs Bradley, who, as his psychiatrist, knew a great deal better than this, held her peace. 'But really,' the woman continued, 'I begin to have my doubts. She does just as she likes with him, madam, and so high and mighty with it as makes you wonder. She's changed several things already that suited the master but don't suit *her* – and that's *before* they're married! Why, the other day, she even went so far as to countermand his orders to Mrs Pearson, and when Mrs Pearson referred the matter back to him he give her the most terrible shock by telling her to do as Miss Campbell said. I doubt if Mrs Pearson will stop here very much longer. If she could get a parallel sort of place, I wouldn't be surprised if she wouldn't pack her bag to-morrow!'

'There are not a great many housekeepers' posts of this kind in these days,' Mrs Bradley gently pointed out. 'There isn't the money about.'

'Folks have their pride, madam,' Mrs Call retorted, 'and there's some things even beggars can't abide.'

Mrs Bradley, who had come up to get her fur coat, for it was a brilliant moonlight night, intensely cold, and she proposed to take a turn in the garden as an antidote to the poisonous mental atmosphere of the house, went downstairs again, and, in the moonlit garden, found Manoel. He was smoking a cigar and was wearing a black Homburg and a heavy overcoat with an astrakhan collar.

'Ah,' she said. 'I shall be glad of company. Let us stroll as far as the lake.'

Manoel, who had been leaning with his back against the terrace parapet so that the light from an uncurtained window was full upon his face, gave her a flashing smile and raised the hat.

'By all means,' he replied. 'You are just the person. I had hoped to see you alone, but did not know how to arrange it. This is contrived by God. You know, I am to go. She wishes it, and my father makes me to obey. I wish she were dead. It would make simple what is now nothing but complication. Why should I go, to please her, but not myself or, I think, my father? But there it is. He has ordered me out of the_house; that house which should one day be mine.'

He spoke passionately although in low tones.

'No one seems very happy about the marriage,' said Mrs Bradley, as they began to walk towards the steps which led down to the garden.

'I do not understand it,' said Manoel. 'No, it is dark to me, this arrangement. If I thought my father would be happy – not that I care for him much – but even that could be tolerated. As it comes' – he made a gesture, the glowing tip of his cigar pointing it – 'there is no happiness for anybody. She does not love him. He does not love her. There is *un engaño* – how do you call it – ?'

'A trick. Some fraud. Some deceit.'

'So I believe. She has . . . no, I have not the English word. . . . I wish to say . . . '

'She has hooked him?'

'The metaphor to catch fish! That is good. I like it. She has hooked him. But how? But why? She is not beautiful. She is not gay. She is not charming. She has good features, but there is no life, no soul. She is *perverso, malo* – bad, bad, bad! How can I kill her, and not be found out?'

Mrs Bradley was neither prepared nor able to offer any sug-

76

gestions. She had once got away with murder herself, but only from the highest motives had that particular murder been committed. She seldom thought about it, and never with the slightest regret. She said to Manoel:

'If you feel prepared to listen to advice, you will do as Sir Bohun suggests – go right away from here and as soon as you can. It does no good to brood over wrongs. You are a young man of talent and determination. Forget your rights and take up your duties. Go out and make another fortune for yourself. Put the sea between you and temptation. For your own sake I urge it.'

Her eloquence, and the beautiful voice in which it was rendered, appeared to mollify the young man. They had reached the lake, and stood for a time looking at the reflection of the moon on its quiet waters. The night was eerily still, and this stillness suddenly seemed to impress itself upon Manoel, for he shivered, turned abruptly and began to walk back towards the house.

'Do you play billiards?' he asked, as Mrs Bradley turned with him.

'Yes. Not as well as you do, I dare say.'

He gave a short laugh.

'I have had plenty of practice these last days. It is the only room, except my bedroom, into which she does not come, I think. And my bedroom – I lock the door at night!'

'A pretty kettle of fish,' wrote Mrs Bradley to Laura when she went to her room that night, 'and I shall not be at all sorry to bring my visit to an end. Expect me on Monday at midday.'

But there were still Grimston and Bell for her to hear. Curiously enough – yet naturally enough, too, considering how wide was her circle of acquaintances and how far-reaching her own reputation – both approached her, although at different times, with the same request.

Grimston came first. He brought in her early-morning tea.

'I collared it from the maid because I particularly wanted to see you alone and where we wouldn't be overheard,' he said. 'I say, I'm sorry about that three in the morning business. You've forgiven me, haven't you? Please!'

'Forgiven *you*, but not forgotten the unwarrantable intrusion,' said Mrs Bradley solemnly. 'Why, you might have murdered me in my bed, and I none the wiser!'

Grimston laughed, a sincere and youthful sound; then his face darkened as he said:

'Not to beat about the bush – and I do hate asking you; please believe that; but – could you? – I mean, I shan't be able to stay here with Philip once Linda takes command. Could you recommend me for a job if I needed a recommendation?'

'I see no reason why I should, nor why I should not, child. In any case, my recommendation would be of no value. I know nothing of your qualifications, nor of the needs of boys who have a tutor instead of going to school. Why cannot you apply for a post in the usual way, through a scholastic agency?'

'I'm black-listed. I let a boy die.'

'You let a boy die? How was that?' (The suicidal tendency, if it existed, might be capable of explanation, she thought.)

'Yes. It was my first post after I left the University. I had to take the school swimming. I can swim, but I'm no great shakes. A boy got into difficulties. I was on the bank. I watched him struggling. I was afraid to go in after him. When at last I made myself go in, and got to him, it was too late. I got him out, but he died before we could get the water out of his lungs. There was something in the paper – praising me, you know. I couldn't bear it. I told the headmaster the truth, and gave in my resignation. He wouldn't accept it. Said it would look bad for the school. The fatality (he said) was bad enough, but if the parents gave up thinking I was a hero and realized that I was a poltroon (his exact words) things would be ever so much worse. I tried to commit suicide that night. I did cut my throat, but – but not enough. Then he *did* sack me. I couldn't take another post at a school. I couldn't stand it, for one thing, and, for another, I feel sure my reputation would follow me.'

'Nonsense! Look at it in a practical way. *Why* did that boy get into difficulties?'

'Direct disobedience, of course.'

'Exactly.'

'That doesn't absolve a schoolmaster, you know.'

Mrs Bradley regarded him compassionately, and suddenly promised to do her best for him.

After lunch came Bell with a message from Sir Bohun, who needed a word of five letters to give the Lancashire equivalent of what Columbus said when he sighted the West Indies and spotted an animal. Mrs Bradley suggested 'eland', and Bell, having thanked her, hesitated and then asked her whether she happened to know of anybody who needed a secretary.

'I don't think I shall be staying on here after Sir Bohun is married,' he said. 'There are – reasons why I can't. It's been a pretty good billet, and I don't really want to leave, but I don't think I shall be able to help myself. In any case, I expect things will be very different, and I don't suppose I should like it much if I *did* stay.'

Mrs Bradley nodded thoughtfully.

'I cannot make any promises,' she said. Bell murmured gratefully. She looked at him, then, and asked:

'Have you kept the competition papers, by any chance?'

'Yes, I have. I've had no instructions about them, and when that is the case I usually hang on to things until it's obvious Sir Bohun won't ask for them. Why? Do you want to look at them? I can get them for you if you like.'

'I should like to see them.'

'Morbid psychology?'

'Not necessarily morbid.'

'I'll go and get them at once. You'll let me have them back at some time or other, won't you? – just in case Sir Bohun wants them, you know.'

'They are not confidential documents, I take it?'

'Oh, no. Why should they be?'

'Good. They should make very interesting reading. If I might have them to-day . . . I am going home on Monday.'

## CHAPTER 7

# TWO HOSTAGES OF FORTUNE

> 'They are all innocent and mild;
> No grief nor want amongst them found,
> But all are well and safe and sound.'
> THOMAS WASHBOURNE – *Damon Paints the Joys of Heaven*

\*

As it happened, Mrs Bradley did not even remain under Sir Bohun's roof until the Monday. She had written to Laura on the Friday night to catch the morning post, but just before midday on the Saturday she received a telegram.

> *Grandson John wished on you parents called abroad*
> *what instructions Menzies*

This message did not surprise Mrs Bradley. She had known for some time that her second son and his wife might suddenly go abroad again, and she had agreed to take charge of the little boy provided that she could board him out most of the time and, later on, send him to a preparatory school if they looked like being out of the country for any length of time. She had already made preliminary arrangements for him to stay on a farm. One of her former students at Cartaret Training College, where she had reigned for a short but interesting time as Warden of one of the Houses, had married a farmer, and, by a coincidence which she afterwards recognized as the gift of a beneficent Providence, the farm was not very far from Sir Bohun's house.

'Look,' she said to him, 'my grandson will be lonely, perhaps, without another boy for company. Let me have Philip, and Timothy as well, and Nanny Call to keep an eye on all three of them. John is a lively child, healthy and quite well-behaved.'

Sir Bohun Chantrey jumped at it.

'The very thing!' he exclaimed. 'Beatrice, that's really wonderful. I could not wish for anything to fall out more aptly.'

In consequence of this attitude, Mrs Bradley found herself one frosty morning in early January escorting Nanny Call and three little boys to Joysey's Farm, and, later, found herself leaving them there and reverting to the house in Kensington from which she could get to her clinic.

'What a bit of luck that Alice Boorman decided to wed with a farmer,' said Laura, welcoming her employer home with China tea and biscuits. 'She always *was* a sensible sort of old scout. How often do we go and see how the boys are getting on?'

'Once a week, I should think, but not yet. Let us give them time to settle down and get to know one another. We can leave them alone for at least a fortnight. Our dear Alice seems delighted to have them, and she can be relied on, I think, to be kind but firm. I am not so sure about her husband.'

'Oh, he's certain to spoil them, but it won't matter. And I don't know why *you* should carp and cavil. You *always* spoil children.'

As it happened, the three little boys were not destined to be left for a fortnight without visitors, for the smallest, Timothy, was invited to stay with relatives who doted upon him and who did not care much about Philip, a less sunny, more self-contained child.

'Of course, I'm terribly *sorry* about Tim,' said Philip, when his brother had been removed, 'but it does give us more scope.'

To the horror of Alice Cartwright (*née* Boorman), Mrs Bradley approved openly of this unethical attitude.

'*Of course* it will give them more scope,' she pronounced, 'and I am very glad to know that Philip is not hypocritical. He and John are of an age, and will enjoy themselves far more without having the tiny boy tagging along. John is bloody, bold, and resolute, and Philip is clever, and will soon think of mischief far beyond the range of John's intelligence. I have the highest hopes of the association for both of them'.

The boys apparently had the highest hopes of it, too, and settled down to the winter life of the farm, the society of the farm animals, and to an orgy of quiet devilment conceived chiefly in innocence and because of a thirst for experiment.

Both possessed bicycles, and Alice, with an enthusiasm undimmed by some years of teaching geography to unreceptive audiences, showed them how to read an ordnance map of the district. They went out for short runs in the mornings if the weather was moderately fine, and for longer ones after their midday meal, provided that they promised not to sit on the damp ground. They were also under pledge to keep an eye on the time (measured for them by their Christmas-present wrist-watches) and to return to the farm before the light failed.

Having extracted this particular promise easily enough (since as John immediately pointed out, they would want to be back in time for tea), one mild afternoon Alice saw them off. She had not asked them where they proposed to go, and it was as well, perhaps, that this was so, for she would have felt compelled to forbid them to carry out their plans, which included a visit to two railway stations, one of which had been abandoned and left deserted for several years. It had lost its usefulness when a large housing estate had been opened about a mile and three-quarters up the line. A new station had been built to serve this new estate, and the old station had become a mere dump for heavy iron objects whose use and function could only be guessed at.

The boys were not primarily interested in either station, but the symbols showed bridges. It was their object to sit on bicycles propped against the wall of a bridge, and, from this vantage-point, to do a little engine-spotting. It was not until they reached the first of these bridges that John discovered the fact that the station a little beyond the bridge was no longer in use.

'Philip,' he said excitedly, 'look! *A ghost station!* Let's see whether we can explore it!'

It proved easy enough to do this. The up platform was bounded, where it left the roofed-in, sheltered portion of its length for an excursion into the open air, by a wooden fence very easy to scale. This open fence separated part of the platform from a field. It would have taken far less ingenuity than that possessed by a couple of active, lively children to find a means of admittance. In less than three minutes John and Philip were on the platform and were beginning to poke about.

The far-off sound of an approaching train – the line was only an unimportant branch affair, and trains were infrequent – caused the boys to take cover. There was no lack of hiding-places. Whatever the original purpose of the extraordinary specimens of ironwork which had been dumped on the deserted platforms, they certainly afforded shelter. Each boy dived behind a contraption which looked something like an old-fashioned cannon, and prepared to wait until the train had clanked by, for it was a goods train which was approaching.

Suddenly, from behind John, came a sound which had no connexion with the noise of the approaching train. It was a long, persuasive, pleading, heart-hungry whine. The train clanked through the station and rattled into the distance. John came out of hiding and beckoned wildly to his companion, who was dusting himself down.

'Here, Philip!' hissed John, continuing to beckon. 'In the waiting-room! Quick!'

The waiting-room had been directly behind John's hiding-place. It was a dilapidated ruin. The door had gone, and so had most of the ceiling, and the floor was covered in rubble. At one corner, however, the rubble had been cleared, and in the clearance, tethered to a staple fixed in the fireplace wall, was a gigantic dog.

Mrs Bradley and Laura would have recognized it at once as the spit and image of that same *Hound of the Baskervilles* which had put in such a mysterious appearance at the Sherlock Holmes ball. The boys, of course, had not seen the creature before. John went towards it. Philip said:

'Mind how you touch him. He looks fierce.'

'He ought not to show temper, that kind of dog,' said John. 'He's just fed-up with being left alone and being tied up, I expect. Let's undo him and give him a run.'

Philip looked doubtful.

'Pretty silly we should feel if he ran off and we never saw him again,' he rightly observed. 'Wonder who his owner is? Wonder if he's hungry? Wonder why they leave him here like this? It can't be to guard the station because he couldn't do much guarding if he was tied up all the time.'

'Perhaps he's a police dog, and the police are after some crooks, and will come and fetch him when they want him.'

'Could *be*, I suppose, but he doesn't look much like a police dog. They usually have Alsatians. This one isn't an Alsatian. He looks' – he studied the dog which had now stretched its great length along the floor and was taking no more notice of the boys – '*I* think he looks like a cross between a Great Dane and an Irish wolf-hound –'

'And a donkey,' said John giggling. The dog looked at him and uttered a long, bored sigh.

'Miss Campbell is afraid of dogs,' said Philip. 'She's even afraid of spaniels. She says she was never brought up with dogs. They

83

lived in a flat and weren't allowed to have one. *I* think it's silly to be afraid of dogs, but one isn't supposed to pet them when they're chained up. That's only common sense. How long are we going to stay with him? Time's getting on, and we promised to get back before dark.'

'There's time yet, and I don't like leaving the dog. I think he's lonely. Look here, let's wait another quarter of an hour, and then, if there isn't another train, we'll go. I hope our bikes are all right. I think I'll nip up and see.' Before he could leave the platform, however, there came from the distance the sound of another train. 'Perhaps the dog belongs to an engine-driver or someone,' continued John. 'If so, we'd better scram. He might pull up and jump off to have a look at the dog, or feed him.'

They hid again behind some of the junk on the platform, but nobody got off the train, so they sneaked back over the fencing, the way they had come, and were soon on their homeward road.

'An adventurous afternoon, I trust?' said Mrs Bradley, who had joined the party at tea. The boys, who were not old enough to keep much knowledge to themselves, opened up and told her everything that had happened, repeating all their own conversation *verbatim*, and, in fact, several times. Mrs Bradley listened with flatteringly close attention. Hers was only a flying visit. She was back in Kensington by six o'clock, for she and Laura had tickets for a theatre.

'*The Hound of the Baskervilles*, you think?' said Laura, when the tale was unfolded at dinner. 'And Linda Campbell is afraid of dogs, so *she* isn't likely to be the practical joker – or is she? Hardly, I should say. But I can't understand chaining the dog up like that. He seemed such an excellent animal, I thought. It's bad for him if he's kept tied up in that dismal place, and perhaps not properly fed. I say, how would it be if I tazzed down there and had a look at him? The kids can show me where he is.'

Mrs Bradley thought this an excellent idea. All told, the dog was a mysterious factor, and she knew how much Laura loved to exercise what she mistakenly thought of as her detective faculties. Besides, she had been worked hard since the beginning of the autumn, and a week-end on the farm, even at that time of year, and the society of Alice, with whom Laura had been closely associated at college, would do her no harm at all, Mrs Bradley decided.

Laura arrived at the farm on the Friday afternoon in time for tea, and found the household in its usual flourishing condition. She heard at first-hand the tale of the dog at the station, played with the boys, told them a lurid bedtime story, and then settled down for further gossip and reminiscence with Alice, who had not altered much from the self-effacing, wiry, whip-cord creature that she had been at college except that she had filled out a little, and was inclined to boss the so-far unmarried Laura.

'What are you really here for, Dog?' Alice enquired affectionately when her husband had gone off for his Friday evening couple of pints at the local inn. 'You're not here just to find out how Philip and John are going on.'

Laura explained that Mrs Bradley was interested in the dog which the boys had encountered at the ghost station.

'Oh, yes, they told Mrs Bradley all about it,' said Alice. 'I can't think who owns it, but it's very cruel, anyway, to shut it away like that. Do you really think it's the dog you saw at this Sherlock Holmes party?'

Laura had described the party in some detail.

'I don't know,' Laura replied. 'Anyway, I'm going to investigate to-morrow. I shall have to ask the boys how to get there, but I don't really want to take them with me. I'll be much better off on my own.'

'Oh, I can tell you how to get there,' said Alice. 'The ordnance maps are all on that shelf. I'll get the one you want and show you the way.'

She and Laura pored over the map, spending far more time than was necessary to identify the ghost station, and then, when they had picked out Sir Bohun's house and the spot on the edge of the heath where the *Queen of the Circus* stood, Laura told Alice more about the Sherlock Holmes party than she had so far recounted, and finished up with a character sketch (as she saw him) of Manoel Lupez.

'Why did he want to kiss you? You aren't the kissable type, Dog,' commented Alice with comradely honesty.

'I know,' answered Laura, with equally agreeable frankness. 'I think he was just plain bored. However, I smacked his face for the good of the cause, and he complained about me to Sir B.'

'Why? What did he expect you to do?'

'I've been thinking things over,' Laura replied, 'and putting my detective faculties to work. (Don't groan! I know you don't think much of them, but let me tell you that I've been of inestimable service to Mrs Croc. more than once by applying my brainpower to her problems.) Anyhow, the conclusion I've come to is that Manoel, for some reason best known to himself, wanted to get me, and therefore Mrs Croc. and Gavin, out of that house at that time. He thought that if I were flung out, Mrs Croc. would go, too, in support of her P. Sec., and that Gavin (having, possibly, poked him in the nose first) would follow suit. It may be that he was keener to get rid of the boy-friend than of anybody else, and, of course, if Gavin *had* hit him, there would have been nothing for it but the final leave-taking, apologetic or at daggers drawn as might transpire.'

'Why should he want to get rid of Robert?'

'Policeman, chump.'

'Oh, Dog! Why shouldn't he want a policeman in the house?'

'Curiously enough, dear, because people don't when they're up to N.B.G. and, if you ask me, that's just exactly what that Manoel *is* up to. I'd like to know how often he sleeps in that house o' nights.'

'Nonsense! You've got nothing whatever to go on in saying that!'

'I feel it in my Highland bones.'

'Time your Highland bones had more sense. You're prejudiced against Manoel just because he's a foreigner!'

'I'm not, either! I hate racial prejudice, and all that, just as much as you do. More, in fact, because I've got more imagination than you have. No, it's nothing to do with his being a Mexico-Spaniard (and a bull-fighter to boot). It's because he's definitely anti-Bohun, and I *know* he means to do something about him. Sir B. is terrified out of his life. For some time he's been expecting something to happen to him, and he really had us and Gavin there to guard him.'

'But you told me yourself, when we were talking about the party the other day, that Sir Bohun is a little bit mad,' argued Alice reasonably, 'and the first thing mad people do is to get a persecution complex.'

'All right, all right. Well, look here, I'd better get off while the boys are out of the way and can't pester me to tag them along.'

'You can borrow the car – or there's a horse. It's by-roads nearly all the way.'

'I'll walk, thanks. I can think better when I'm walking, and, anyway, I need the exercise. Back in time for tea. Doing more of those potted-meat sandwiches? – Good! I hoped you were. So long! Be seeing you again by the time it's dark.'

## CHAPTER 8

# THE GHOST STATION

' "You are not afraid, are you?"
"Not in the least," I answered.'
GUY BOOTHBY – *Doctor Nikola*

\*

LAURA still retained something of her childhood sense of adventure and romance. The ghost station fascinated her, with its dumps of heavy iron objects to which she could assign no name. Welded on to her original bias towards the strange and the bizarre were the essays of that interpretive and poetic genius Paul Jennings, and, because of his extraordinary and prodigal vision, she saw more in the ghost station than was actually, pedestrianly, there.

Apart from being unable to name any of it, she could not imagine what was the reason for, or the function of, most of the discarded ironwork she saw about her on the two deserted and dirty platforms. Strange objects on wheels, stranger objects without wheels but having rusty, unconventional rollers, objects with large handles and a kind of amphibian frightfulness as though they were alligators prepared to look like logs, or logs prepared to look like alligators, smothered both sides of the station, a nightmare collection of junk to which she could ascribe no possible purpose, either in the past, present, or future.

The dog was there, all right. Laura made it her first business to establish that as a fact. He whined at her approach, and as she spoke to him he backed away, timid and mistrustful. She continued to talk, and proffered the meaty bone with which she had come provided. The dog wagged his tail (he was indeed a hybrid animal, she thought), looked up at her, then took the bone delicately between his teeth and retired to a corner. At the same time Laura heard the sound of an approaching train and, her business with the dog being satisfactorily concluded, she went out to see it go by.

As, however, she was undoubtedly trespassing, she decided that to take cover while she watched might be prudent if somewhat

88

inglorious, and glanced round for a sniping post. As it happened, the station was approached by a considerable bend in the direction from which the train was coming, so that she had plenty of time to leave the ruined waiting-room, and take up a strategic position behind some Emmett apparatus before the train entered the station.

The train passed through at about thirty-five miles an hour, and Laura was about to emerge when an unusual sight caused her to go hastily back into hiding. This apparition was that of a girl on a bicycle who was riding along the yard-wide flattened verge at the side of the railway track.

When she drew level with the ramp which formed the end of the platform, the girl dismounted, pushed the bicycle up the slope and along the platform, and then propped it up against the wall. From the carrier she unstrapped a petrol can, and from a basket on the handlebars she extracted a parcel.

Laura, startled, recognized her as Celia Godley, Sir Bohun Chantrey's twenty-two-year-old niece. She did not know what to do. She did not want to spy on the girl, but she did not intend to disclose her own presence. She found that there was nothing for it but to watch what Celia did, and it was soon clear that the object of the girl's visit to the ghost station was to feed the dog and give it something to drink. These humanitarian activities concluded, she came out of the waiting-room, looked about her, then walked back to where she had left her bicycle. She carried the petrol can, swinging it easily, strapped it on to the carrier, put a screwed-up piece of paper in the basket on the handlebars, and soon was pedalling back by the way she had come.

Laura came out of hiding and dusted her skirt with her hand. She could make nothing at all of the incident.

'Hm!' she said aloud. 'Doesn't look as though my bone will be as good an introduction to a beautiful friendship as I'd hoped. However, this is most intriguing. If it's her dog, why did she streak away from him with the rest of them at the ball? – and why does she keep him in such a peculiar place as this? And if it *isn't* her dog, who's she stooging for?'

She marched up and down the platform for a bit because she was cold. Then she went into the waiting-room to see what the dog had done with her bone. The dog was lying down. His bowl of water, supplied, she felt certain, from the petrol can, was half-empty. Laura glanced round for the bone. A tail wagged half-uncertainly, and the bone was disinterred from beneath an old sack. The dog then lay with it between his paws and looked at her with sagacity. Satisfied that the fresh-looking bone had not been allowed to betray her presence, Laura left the station and walked back to the farm. It was a considerable distance away, and the walk allowed time for thought, but the more she thought, the more puzzling became the whole affair.

Mrs Bradley listened in silence over the telephone to the tale when Laura rang her up that evening, but that she was interested Laura had not the slightest doubt. When the brief narrative was ended, Laura asked the obvious question.

'What do you make of it all?'

'Only one thing seems clear at present,' Mrs Bradley replied. 'The dog does not belong to Celia, but she helps to look after it by taking food and water. It is a mystery, this dog. I should like to find out more about it, I confess. Since, however, it is not our business, I think we shall have to leave matters as they are. The dog has been a mystery from the time of his appearance at the party.'

'I am going there again to-morrow, at the same time, to see what happens. It won't be much trouble to keep away from Celia, and as soon as she has gone I'm going to let the dog loose for a bit. It's cruelty to keep him tied up in that beastly waiting-room. He isn't savage, he's only puzzled and lonely.'

'Well, kindly remember that if he eats you I disclaim all responsibility. However, if I really believed he was dangerous, I should forbid you to go there again. When next I see Sir Bohun I will find out what I can about Celia, but I shall not mention the dog,' said Mrs Bradley. 'How is Alice? Quite well? And how are the little boys?... Excellent, Good-bye, then. Robert is going to drop in on you when his duties permit. He dined here last night and thinks the Gunter case is breaking very nicely. They are pretty sure of a conviction. Once they had interpreted correctly the clue of the dining-club tea-cloth, everything fell into place. Good night, dear child. Sleep well.'

Laura slept as well as she usually did – that is, for the three to four hours which seemed all that was necessary to restore the energy she used up during her day. For the rest of the night she turned over and over in her brain the extraordinary matter of the railway-station *Hound of the Baskervilles*, but this proved to be a waste of time, for she could come to no conclusion at all which made any kind of sense.

She put the matter out of her mind on the following morning, and took the boys out for a ride. The boys were anxious to visit the disused station again, and expressed deep disappointment when she refused to go there with them. Alice backed her up firmly.

'It's no business of yours,' she said, 'and you've no right to poke about where you're not wanted.'

'We could take it a bone when we've got one,' said Philip hopefully, when they got back after their ride. 'When will there be another bone, Aunt Alice?'

'Not for a long time yet, dear,' Alice replied, 'and the dog will be gone by then. They can't keep him there very long. I expect they've nowhere to put him until his kennel arrives, or perhaps the people live in a flat and are leaving him at the station until they move into a house.'

'I only hope your suggestions are not the truth,' said Laura, when the boys had gone to bed. 'That dog is my pet mystery at the moment, and I don't want it to make sense of that sort.'

'You're an incurable romantic, Dog,' said Alice serenely. 'You'd make a mystery out of a steak and kidney pudding!'

'Probably should, at that,' agreed Laura gloomily. 'Never made or cooked one in my life!'

Alice laughed. Laura said soberly:

'Keep the kids busy while I slip away after lunch. I'm going to see that dog again. I shall probably give him a run.'

'Oh, dear! But isn't he savage? The boys said he wasn't, but with John what he doesn't want doesn't exist. You'll be careful, won't you?'

'Oh, yes, but he isn't at all dangerous. I'd love to know how Celia Godley comes into it, though.'

'There's a piece of liver you can have, and I'll mix him up some vegetables and gravy.'

'Shouldn't bother. He seems to be fed and watered. I'll have the liver, though. Let's hope he fancies it.'

When she was ready, she borrowed a strong leather lead, and, the boys having been taken to help the pigman with a boiling of small potatoes, she escaped on to the highroad without difficulty.

The procedure was as it had been the first time. Laura gained the station and took cover. The train went past as before, and at a reasonable distance in its wake (presumably so that she could not be seen from the guard's van) came Celia on her bicycle with food and water for the dog. Laura gave her plenty of time to get away, and then went into the waiting-room. The dog made two gulps of the liver, wagged his tail, and allowed himself to be stroked. Laura released him from his chain, hooked the lead on to his collar, and said encouragingly, 'Come on, then.'

The dog gave a yawn and then a slight snort, and followed her meekly on to the platform. At the sound of an approaching train she dragged him into the waiting-room again, but after the train had passed they resumed their exercise. After a bit she took the lead off. The dog came to heel, and she took him out of the station and on to a rough field for exercise.

'There!' she said, at the end of half an hour. 'That's all for to-day. I'll come and see you again to-morrow. Come on.' He followed her with the greatest docility to the waiting-room.

She kept up this errand of mercy for nearly a fortnight, and usually took the boys with her, for it was clear that the dog was harmless. Her conscience troubled her for leaving Mrs Bradley so long, but every time she telephoned to suggest coming home, her employer emphatically forbade her to do any such thing, adding untruthfully that there was nothing to do in London but go to the pantomime. The weather remained mild and fairly dry, and Laura was only too glad to receive Mrs Bradley's reassurances and remain with Alice and the boys in the country.

At the end of the fortnight she received a disappointment. The boys had driven in to the town with Alice's husband, and so Laura went alone to feed and exercise the dog. She was considerably later than usual because she had waited to get the boys out of the way, so she decided that it would be as well to let the train and Celia come and go before she went into the waiting-room.

The train duly appeared and disappeared, but there was no sign of the girl. The evening, which promised to be misty, began to creep closer. The air was chilly and damp. Laura decided to risk matters, and went towards the waiting-room, speaking to the dog as she went. But the dog was gone and so was the chain. Only the staple to which the animal had been fastened remained to show that he had been there. The waiting-room had been cleaned out and someone had opened the window.

'Well, I'm dashed!' thought Laura. Then an obvious explanation came to her. 'Celia must have got there earlier than usual and taken him out for a walk,' she said to Alice when she got back. 'I'll pop over again to-morrow and make sure.'

The next day she went very much earlier and stood by the waiting-room window. It was still open. There was still no sign of the dog. Laura was considerably disappointed and turned away.

'Was my journey really necessary?' she said aloud. In the utter stillness of the silvery pale of the afternoon whose sunshine seemed to make the station more dingy than usual, her own voice startled her. The station suddenly seemed not only grimy but evil. She glanced about her, shrugged off the unaccountable feeling and walked back along the platform to climb the fence and go home. Suddenly she stopped short, staring at some ominous-looking blotches.

'Good heavens, the brute has savaged someone!' she said. 'Wonder whether it was Celia he went for? Shouldn't have thought he'd go for anybody. By the look of this blood he must have turned pretty grim.' Feeling decidedly grim herself, she searched the platform and looked into a decrepit office where porters had once had their mysterious lair. Then she crossed the line in contravention of the bye-laws and searched the opposite side of the station. There were some stairs which led to the booking office above. She went half-way up, listened, heard nothing, and so returned to the farm.

'Hallo, Dog,' said Alice when Laura appeared. 'Anything interesting happened? You look het up.'

'The dog's gone,' said Laura, 'and before he went he bit someone fairly badly. There's blood about on that platform.'

'Good gracious! Suppose it had turned on you or the boys! I wonder who it went for?'

'There is no evidence to show, duck. Let's hope it was its owner. Anybody who tied a dog up in that disgraceful hole deserves to be bitten, I should say. One thing I can establish – '

'What?'

'I can ride over to Sir Bohun's place to-morrow and find out whether the dog bit Celia Godley.'

'Even supposing he did, I don't see what good it will do to find it out.'

'Knowledge is power,' said Laura owlishly. Directly after the midday meal next day she resisted all the blandishments of the boys, who wanted her to play football with them in an exceedingly miry paddock (for the frost had gone by that time) and rode off to Sir Bohun's house on the excuse of giving him news of Philip's well-being. She found Sir Bohun in an excited state compounded of anxiety and testiness.

'She still isn't back!' he said. Laura was interested to note that Celia Godley, unscathed, was still staying at the house.

'Miss Campbell?' Laura enquired. She thought Celia looked particularly blooming. ('Might be in love,' decided Laura, who fancied herself as a psychologist.)

'Confound her, yes! Well, this is the last time I put up with it! Her explanation was pretty thin before. This time I shall tell her I'm through,' declared Sir Bohun in violent tones. 'Damn it, it's not respectable, all this staying out at night, and I'm determined not to stand for it. Hang it all, it makes me a laughing-stock! No, she's cut her stick once too often. I've had enough of it.'

'I don't blame you, uncle,' said Celia demurely.

'I suppose,' said Laura, 'she couldn't have been bitten by a dog?' Out of the corner of her eye she saw Celia start. There was an audible gasp, too, from that corner of the hearth.

'Bitten by a dog? Why the devil *should* she be bitten by a dog?' Sir Bohun demanded.

'There was such a thing as the *Hound of the Baskervilles* here on the night of the Sherlock Holmes party, if you remember.'

'Hound of the – Look here, young woman, this is no time for nonsense!'

Laura looked at him, and then at Celia. The latter had recovered and was smiling. Laura said no more upon the subject. Instead, she gave such news as there was of young Philip, and took her leave, refusing Sir Bohun's invitation to stay for tea. She went to the nearest call·box and telephoned Mrs Bradley.

'The *Hound of the Baskervilles* has savaged somebody at that derelict railway station. Linda Campbell is missing again. Could there be any connexion?' she suggested.

'Why should there be?' Mrs Bradley mildly enquired.

'I don't know. It's just a thought. The dog isn't at the station any more. He must have been released. He didn't slip his collar, or anything. I wish you'd come down and look into it. There's blood half-way down that platform. The dog may be a killer, for all we know. In fact, I feel in my bones that he is.'

'Very well, dear child, I will come, but I think that your Highland gift of second sight may be myopic for once!'

'Good heavens!' cried Laura, horrified. 'I haven't the Gift! It's just a hunch I've got that all is not well with L. Campbell.'

'Mr Grimston had the same hunch when he told us his dream, child, yet nothing appeared to be wrong.'

'I can't help Grimston's troubles. He's a queer fish, anyway. When shall I tell Alice to expect you?'

'Not at all. I shall go straight to Sir Bohun.'

'You *do* take it seriously, then? Do you mean about the dog, or Linda C.'s disappearance, or both?'

'There is no need to jump to conclusions. Obviously there is more in Miss Campbell's life than her duties as nursery governess or fiancée, but that is as far as we can go. When I have seen Sir Bohun I will contact you again.'

'What do you make of it, Alice?' asked Laura, after the boys had gone to bed.

'Nothing. Why should I make anything of it?' Alice enquired serenely. 'I don't know Miss Campbell. I don't even know the dog. Can you take onion soup for your supper?'

Laura went to bed that night full of onion soup and, as she herself expressed it afterwards, very strange forebodings. Such strange forebodings did she have that she got up as soon as it was light, made tea, took some up to Alice, and announced her intention of taking a stout stick and returning to the ghost station.

'Not without *me*,' said Alice. 'Wait a bit, and I'll get us both some breakfast.'

'What's up?' asked her farmer husband sleepily; and when he was told he said, 'We'll all three go. If the dog has turned savage and happens to be anywhere around – '

'He can't be,' said Laura; but, for once in her life, she let the other two have the last word.

# CHAPTER 9

# DESDEMONA?

'And I have done a hellish thing,
And it would work 'em woe:
For all averred I had killed the bird
That made the breeze to blow.'
SAMUEL TAYLOR COLERIDGE – *The Ancient Mariner*

*

IT was a strange little procession that went to the ghost station
that next time. There was mist everywhere, for the landscape was a
patchwork of sand, gravel, and water. A river wound, between
banks clothed with nondescript, uninteresting bushes, near to
Alice's farm and the railway, its natural sluggishness quickened
into some sort of life by a lasher beside a mill. In the gravel pits the
wastes of water stretched like lakes of the dead beneath a canopy
of ghostly miasma. The only natural pond in the neighbourhood,
bordered by short winter grass (startlingly emerald even at that
hour of the morning), could have been the mere to which Sir
Bedivere consigned Excalibur. A cow or two loitered near its
border, and sedge and a clump of bulrushes gave an unreal, picture-
postcard effect. This, and the mist, reminded Laura of angel-choirs
in American films.

'That's where the local mosquitoes breed,' said Alice, turning
her head. 'Come on, Dog. Don't loiter. I want to get back and
cook the breakfast.'

They reached the station and slid down the bank on to the platform. Laura found herself glad to have the other two with her. She
had a sixth-sense impression that, even apart from themselves, the
station was not deserted.

'What exactly do you expect to find here, Dog?' enquired her
matter-of-fact and agile friend, joining her on the platform and
looking round for her heavier, more slowly-moving husband.

'I don't know,' Laura replied. She still felt thoroughly uneasy.
'I don't like the thought of that dog. If the person he savaged was
alone – '

96

She led the way towards the covered part of the platform and pointed out the blotches of blood. Alice's husband bent to examine them.

'Wish I'd brought Bruce,' he said. 'He'd probably trail the chap so that we could find out what happened to him. But, you know, Laura, I shouldn't think a dog of the sort you described – a Great Dane, wasn't he? – would maul anybody to this extent. There's a lot of blood here, and it looks as if it spurted from a wound. It isn't just drops of blood, such as you'd get if a dog bit you. Let's look about us. I shouldn't think anybody who lost that amount of blood could have got very far without help. What's up these stairs?'

'Don't you go,' said Alice, darting ahead. 'Your two tons might bring the woodwork down!' She leapt up the stairs at top speed, Laura after her, and the heavy young farmer, slower off the mark but willing to risk his neck, followed in the rear.

The stairs proved perfectly sound, and the farmer's hunch was justified. Lying close up against the locked doors of the disused booking-office was the body of Linda Campbell. Alice, in the van, gave a groan. Laura knelt down and picked up a limp hand.

'*Rigor* over and done with, I suppose,' she said, gently replacing the icy hand beside the pathetic body.

'The telephone from here is bound to be disconnected,' commented the taciturn farmer. 'Laura and I had better stay, Alice, love, while you go off and phone a doctor and the police.'

There was no necessity for argument, so Alice went down the stairs at once, ran along the platform, climbed the bank and, remembering that there was a public telephone very near the ghost station, she made for that instead of taking the longer route to the farm.

It was not the first time that Laura had seen unnatural death. She and the farmer turned their backs, as by tacit agreement, on the dead girl, and gazed out of a dirty window on to the railway line below. Neither spoke.

After a short interval Alice reappeared.

'I've telephoned Mrs Bradley as well,' she said. 'I didn't know whether I ought to tell Sir Bohun Chantrey, but I thought it better not. It would be the business of the police to tell him, no doubt. Besides, from what you've said from time to time, Dog, it seems possible that someone at the house is responsible for – this.'

Unlike the others, she had been gazing at the body, but with compassion, not with curiosity. Death had given Linda Campbell a softer, more youthful appearance than had been hers in life, although Alice, who had never encountered her then, did not realize this, but only wondered that Laura, who was tolerant, should have disliked the dead girl so much.

Laura, staring out through the grime and the cobwebs, was thinking her own thoughts. There was not much doubt as to the cause of death. As soon as she had knelt down beside the body, she had seen the tear in the transparent mackintosh and the tear immediately below in the cloth of the light-grey suit. She had marked, too, how the blood had stained both garments. Stabbed to the heart – a phrase with an olde-tyme flavour which, in less dreadful circumstances, would have made Laura smile – was the obvious description of the manner in which Linda Campbell had come by her death.

But if the means by which the death had been accomplished were obvious, the identity of the murderer was not obvious at all. (That Linda had been murdered Laura had no doubt whatever. The absence of the weapon indicated murder quite clearly, for accident seemed out of the question.) There was only one crumb of satisfaction to be got from the whole shocking business – at any rate the dog was not to blame! At least – Laura swung round and stood gazing intently at the body – it did not *look* as though the dog was to blame. The nylon stockings – Laura gingerly raised first one of the legs and then the other – were very slightly mud-splashed but there were no rents or tears. The same, so far as Laura could see without turning the body over, was true of the clothing. Except for one thing, the bloodstained slits in the waterproof and the suit were the only evidence of violence.

What the one thing was Laura did not discover until Mrs Bradley arrived at the farm. The police took statements from the three who had discovered the body, and heard the tale of the dog on the station. They appeared to attach no importance to it.

'That wasn't done by a dog, Miss,' said the inspector who took Laura's statement. 'Not even the broken breast-bone.'

'What did he mean by that?' asked Laura, when Mrs Bradley came to the farm later on in the morning.

'Whoever stabbed Linda Campbell must have had to press on

the breast-bone to detach the weapon, I imagine,' Mrs Bradley replied. 'I am surprised that the police made mention of it to you.'

'I bask in the reflected light of Gavin's glory. That's why they unleash their tongues. Seriously, I think the man was probing for information. I don't mean that they suspect me, but they can't see why I ever went to the ghost station at all.' She paused and looked troubled. 'I suppose I'd better stop calling it a ghost station now. I take it she was killed where I saw the blood on the platform?'

'There does not seem any doubt of that. The police would not suspect you of guilty knowledge. The broken breast-bone is a matter of interest. The weapon, which would have had a very sharp point, must have passed completely through the body. It must have taken tremendous force to run the girl through like that. No wonder the murderer broke the breast-bone to get the blade out again.'

'You mean he had to put his foot on her as she lay there?' asked Alice, horrified by this picture.

'Undoubtedly so.'

Laura spent the remainder of the day racking her brains as to the significance of this observation. Mrs Bradley, after the midday meal, went off to see how Sir Bohun Chantrey had received the news of the death. She found the baronet in a state of great agitation, but not on Linda Campbell's account.

'Now what do you think, Beatrice?' he exclaimed. 'I had that young Grimston in to tell him I was dispensing with his services and here was fifty pounds in lieu of notice, don't you know – ?'

'In lieu of notice? Why, what had he done that you wanted to get rid of him like that?'

'Nothing, except to keep on bleating about poor Linda and repeating his stupid dream. The police have been here, and he's been fool enough to tell it to them as well. They'll run him in if he persists. I'm sure they'll run him in, and I'm positively sure he didn't do it. He's a silly fellow, it's true, but he's not as silly as that!'

Mrs Bradley admired the choice of adjective very much.

'Silly?' she repeated thoughtfully. 'Is he a silly fellow, then?'

'Damn' silly, I should say. But, apart from that, who'd want to kill Linda, anyway? She wasn't worth it.'

'But she was worth marrying?'

'Hardly the same thing, Beatrice. Anyway, if they do run him
in he'll go to bits. Probably confess to it as soon as not, just to shut
them up and keep them quiet. The devil of it is that I don't know
how to help him. I wish you'd have a word with the chap. He's
nearly off his head. Keeps saying that Manoel must have done it!
What would Manoel do a thing like that for, I should like to
know?'

Mrs Bradley, remembering her conversations with that brier on
Sir Bohun's rose-bush, could have told him very easily, but she
held her peace, except to say:

'So the police suspect murder, do they? Did they tell you that,
as well as the fact of the death?'

'They haven't much option, Beatrice. Apart from the fact that
the poor girl has been spiked right through the heart and out the
other side, the breast-bone is crushed. It's a most terrible business.
My own view is that one of those gangster thugs attacked her. Her
handbag and her watch (cost me a hundred and twenty pounds,
that watch – engagement present – so I knew it was worth stealing)
have both disappeared. The police are only on to Grimston because
he *will* keep babbling about that ridiculous dream. They've decided
he isn't right in the head. Mind you, I could have told them that
myself. Never *has* been right in the head, so far as I'm aware, and
took it hard when Linda turned him down.'

Mrs Bradley clicked her tongue sympathetically.

'I should be interested to talk with him,' she said. Then she
added with unusual abruptness, 'I have never been able to see why
you kept him here once Philip had gone away.'

'Oh, that? Well, the terms of his engagement weren't up, and
one likes to be fair.'

'There was no need to keep Mr Grimston under the same roof as
Miss Campbell, though, was there, when once the engagement
was announced? It seemed rather unkind.'

'I never thought of that. Grimston knew what had happened
and didn't give his notice, and I've had Mrs Dance here all the
time to keep things head to wind.'

'Your niece, Miss Godley, too, I understand. Laura Menzies
met her here the day she called.'

'Celia? Yes. I don't pretend to understand young women. She
was supposed to be off to Switzerland for the winter sports, but,
instead, she decided to stay on here. I'd be flattered if I weren't

perfectly certain there was an ulterior motive. You don't think she's fallen for Grimston or Bell, I suppose?'

'Nothing but a love affair – preferably a clandestine one – should keep a girl of her age from toboggans and skis, I feel.'

'My idea, exactly. It's wonderful how great minds think alike.'

Mrs Bradley, who did not claim a great mind for herself, and who was quite certain that Sir Bohun did not possess one, assented gravely.

'I have often noticed it,' she said. 'When can I see Mr Grimston?'

Grimston, when interviewed, was gloomy.

'I haven't a dog's chance,' he said. 'They've got chapter and verse, all right. Somebody's told them the tale, and I'll wager it wasn't Sir Bohun. He's an old fool, take him for better or worse, but he isn't a two-timer.'

'Your slang is out of date, Sir Bohun is not old, and your choice of words from the marriage service is enlightening, Mr Grimston. What makes you think the police suspect you of murder?'

'Well, about myself and Linda . . . my feelings for her were well-known in this house.'

'But in that case you would have killed Sir Bohun, not Miss Campbell, wouldn't you?'

'Difficult to say.' He frowned, trying to work it out. 'And, of course, I *did* find the body, didn't I?'

This statement impressed Mrs Bradley.

'I shouldn't worry,' she said, and in such dulcet accents that Grimston looked at her gratefully.

'I know that's just bromide,' he said, 'and yet I believe you really mean it.'

'Did you,' asked Mrs Bradley earnestly, 'recently go to see a man about a dog?'

'I?' He looked puzzled. 'What do you mean?'

'Nothing, if you do not know what I mean, child. Now tell me all about the body.'

'Finding it?'

'And all the rest. Once you have told it to a sympathetic listener, you can forget it. Come, now! All the details, including the way in which they struck you at the time.'

'The details?' He appeared to lapse into deep thought.

'He is wondering what to leave out,' said Mrs Bradley to herself.

'I hope I shall not be given exactly the same story as the one he has given to the police.'

Grimston soon made up his mind.

'I had better begin with my dream. You remember my dream?' he said.

'Very clearly. Astonishing that it should in some measure have anticipated the facts.'

'Not only astonishing, but awkward,' Grimston retorted. 'The police don't like it a bit. I knew something would happen .to Linda,' he went on in a different tone. 'She was playing the fool all round.'

'So your so-called dream was nothing of the sort, but was intended as a warning to her. I think that must be what you mean.'

'That's about the size of it. She'd told me I'd got no chance with her, and I knew she was angling for Sir Bohun. At the same time she was trying to run Lupez, who's dangerous – I've tried to drop a word to young Celia Godley, but she won't listen – Bell, who didn't want her; she embarrassed him; and Dance, who's ready for anything because he's rather in despair, poor chap; doesn't want his divorce to go through; still in love with that box in which sweets compacted lie, that fascinating little devil Brenda. Why, Linda even tried to fasten on to that C.I.D. chap who came to the Sherlock Holmes thing. Didn't you notice? She got the brush-off there all right! I suppose handsome, manly policemen have to learn to protect themselves from designing women, don't they?'

'Undoubtedly. But tell me about the body.'

'The body!' He laughed. 'That's about all Linda ever was, I suppose – a body!... It was this way: I've been at a loose end, as you can understand, since young Philip has been at the farm. Sir Bohun has continued my usual salary, and has given me the library to catalogue, but I can't spend all day doing that. I've got into the habit of taking a morning walk, whatever the weather. I intend to do some pot-holing in the summer, so I thought I'd toughen myself up.

'Well, around here, of course, the heath is the obvious place for rough walking, so that's where I began to do most of my training, with some road-work thrown in for good measure. Sir Bohun left me to my own devices, so I'd leave the house at half-past seven or even earlier – before it was really daylight, you know – and do my trot around for perhaps a couple of hours.

'Most mornings it's been misty. I've always been fascinated by mist and fog. This side of the heath it's swampy, and the miasma over that, these winter mornings, has been like something out of a ghost story or the more horrifying sort of fairy tale. It's generally pretty misty over the gravel pits, too – I suppose because of all that water – so I usually made for that big pit on the path to the village of –'

'Common Row?'

'That's it – Common Row. I don't know what's come over my memory for names since this rotten business blew up.'

Mrs Bradley could have given him two explanations. She wondered which was the correct one in his case. Either he had some sufficient reason for subconsciously deleting the name of the village from his mind, or else he was trying to substitute Common Row for a name with guilty associations, the very fact that these *were* guilty being sufficient reason for his not being able to produce the substituted name as quickly as he might have wished.

She made no comment upon his last remark, and waited for him to continue.

'Well, I was jog-trotting along on the grass at the side of the track – the path itself was slippery – and I remember thinking, as I've often thought before, how much like the superstructure of a battleship some of that excavating machinery is. I was following the track where it turned off towards the workings. At that time in the morning – it was only just beginning to be really light – the chaps who worked there hadn't come on the job, so it was all very nice and private. Well, the first shock I had was seeing on the ground a very nice silk scarf, a yard square at least. I picked it up. It was damp from having been out all night, and while I was wondering where I'd seen it before, I found Linda. I literally fell over her, and went sprawling. I couldn't believe she was dead, but there was no doubt about it. I left the body where it was. Of course, the silk scarf was hers. I must have seen her with it dozens of times. I don't think there's any more to tell. I rang up the police, of course, and told Sir Bohun, and – well, that's about all, except that Sir Bohun has dismissed me.'

'Thank you,' said Mrs Bradley. She gave him a keen glance. 'She couldn't have been the victim of a suicide pact, by any chance?'

'Suicide? Oh – oh, surely not! Do you mean Bell funked it, and made off? What makes you think that?'

'I do not know that I *do* think it. It was just a passing idea. I don't think she *wanted* to marry Sir Bohun, you know. The money and position attracted her. I think that was all.'

'I know it was! The damned little fool!' He turned away. He was in tears.

'Well, well,' said Mrs Bradley to Sir Bohun, as soon as they met. 'So your Mr Grimston found the body, did he?'

Sir Bohun looked startled.

'You know, I was told he'd said that. The shock of hearing about poor Linda's death on top of my giving him notice has sent the poor chap off his rocker. You'll have to look after him, Beatrice. Get him away from here quick. What a blessing it's been discovered before he got at young Philip again! Homicidal, probably. Poor Linda! She played with fire there! Bless my soul! Poor fellow! Mind you, I've suspected it before. By the way, you'll stay the night, Beatrice?'

'No, thank you. I am staying at the farm. Laura will be there with my correspondence. To-morrow we shall go for a walk, I expect, and talk about poor Mr Grimston.'

'Why do you think the poor fellow thinks he found the body?'

'I think the heath has certain associations for him.'

'With Linda?'

'Yes. It is associated in his mind with guilt. I think he seduced her by those gravel pits. There is plenty of cover among those bushes.'

'She seduced *him*, you mean, the poor young fool, and drove him off his rocker afterwards!' said Sir Bohun. 'Well, I hope she left Bell alone, that's all. I feel I've had a lucky escape, but that's not a respectful thought, I'm afraid, now that the poor girl is dead.'

# CHAPTER 10

# CONTACT

'Oh, who be ye would cross Lochgyle,
That dark and stormy water?
Oh, I'm the Chief of Ulva's Isle,
And this Lord Ullin's daughter.'
CAMPBELL – *Lord Ullin's Daughter*

\*

THE morning's walk was long and, to Laura, at first incomprehensible. It was pleasant enough, however. There was a cold snap in the air conducive to exercise, and the ice on various puddles crunched purposefully beneath the feet of the walkers as they tramped in amicable accord along the road which led to the heath and the *Queen of the Circus*.

About a mile and a half from Alice's farm they came to the meandering little river which here bordered a marsh. 'I don't think we can explore the swamp with any advantage either to ourselves or to the enquiry,' Mrs Bradley remarked. 'Let us try the banks of the river.'

A narrow path ran beside the stream. At the foot of the bridge there was access to this path down a shelving bank. They gained it and followed it for about a mile and a quarter. Mrs Bradley then looked at her watch.

'What are we looking for?' asked Laura.

'Possible ways to the abandoned railway station, child.'

'Well, there hasn't been a bridge, and we're on the wrong side of the stream.'

'Very true. Let us return to the highway. Keep your eyes open, won't you?'

'If only I knew what I was supposed to be looking for!' Laura exclaimed.

'It is better that you do not know. Report to me anything which strikes you as being out of the ordinary,' her implacable employer replied. They tramped along the highway for another quarter of a mile. The peculiar mixture of urban and rural scenery was both

interesting and repellent. On the one side, once they had passed
the swamp, was the outline of a factory building. Almost opposite
this was a small market garden. At the entrance to this garden Mrs
Bradley halted.

'It says we're to beware of the dog,' Laura pointed out.

'And since when have you and I been afraid of dogs, child?
Remember the heroic front we displayed when confronted by the
*Hound of the Baskervilles!*'

'You think the *Hound of the Baskervilles* might live here? I
should hardly think so, you know, right on a main road like this.'

Mrs Bradley made no reply, and Laura went with her up to a
very small bungalow. A woman with a deeply suspicious expression
opened the door.

'We're not selling,' she said flatly, 'so get out.'

'I am extremely perplexed,' said Mrs Bradley. 'Is not this the
Curlew Kennels? I want to buy a dog.'

'We've only one dog here,' said the woman roughly, 'and he
don't take to strangers. Didn't you see the notice? Can't you read?'

'Is your dog homicidal, then?'

'He might be – given the chance!'

'Perhaps we ought not to provide the chance,' said Mrs Bradley
hastily to Laura. The woman snorted sardonically. Laura laughed
aloud, and the woman's face changed suddenly.

'If you want to buy a dog,' she said, 'you better try Jim Reynolds'
place. I never heard of those kennels you mentioned.'

'And *I* have never heard of Jim Reynolds,' said Mrs Bradley.
'How do we find him?'

The woman gave directions.

'Bit of luck it's on our way,' said Laura as they departed. 'I
should have been most put out if we'd had to turn in our tracks.
Why did we annoy her? And what caused us to knock at her door
in the first place?'

'Instinct,' Mrs Bradley replied, 'and it has played us false, as it
so often does. Man is a reasoning animal. So much for civilization.'

'In other words,' said Laura, with her usual shrewdness, 'you
know the answer, and you're looking for proof. I suppose it's of
no use to ask you who did kill Linda Campbell?'

'I know who, and I think I know why. I know – or can guess –
how, and, of course, from the medical evidence, we all know
when.'

'Then what *don't* you know?'

'As you yourself suggested, how to bring it home to the guilty person.'

'Are we going to visit Jim Reynolds?'

'Oh, no. If you feel adventurous at any time, you might come back to this woman's place, and take a look at her dog. I should like to be perfectly sure.'

'Then you think – ?'

'I think it was interesting that she would not allow us to see him, but I attach no particular importance to the fact. Now for the *Queen of the Circus*.'

But before they reached the road-house it was evident that Mrs Bradley had another port of call. She passed by the gipsy encampment (one of the caravans, Laura noted, possessed a television aerial), and also by a rubbish dump where a man and two youths were sorting cardboard boxes, old iron, and newspapers; but she stopped outside a tall, double-fronted house whose broad door was approached by a flight of stone steps.

'Every window,' she pointed out to Laura, 'has a different kind of curtaining. What do we deduce from that?'

'A sort of respectable lodging-house, I suppose.'

'Exactly, and for women only, I have discovered. I propose to knock on the door and enquire whether there is a room to let.'

'Whatever for?'

'I have no ideas beyond dogs, child.'

She gave her secretary a nod, and walked up the steps. Laura strolled a few yards further along the road. From a side view the house seemed to go a long way back, and still in no two rooms was the curtaining quite the same.

'What a rabbit-warren of old tabbies it must be,' thought Laura, in confused metaphor. She heard the front door slam, and strolled back. There was no sign of Mrs Bradley. 'Copped behind the Iron Curtain! Wonder how long she'll be?' Laura always thought in words, the fruits, she was fond of explaining, of having been exceptionally gifted in essay writing at school. She wandered away.

Mrs Bradley had been admitted by a nervous-looking middle-aged woman who was wearing a uniform which appeared to be a cross between that of a hospital nurse and of a nun of the Anglican Church.

'Come in, by all means,' she said, 'but I'm afraid I can't promise

107

you anything, as I told the Reverend Stopley. We're quite full up,
I'm afraid. I'm afraid we shall have to ask you to wait for a little
while. I don't think it will be very long, if you could manage until
then. Old Mrs Finch is failing, Doctor says, but, of course, he can't
set a time limit. Perhaps you would like to have a look round while
you're here.'

'I seem to be here under false pretences,' said Mrs Bradley.
'I am connected with the Home Office.'

'Oh!' said the woman, dismayed. 'But there's nothing of that
sort here! Oh, dear me, no! We take only the most *respectable* poor!
I am afraid you have been misinformed. Our boarders have never
been in *any* sort of trouble, I can assure you! We take only recommendations from clergymen, you know, and they are quite, quite
aware of our rules.'

'I think we are still at cross purposes,' said Mrs Bradley with
her mirthless grin. 'The Home Office is not in the least concerned
to look into the private affairs of this excellent institution which is
doing such invaluable work. No, indeed.' She stopped, and
regarded the matron of the home with the loving smile of a shark
as it turns on its side and opens its mouth for prey.

'I – I see,' said the woman. 'Then – what – ?'

'Exactly. I wonder whether we might go somewhere where we
shall not be overheard?' (She had become aware of a stealthy
footstep on the stair and had seen a shadow appear where the thin
winter light picked out the banisters.)

'By all means.' The matron led the way to a door which opened
off the right-hand side of the hall. The room to which it admitted
them was furnished as an office, but contained a couple of ancient
easy-chairs. The matron closed the door, indicated the slightly
less worn of the chairs to her visitor and seated herself in the other.
'And now, Mrs – '

'Bradley. Doctor Beatrice Lestrange Bradley. I see that you have
never heard of me. I had better produce my credentials.'

'Oh, not at all! Not at all, Doctor Bradley!'

Mrs Bradley, who would have been hard put to it to produce
anything except the small notebook which was her invariable
companion, nodded amiably and fixed the matron with a basilisk
eye.

'Well, now,' she said, 'to explain my business here. You have
read in the newspapers, I take it, that the dead body of a young

woman has been found on a deserted railway station not so very
far from this house.'

'I did not read of it myself – I don't read the newspapers – but
Miss Galbraith has been full of it. *Not* our best type, I'm afraid.
In fact – difficult. Very difficult. She has been on the stage, and she
finds it hard to settle to the kind of life we lead here. If it had not
been for the Reverend Snaith, who happens to be very sorry for
her, I would have preferred not to take her. She is not very
manageable, I'm afraid.'

Mrs Bradley had begun to be fascinated by the numbers of
things of which the matron appeared to be afraid. Like that
humane genius Sigmund Freud, Mrs Bradley did not believe that
people used words at random. Censorship was always present,
but the subconscious mind was desperately honest in the sense
that it was apt to produce the truth at very awkward times. The
matron certainly *was* afraid – afraid of responsibility, most probably – and her constant use of the word, in contexts where it
appeared to make nonsense of itself, was revealing.

'The less inhibited your Miss Galbraith is, the better for my
purpose,' said Mrs Bradley briskly. 'You say she has read about
the case?'

'In *all* the Sunday papers, I'm afraid. The Sunday papers and
her daily ten cheap cigarettes are what she spends her money on.
Her nephew pays for her keep here. We charge very little, of course,
as we have connexions with various charitable organizations, but
I'm afraid he can ill spare the money.'

Mrs Bradley wagged her head solemnly. A knowledge of the
significance of most apparently altruistic actions caused her to
suppose that the nephew, whoever he was, might prefer to make
considerable financial sacrifices rather than have an aged and
slightly disreputable aunt to live with him. She did not mention
this view to her present audience, but remarked cheerfully:

'She sounds just the kind of person who might be very useful
to us.'

'Yes, well, I'm afraid she's out at present. She goes for a walk
on the heath every fine morning with her dog.'

'Her dog?' The matron did not understand Mrs Bradley's
prompt reaction to this word. She nodded unhappily.

'She refuses to be parted from it. Pets are not allowed here
except for cage-birds, and not many take advantage of that. I my-

self had a dear pussy, but when this great dog came along I had to get rid of her. She would not have been safe. I'm afraid I have sometimes harboured very uncharitable feelings towards Miss Galbraith.'

'I am sure you must have, done. Oh, well, if she is not here, I won't detain you any longer. By the way, I suppose Miss Galbraith's dog hasn't had a *holiday* recently?'

'A holiday? Not exactly a holiday. He was hired to take part in a film, I understand. I don't know what they paid her, but I suspect her, I'm afraid' – the matron lowered her voice – 'I *suspect* her of having smuggled *drink* into the house. Of course, if I had been able to prove it, she would have had to go. We couldn't begin *that* sort of thing!'

'Of course not. Of course not. Well, good-bye, Matron.' Mrs Bradley rose.

'I'm afraid I still don't know why you want to see Miss Galbraith,' said the matron. 'Is it secret official business?'

'No, not secret. Official, of course.'

'Oh, yes. Oh, I see. Well, thank you so much for calling. Might I – might I use your name when I write to our Committee?'

'Certainly. I will give you one of my cards.' She had just remembered that Laura had pushed two or three of these misleading, grandiose objects inside the cover of the notebook. Mrs Bradley left the matron to study the card. The matron looked awe-stricken. Laura, who had had the cards printed, had not stinted Mrs Bradley's share of honours.

'*Dame!*' murmured the matron ecstatically. 'Not only *Doctor*, but *Dame!* Dame Beatrice Adela Lestrange Bradley – ' She continued to peruse the card, mouthing the formidable degrees which followed the aristocratic announcement. Mrs Bradley turned at the gate and bowed. The matron returned the bow, looking slightly dazed; then she skipped down the steps to the gate. 'You *will* come and see us again, won't you, Dame Beatrice? Any time at *all!* We shall be *honoured* to meet you.'

'Such is fame!' said Laura, grinning, when, as they pursued their way towards the road-house, Mrs Bradley gave an account of the interview. 'Makes you think a bit, though. After all, anybody could have one of those cards printed, I suppose, and most people would be boobs enough to fall for it, whether it was true or not.'

'You terrify me, child,' said Mrs Bradley. 'Now, as soon as we get on to the heath, keep a watchful eye open.'

'I thought we were going to have lunch at the *Queen of the Circus!*'

'We are, but I am anxious to meet a Miss Galbraith, who resides at the house I've just left. According to the list which I read in the matron's office, lunch is served at twelve. It is now half-past eleven, so I imagine that Miss Galbraith should soon be approaching the house. Elderly ladies dislike to miss their food.'

'So do younger ones,' retorted Laura. 'I'm already dying for mine. I wonder what sort of a meal the *Queen of the Circus* can produce?'

'My own experience there was pleasant, I seem to remember.'

'I say,' said Laura suddenly, 'do you see what I see?'

'How can I tell, child? What I see are several automobiles, a motor cycle, three bicycles, a young woman accompanied by two children and – '

'The *Hound of the Baskervilles!*' cried Laura. 'It must be! There couldn't be two!'

'I was about to add that I can also see an elderly woman and with her a large and apparently even-tempered dog.'

'I say! This seems to add up! What do you want me to do?'

'I want you to stroll on ahead of me, and go into the *Queen of the Circus.*'

'Good-o! I say, the old girl's pretty hearty if she takes the hound out for walks in weather as cold as this.'

'She is not only hearty. She may be in considerable danger, if what I suspect is true,' said Mrs Bradley.

'I thought you had some idea that the dog we weren't allowed to see might qualify.'

'There is nothing to show that there was only *one Hound of the Baskervilles*, child.'

'But the dog at the station was the very spit and image of the one which turned up at the Sherlock Holmes party that night, you know.'

> '*And, which was strange, the one so like the other*
> *As could not be distinguished but by names.*

It is not only the twins in the *Comedy of Errors* who could not be told apart. Two puppies of the same litter may be widely different in temperament, but in appearance – '

111

'So *that's* what you think!' exclaimed Laura. 'Miss Galbraith's dog was the original *Hound of the Baskervilles* at the Sherlock Holmes party, and the market garden dog was the one I saw at the railway station! Oh, I say! That explains a lot!'

'It explains nothing at all,' said Mrs Bradley. 'And now you would like your beer. Go along, and don't hurry. I will just pass the time of day with Miss Galbraith, if this is she.'

Laura walked on ahead. When she came to the woman with the dog she stopped. The dog stopped, too. Laura fondled his head and patted him. When she straightened up the enormous animal stood on his hind legs, put his paws on her shoulders, and licked her cheek. Mrs Bradley came up as Laura, sturdy though she was, staggered under the impact.

'Dr Livingstone, I presume?' she said to the owner of the dog, as Laura, recovering her balance, removed the huge paws from her shoulders. The raddled lady looked puzzled.

'I'm sure I haven't the honour,' she replied, 'though I seem to have seen you before.'

'I have just come from your lodgings,' said Mrs Bradley. 'I passed you some time in November out on the heath. I am delighted to make your acquaintance, Miss Galbraith. I believe that is not your stage name, though?'

'Yolanda Fleur, dear. What exactly was it? If you're the Income Tax, I don't have any income while I'm resting.'

'I have no connexion with the Income Tax authorities, my dear Miss Galbraith. It is in connexion with your profession that I have come to see you. I enquired at the –'

'At the Cats' Home?' Miss Galbraith supplied, with a gurgle of laughter. 'Oh, did you, dear? And to what exactly – ?'

'We were wondering whether you would care to appear in a play. You would have to go north, I'm afraid, so perhaps it wouldn't interest you.' She motioned Laura to be off.

'North? How far north?' Miss Galbraith's decision to accept the offer could be taken for granted, Mrs Bradley noted.

'The north-east of Scotland. The theatre is in Aberdeen.'

'Would there be a job for Dusty there?'

Mrs Bradley inspected the enormous animal with interest.

'If he could please his previous employers he could please us. I do not doubt it. I have the highest reports of his work.'

'I understand all right about the film people,' said the old actress, 'but I still wonder what that little caper was in November. You wouldn't know about that. Some young woman came along and asked me to hire Dusty out for a party. I said the dog wasn't used to children and I wouldn't have him pulled about, but she said it wasn't children and that I could come with him if I liked and make sure everything was all right. Ever so nice she was, and offered three guineas. There was only one thing I didn't like. She wanted to touch him up here and there with luminous paint. Still, I felt sure she wouldn't hurt or frighten him. I suppose she wanted him for charades or something of that sort. Anyway, I agreed so long as she promised to fetch him and bring him back, and chain him up quietly as everybody at the Cats' Home was certain to be in bed. I was a bit worried when it turned so foggy, but a gentleman turned up to fetch him and I don't know who brought him back, but he was there all right in the morning.'

'That is extremely interesting,' said Mrs Bradley. 'Now, is it convenient for you to travel to Scotland to-morrow? It is? Splendid! The matron at the hospital will vouch for me. I will send a taxi for you, then. You will need a letter of introduction and the address of the repertory company in Aberdeen, and I had better, perhaps, provide for your expenses now.'

This unusual series of arrangements appeared not to surprise Miss Galbraith. She seemed to be accustomed to extraordinary transactions. She took the pound notes, counted them and merely observed:

'I dare say you'd like a receipt.'

'You can send it to me from Aberdeen. Here is my card,' Mrs Bradley replied, extracting one of these impressive recommendations and handing it over. 'And now I wonder whether you can describe the people who hired Dusty?'

But Miss Galbraith was vague. Her description of the woman could have fitted Linda Campbell, Brenda Dance or, at a pinch, Celia Godley. About the men she was a little clearer. The first man she had seen was middle-aged and spoke with a thick foreign accent – German, she thought, but she 'wasn't much up in languages'. The man who had hired the dog for the film people was English, was much younger than the first man, did not give the idea of being on the stage – 'you can't often mistake them, dear, if you've been in the profession as long as I have' – but, Miss Galbraith was almost certain, had been wearing a wig.

The conversation continued until Laura reappeared and joined them, the dog showing the same affection for her as he had done when they had met before. With mutual expressions of friendliness, Miss Galbraith and Mrs Bradley parted, and, as they walked onwards for lunch, Mrs Bradley gave Laura details of what had proved to be a most interesting and, in some respects, a most enlightening conversation.

'Poor old party,' said Laura. 'What happens when she gets to Scotland?'

'She will find the company avid to receive her. *The Argonauts* are on tour with *Peter Pan*, and their producer is a personal friend of mine. He will use Miss Galbraith and keep her busy for a week or two whilst we obtain the facts we need. As soon as I realized how the murder had been committed, and by whom, I foresaw that the owner of the *Hound of the Baskervilles* might, at some time, need protection.'

'Well, I'm dashed!' said Laura. 'What *don't* you know?'

'Exactly what went on in the Cities of the Plain, child. Even allowing for all the sources and idiosyncrasies of human behaviour which modern psychology has laid bare, it is difficult to conceive of a state of things so far removed from normal conduct that the cities had to be destroyed in so uncompromising a fashion. One thinks of post-1918 Hamburg; one thinks of the port of Suez; one thinks unutterable thoughts; and, after that, imagination boggles, as the master of the comic novel has said.'

Laura regarded her employer sideways and with distrust. They repaired to the dining-room of the *Queen of the Circus* for lunch. When it was over, Laura said:

'I suppose my next assignment is to see Miss Galbraith off on the *Royal Scot* to-morrow.'

'It is safer for her if we appear to have no connexion with her. I will send a taxi for her. I have given her the money for her fare and a little over. And now for a stroll on the heath,' said Mrs Bradley.

# CHAPTER 11

## TO SEE A MAN ABOUT A DOG

'All this propaganda had its effect.'
HELEN SIMPSON – *The Spanish Marriage*

*

WHEN they had left the *Queen of the Circus* well behind them, and were out on the open heath and heading towards the gravel pits, Mrs Bradley said cheerfully:

'Well, that disposes very nicely of Miss Galbraith and her innocent dog.'

'Why do you call him, rather deliberately, her *innocent* dog?' enquired Laura.

'For the best of reasons, child.'

Laura recognized the note in Mrs Bradley's voice which meant that no more information would be forthcoming at that moment, and they walked on in silence until Laura asked:

'Are we going to walk over to the village?'

'Such was my intention,' Mrs Bradley replied. 'I have questions to ask there.'

'Questions? Of whom?'

'Of the vicar. I wish to ask him what he thinks is the probable date of his font. Then I shall digress by referring to the not highly original *rebus* of one Boddy, which I shall pretend I saw in the church when I visited it, and from that, I hope, the conversation will take a turn towards bodies in general and that of Miss Campbell in particular. When I have spoken of these things I propose to talk about dogs.'

'To the vicar?'

'Why not? He is in as good a position as anyone else to tell us what kind of dog is kept by the people at the market-garden. He *should* know the dog. It happens to reside in his parish.'

'I agree. What's more, we'd better hurry. Time marches on and I can't say I fancy these wide-open spaces after dark.'

The vicarage was a house two hundred years old, and the vicar

115

a worried-looking man of fifty, who welcomed them dubiously. He was eloquent, however, on the subject of the font, and insisted upon showing them the parish registers, although these were of only moderate interest since every entry before 1791 had been destroyed either by vandalism or by fire. He also offered interesting, if occasionally redundant, footnotes.

Mrs Bradley made some pertinent remarks, Laura some appreciative noises, and they began to walk towards the very fine effigies of a knight and a lady.

'The significance of the dog as a foot-rest escapes me,' Mrs Bradley began, as they stood beside the recumbent figures. The vicar was about to refresh her memory when Laura, deducing that she had received her cue, said brightly:

'Miss Galbraith's dog would make a pretty big foot-stool – big enough for both those people, I should think.' It was clumsily phrased, but she could decide upon nothing more graceful on the spur of the moment. It sufficed, however. Mrs Bradley followed it up before the vicar could get a word uttered.

'Ah, yes,' she said. She peered at the dog of stone. 'Not quite the same breed as this one, I imagine. An enormous animal, vicar, and as tame as a puppy. You have seen it about, I dare say?'

'Poor Miss Galbraith,' said the vicar. 'Such a lonely soul, I'm afraid, and so fond of that great creature. It would have broken her heart to have been parted from it. I used my good offices with our dear hostel matron, but I doubt whether they would have prevailed had not that fortunate offer come along. Even then, Miss Galbraith needed some persuasion before she would part with the dog. I pointed out, however, that if the good matron was prepared to have the dog at nights, and one pound a day was being paid by the film people for its services, she should try to be content, but she missed the daily walk on the heath. She said she did not feel safe without its company. One can understand that, of course. But how long the matron can be required to have it at the house all day long is another matter.'

'What about its twin?' asked Laura bluntly, as they walked towards the south door.

'Its twin? I'm afraid I have no idea. Miss Galbraith was given the dog by a publican in Pimlico, I believe. She lived there before she came out here. She rented a place in this village for some years, and brought the dog with her, but her little cottage had to be condemned, and there was nowhere else in the village for her to be. It was fortunate indeed that there was room for her in the hostel.'

'Doesn't help us,' said Laura, as she and Mrs Bradley struck on to the path which led back across the heath to the *Queen of the Circus*. 'What next? My burglarious entry into the fastness where the other dog is?'

'Quite unnecessary. Miss Campbell was killed by a human being, not by a dog. The second dog is immaterial.'

'Then why wouldn't the woman let us see it? I'm going to get a squint at that dog, come what may. I have a hunch it is germane to the issue.'

'I have a hunch that by the time we get back to the *Queen of the Circus* we shall be ready for tea and then can watch their television screen until cocktail-time, after which I will treat you to dinner,' said Mrs Bradley. This simple, satisfactory programme was carried out, but as they were going into the cocktail bar, Laura leading, as usual (for she held a chivalrous theory that her employer should be protected, as far as possible, from the rude gaze of the road-house frequenters), an unexpected apparition waved a pleased hand in greeting. It was Toby Dance, who had left Sir Bohun's house soon after the Sherlock Holmes party, leaving Brenda, he explained, to stay on for a bit, as there seemed some idea that Sir Bohun wanted someone to play chaperone.

'Oh, hullo,' he said when Laura came forward. 'You still here?'

'More or less,' Laura replied. 'What's that you've got?'

'Dry Martini. You can have it. I haven't begun it. I'll ask for another. The barman's removed the doings, otherwise I could give you one.'

'No, we'll have sherry,' said Laura. 'You might shout for me. Pete's in the other bar.'

Mrs Bradley came forward.

'Ah,' she said, favouring Dance with a grin. 'Chivalry, I perceive, is not dead. This would appear to be the gesture of a Galahad, a white man, a *pukka sahib*, would it not? The return of one who has the instincts of a gentleman and a sportsman!'

Dance laughed and fingered his tie.

'You're right,' he said. 'S O S from my wife. As you say, a gentleman by instinct (if not by birth and breeding), I responded in the only possible way, and came along.'

'I congratulate you. The police have not yet finished their interrogation, I believe. Your presence here should help to show that you, at least, are persuaded that Mrs Dance did not take the shortest cut to Sir Bohun's bed and board.'

Dance looked slightly taken aback at encountering this crude view of the situation. Then he laughed again, tossed off his drink, and took another which the barman pushed towards him. He recovered at once from what appeared to be a momentary shock, and raised his glass in mock salute.

'I do like people to call a spade a damned shovel,' he said. 'It usually is, unless you can't be bothered to dig up the past. You are quite right, of course. The police are bound to find out all sorts of little secrets which have the makings of shame in them, and I didn't want my divorce proceedings to be one of them. I hadn't filed my petition, as it happens, so when I got Brenda's frantic note I telephoned Chantrey and was invited to come along. He's a decent sort of chap in his way, and, between ourselves' – he lowered his cheerful voice – 'remarkably thankful to get that chap Grimston out of the house. You knew he had gone, I suppose?'

'Sir Bohun dismissed him with a cheque in lieu of notice, I believe. I wonder what he will do?'

'Oh, he'll get another job all right, an intelligent fellow like that. Let's all have another. I'll have to be off pretty soon. Chantrey has very decently invited me to dinner and to put up there for a night or two. By the way, did you ever see any more of that chap Mildren? Quite a bright lad, I thought. I've always been interested in anybody on the stage.'

'What was he like as an actor?' asked Laura suddenly. Dance chuckled.

'Pretty hot. Character parts, you know. Brenda could tell you better than I can, I should say. But I saw enough to know he was good. While you girls were changing your reach-me-downs for that Sherlock Holmes treasure hunt, old Mildren was taking off the various members of the house party. He did Chantrey and Bell, poor old Grimston, Lupez, you, Miss Laura, the fair Celia, you, Mrs Bradley, I'm afraid, the impudent hound – '

'Didn't he do *you?*' demanded Laura. Dance shook his head.

'He said I was only a type, not a real character,' he answered. 'The same went for Gavin.'

'Oh, *did* it!' snorted Gavin's fiancée.

'I should like to have seen him,' said Mrs Bradley sincerely.

'That gives me an idea!' exclaimed her secretary. Her apprehensive employer hastily ordered her another drink.

They got back to the farm after a very early dinner at the roadhouse, and a little later Laura, finding that the coast was clear, decided to carry out her plan of getting a glimpse of the animal which, in spite of what Mrs Bradley had said, she felt sure had been substituted on the station for Miss Galbraith's affectionate and amenable pet.

She tied up her head in a dark silk scarf, wrapped up warmly, for there was a weather report of a freeze-up, put a small electric torch in her pocket, and slipped out. After a sharp walk she came to a narrow stone bridge over the river and walked into the thickish mist which covered the marshes. These swamps stretched for almost half a mile alongside the road. Opposite was a small copse and beyond that lay the gipsy encampment. One or two lights from the caravans penetrated the mist, and further on the mist thinned out again to disclose the house where the market-gardeners lived with their dog.

She walked past it very slowly, listening hard. From behind the side gate she heard the dragging sound of a chain which proved that the dog was there.

'Now or never!' thought Laura. 'He's certain to bark as soon as I get close to him. One thing – as he's chained up he can't go for me!'

There were no lights at the front of the house. She walked along past it and then switched on her torch to look at her watch. It was almost ten. It was too early to expect that the people would have gone to bed, and there had been no sound of the wireless. Perhaps they were out, although she doubted whether the woman she had seen on the previous visit was the type to patronize the *Queen of the Circus*. If so, she would soon be on her way home because of the licensing hours.

'Here goes,' thought Laura. Torch in hand, but switched off, she returned to the house and crept up to the side gate. A low growl and further dragging of a chain came from behind it. Laura switched on her torch, fumbled with the catch of the gate, pushed the gate open and shone her torch on to a small shaggy terrier who leapt the length of his chain to get at her, and fell back half-choked. By the time he was giving tongue Laura was outside the front garden gate and was walking briskly up the road. She felt rather a fool.

'Never mind. There's one thing I *can* do,' she decided. 'I can check on Miss Galbraith. I'll do it to-morrow morning, unless Mrs Croc. says no.'

Mrs Bradley had no objection to the plan.

'Do not ask leading questions,' she said. 'What we want is a description from the matron of the people who hired the dog. Of course, she may not have seen them, but, as she seems to act as doorkeeper, it is most likely that she did. I believe Miss Galbraith entirely, but confirmation of evidence is always valuable, so off with you early in the morning.'

So, before the sun was up and while the ground was like iron with the frost, Laura stepped out along the road. The mist was not sufficient to slow her down, and it was a matter of minutes only before she found herself at the flight of steps which led up to the front door of the hostel. There was a dim light in the hall and one or two rooms were also lighted. Encouraged by these signs that the household was already stirring, Laura careered up the steps, and knocked at the door.

A grille, like that on the outer door of a convent, was pushed aside, and two eyes glinted at Laura.

'Who is it?' demanded the official (although slightly nervous) voice of the matron.

'Dame Beatrice Lestrange Bradley's secretary,' proclaimed Laura, rightly judging that this information would have the effect of an *Open Sesame*. So it proved. There was the sound of bolts being drawn and a chain being removed. Then the light – gaslight, obviously – was turned up, and the front door was held ajar.

'It's rather early for callers,' said the matron, half apologetic and half accusing. 'We were really not unlocked from last night.'

'I'm so sorry,' said Laura cheerfully. 'There was just one point about Miss Galbraith and her dog. We met the vicar, you know, and he said something about a film.'

'Certainly. Miss Galbraith was able – but won't you come in, Miss –'

'Menzies. Spelt the Australian way but pronounced as in Scotland. Thanks.'

She was ushered into the matron's own room and was aware of

more than one elderly head being craned over the banisters.

'The vicar persuaded me, against my will, to accept the creature,' went on the matron, when Laura was seated, 'and it was a relief to me, I confess, when it was required by the film people. One of them, obviously a foreigner, called for it and took it away with him.'

'Can you describe the man?' asked Laura.

'The most noticeable thing about him was his accent, which was guttural and foreign,' replied the matron.

In spite of the warning from Mrs Bradley against asking leading questions, Laura could not resist trying one of these.

'Could he have been a Spaniard?' she enquired.

'I have really no idea. He was a middle-aged man, rather grizzled, and with his hair receding from the brow and cut extremely close.'

'Not black-haired?'

'Oh, dear me, no. Apart from the greyness, I should say he was a fair-haired man. He had grey-blue eyes, I think. Why, is there anything wrong?'

'No. Mrs Bradley is making a psychological study of one or two film people, that's all.'

'But this man, and the young woman who came with him, were not film people. At least, I don't think so. They came to hire the dog to go to a party. No, the film actor turned up at the beginning of this month and wanted the dog daily. Miss Galbraith let him go, but she was not altogether satisfied, for some reason, and found out where the young man was taking him. And where do you think they were filming?'

'When I saw them,' said Laura, 'they were on location at that disused station just this side of the new estate at Dilcocks.'

'Oh, of course, if Dame Beatrice is interested in them, you *would* know,' said the matron, in a slightly disappointed tone.

'How many times did Miss Galbraith go to the station?' Laura asked.

'Only the once. The young man who had come to hire the dog was there, and said that the cameras would be along at any time and that they couldn't have people on the platform when they had begun work. She saw that point, of course, and had to be satisfied to come away if she wanted her money. And, really, she drinks and smokes so much, and pays so much for that animal's food, that she needed the money very badly. Anyway, he made her promise faithfully not to go there again.'

'And this young man? Can you describe him, too? Mrs Bradley is particularly interested in a dark, hard-faced, black-eyed man. Is that the one who came here at the beginning of the month?'

'Oh, no, nor the second one, either. The film man who came had hazel eyes and dark-brown hair. Miss Galbraith said it was a toupée, but I only saw him with his hat on, and, in any case, I am not the one to question whether a person's hair is really his own. But really dark – oh, no, I can be definite over that, and the first one who came was grey-haired but must have been fair.'

Laura had one more question to ask.

'The dog,' she said. 'He seemed a reasonable enough animal to me. Did you ever know him turn savage?'

'*Dear* me, no! I wouldn't have kept him a *day* if I thought him savage. He was, I must admit, a singularly docile animal.'

'Miss Galbraith has gone to Scotland, I believe?'

'A taxi came yesterday evening. I am not too happy about it. Miss Galbraith had retired from the stage. If she had not, I could not have taken her in. This house is not intended for people in active life. However Dame Beatrice rang up and arranged for the rent to be paid and I could hardly affront a D.B.E.'

'Certainly not,' agreed Laura. 'There is only one point not clear. Apparently the dog was on *daily* hire to the film people. What exactly does that mean?'

'Miss Galbraith had it back every night.'

'The film people brought it back here? You said that Miss Galbraith had to promise not to go to the station while they were filming. How did it get itself returned?'

'Dear me!' said the matron. 'I have no idea how it came back here each night. I should think, after the first time, it probably found its own way.'

'Oh, yes, of course. It doesn't really matter, anyway. It has nothing to do with Dame Beatrice's psychological studies,' said Laura carelessly.

'Of course not. But little mysteries do nag at one so,' remarked the matron sympathetically.

# CHAPTER 12

# OFFICIALDOM

'Oh! think of all the happy days we have had together,
before these terrible misfortunes came upon us . . . and you
cannot leave us to bear them alone . . . '

CHARLES DICKENS – *Nicholas Nickleby*

*

MANOEL sat down at the Superintendent's invitation, crossed one
shiny, black-trousered thigh over the other, and nodded.

'You wish to know all that I can tell you of Linda Campbell's
death? Very well. Please to go ahead and ask questions. That,
I believe, is the method.'

'Did you call her by her Christian name, then, Mr Lupez?'

'In my country it would not be proper, but in England it is the
custom, when one has met a lady twice, to call her by her baptismal
name, I think. One is not formal over here.'

'It depends. Had she any enemies, as far as you know?'

'Oh, yes. There was myself, also Mrs Dance, Grimston, Miss
Laura Menzies – '

'Miss Laura Menzies? But she was a comparative stranger to
Miss Campbell!'

'But not to Chief Detective-Inspector Gavin,' said Manoel, his
face impassive.

'What do you mean?'

'It was seen that Miss Campbell had cast eyes – you say that,
I think? – towards Mr Gavin, and Miss Campbell was truly more
favoured with beauty and with charm than is Miss Menzies. Me,
I like not big, strong girls.'

'That's as you find them,' said Collins. 'I didn't see Miss Campbell until after she was dead, so perhaps I'm no judge of their
respective looks. I think we can forget Miss Menzies, you know.'

'In Spain we should not dismiss from our calculations a woman
with a lover to be stolen.'

'Never mind that for the moment, sir. Just now you mentioned yourself. I take it you were joking, and I've no time to spend on jokes.'

'Joking? But no. As everyone will have told you by this time, I have expectations of money when Sir Bohun Chantrey dies. These expectations would be the horse that does not go if he should marry again and have sons. He was proposing to marry Miss Campbell. What more natural, therefore, than that I should say to myself that it would be better if there were no Miss Campbell at all? It seems to me logical, that.'

'Quite so. I see what you mean. What about Mrs Dance?'

'Mrs Dance will have told you about Mrs Dance. She is dangerous, that woman, and scruples not to obtain what she wants. I think she would be divorced and marry Sir Bohun for his money, if she could. And perhaps if I were a little older, I would ask her to marry *me*. But not if she is divorced! You see?'

'It's a theory, certainly, Mr Lupez. And Mr Grimston was jealous because Miss Campbell was engaged to Sir Bohun, eh? We've heard that one before, and there's probably something in it. By the way, where were you on Thursday afternoon, January eleventh, and what were you doing?'

'You think that was when Miss Linda Campbell was killed?'

'Yes.'

'I was showing my natural father how we use the *espada*.'

'What's that?'

'The sword we bull-fighters are using.'

'So you and Sir Bohun were together?'

'Of course. A loving father and a loving son – what else?'

'Where was this sword-play going on?'

'In my father's library. The good Bell, who makes my father write letters, was on holiday, so we pushed away the big table and we took turns to be the bull – and to be the *toreador*, too, of course.'

'I see. Thank you, Mr Lupez. I take it you'll be staying on here for a bit? Not going back to your own country yet, I mean? We may need you again. You understand?'

Manoel accepted this dismissal graciously, smiled, and walked quickly from the room. Collins gazed at the closed door speculatively for a moment, then crossed to the fire and warmed his hands.

'What do you make of him, Baines?' he enquired of the sergeant.

'Could bear watching, sir. The only thing is – ' The sergeant, who was young, keen, and modest, hesitated.

'Go ahead, lad.'

'Well, sir, he gave us a pretty sound personal motive for putting Miss Campbell out of the way, but I'd be inclined to think that, if he did it, he did it for another reason.'

'I should have thought Sir Bohun's money was a pretty sound reason.'

'Yes, sir. But everybody seems to know about Lupez and Sir Bohun's money, and I don't think he's a fool, sir. Besides, from what gets around, he's got plenty of money of his own.'

'Granted. All right. Go on.'

'I think his motive would have been dog in the manger, sir.'

'Come again? I don't think I get it.'

'His view that Miss Campbell was more attractive than Miss Menzies seemed to me to be a genuine opinion, sir. Isn't it possible, then, that he decided, when the engagement to Sir Bohun was announced, that if he himself couldn't marry Miss Campbell, nobody should?'

'Bit romantic for nowadays, Baines.'

'Even in the case of a Spaniard, sir, do you think?'

'Hm! That might very well make a difference. Odd chaps, these Latins, although the Spaniards aren't like any others. Anyway, I'll keep the point in mind. Anything else strike you?'

'Only that, with him, honesty, he thinks, is the best policy *up to a point*. People whose minds work like that are even less to be trusted than the out-and-out liars, sir. They're a whole lot cleverer, for one thing.'

'So you think Lupez is our man?'

'It's only a hunch, sir. But I don't like him, so I may be prejudiced.'

'Hm! It's something that you recognize the fact. Go and get Grimston. He should have been brought back by now. I can't think what possessed Sir Bohun to let him go away from here at a time like this.'

'He sacked him, I understand, sir.'

Grimston entered with an air of having screwed himself up to make a speech, but Collins, sensing this, cut briskly across his first words.

'Good morning, sir,' he said. 'I know you've been put about, but I'm sure you'll understand that it has been in your own interests for us to have you back while we make our routine enquiries.'

Grimston sat down in the chair which the Superintendent indicated, but jumped up almost immediately. He strode to the window and back, picked up a book which was lying on the table and replaced it with exaggerated exactness in the centre of a panel of the wood. Collins nodded to the sergeant.

'Now, sir,' he said, 'where were you, and – '

'I want to speak to you particularly,' burst out Grimston. 'It is quite wrong for you to trust me. I am the man you want for murder.'

He paused, his lips parted. The Superintendent nodded indulgently.

'Yes, sir, I see,' was all that he said. Grimston stared at him in perplexity.

'Didn't you hear what I said?' he demanded.

'Yes, I heard what you said, sir. You claim to have been the murderer of Miss Campbell. You will need to convince us of that, sir. What evidence can you bring to prove it?'

'Evidence? Isn't my confession enough for you, then?'

'Not by itself, I'm afraid, sir. So many people confess to murder. We've had seventeen confessions and four eye-witness' reports already. All bogus. Wouldn't stand up even to a preliminary investigation, more's the pity. It would save us a lot of time and trouble if we could get just one genuine confession instead of a lot of blah from all these people who want to sell their story to the Sunday papers.' He regarded Grimston tolerantly.

'But my confession is the genuine thing!' cried Grimston. Collins drew out a notebook, and settled his solid frame more comfortably in his chair.

'Go ahead, then, sir,' he said. Grimston took out a cigarette lighter and fiddled with it. 'Smoke if you want to, sir. It's as well to relax when we can.'

'No, no. Look here, Superintendent, you remember that dream of mine? Well, of course, it wasn't a dream. I mean, I never dreamt anything of the kind, as no doubt you guessed. That dream was a bit of wishful thinking. I had proposed to Linda – to Miss Campbell – and she had turned me down. Well, I don't overrate myself, but the way she did it – contemptuously, you know – got under my skin. I may be a poor blasted usher, but she was only a nursery governess, after all. I saw red. I invented the dream, hoping it would sublimate matters for me and take away the wish to kill, but, far from that being the case, the urge became stronger and stronger, and at last – well, I did it. I killed her.'

'Yes, sir? Can you give us the details?'

'Certainly. I have been thinking things over and I've decided to make a clean breast of everything. It was Fate playing into my hands, I think. I knew that Linda was in the habit of going to the *Queen of the Circus* to meet her brother. He was a bit of a no-good, I gathered. In with a bookmaker's gang. Shady doings on the turf have never interested me, although I like a flutter with anybody in the normal way. She had told me about this brother. He used to give her money. He was good to her that way, because her pay here wasn't very much. I found out about the brother first because I followed her once or twice, thinking she was meeting a lover. However, she satisfied me that that was not the case, and sometimes I would walk with her as far as the road-house and buy myself a drink in the public bar while the two of them chin-wagged in the saloon.'

'Did you ever overhear their conversation, sir?' Collins had heard from Gavin, who had had the information from Mrs Bradley, of the man whom Linda Campbell had met in the road-house saloon lounge, and he was anxious to know more of him. But Grimston shook his head.

'Once I was certain there was nothing involved that would worry me, I took no more interest,' he explained. 'Besides, it had been understood from the beginning that I was not to interfere in any way.'

'Yes, I understand, sir. You were saying – '

'I was going to tell you about that particular morning. I hadn't been sleeping at all well since the Sherlock Holmes party. It was that night when Linda finally gave me to understand that I could give up all hope of marrying her. I've learnt since that some of our conversation was overheard by one of the guests. Detective-Inspector Gavin told me that Mrs Bradley caught the drift of what we were saying, so there's your proof, if you want it.'

'Proof of the fact that Miss Campbell told you she did not intend to marry you, coupled with strong supposition that she intended to marry Sir Bohun, sir? Proof that you made up your

127

mind to kill her? Exactly how did you set about it? That's what we should very much like to know.'

'She went off to the road-house before breakfast on the day of her death. I went out after her. She had hinted of terrible trouble, and I was afraid she might have decided to take her own life. When she reached the road-house she turned down the lane beside it and went on to the heath. It was my opportunity. I followed her, keeping to the bushes. I had the weapon with me. I always carried it. It was a long, two-edged knife, razor sharp and rather heavy. I bought it in London. I can't show it you. I've thrown it away.

'Just as she approached the gravel pits she looked round. I supposed she had heard me, so I crouched down behind a bush, but the early morning was inclined to be foggy, and it did not seem as though she could have seen me. Suddenly she pulled out a gun, but before she could use it I was on her and had knocked it out of her hand. She gave a little scream and I pulled her towards me and shouted out that she must marry me, or something to that effect. She pulled away, and said some things to me which I forget, but I know they maddened me. I said: "All right, then, Linda, you've bought it. I'll show you whether I'm as weak as you think." With that I swung her round so that her back was towards me, and then I stabbed her through the breast.'

'How many times did you stab her, sir?'

'I think it could only have been once.'

'What did you do after that?'

'Nothing. I ran towards the flooded gravel pit and threw the knife in. You'll probably find it if you drag. Then I walked about for a bit, and then I came back here. That was all, I think, but my mind is still rather confused. I've tried to reconstruct the scene, but there are bits which seem quite blacked-out. I don't think I can add any more.'

'Thank you, sir. Got all that down, Sergeant? All right. Type it out, and perhaps, later on, we'll get Mr Grimston to sign it.'

'I suppose I am to consider myself under arrest,' said Grimston. Collins shook his head.

'All in good time, sir,' he said. 'We shall have to check this statement of yours very carefully. Either *you* have slipped up on one or two points, or *we* have. But, of course, as you say, you are rather hazy as to details. You won't go too far away, sir? We may need you again later to-day.'

'Don't you believe me? Hang it, Superintendent, you've jolly well got to! Would I confess to the murder if I hadn't done it? Use your common sense, for goodness sake.'

'Very good, sir. Just give us time to find the weapon. The jury always like to see the weapon in these cases of sudden violence. Gives them an idea of whether there might be extenuating circumstances, or so I'm told. I wonder, when you go out, sir, whether you would be kind enough to ask Mr Dance to step this way? I understand that he is staying in the house. Well?' he demanded of the sergeant when Grimston had gone.

'Mad as a March hare, sir. *He* didn't do it! Doesn't know a thing about it!'

'I'm not so sure, my lad. It may be a way of trying to throw dust in our eyes. I'm keeping a very open mind for the present about Mr Loony Grimston. As I see it, he's a dark horse, and there's no doubt at all that he was very sweet on the girl. Sir Bohun Chantrey is certain of that. It's no new thing for a jealous man to kill a girl if he can't have her.'

The sergeant said, 'Yes, sir,' but not in the tone of one who has been convinced. There came a tap at the door. The sergeant got up and opened it to admit Toby Dance.

'Ah, thank you for coming along so promptly, sir,' said Collins. 'Take a seat, will you? There are just one or two points over which you may be able to help us. I understand that you were not staying in the neighbourhood when this shocking business took place?'

'No. I was living in Town.'

'Your wife was staying here, I believe?'

'Yes. Sir Bohun Chantrey thought it would look better to have somebody else here when his engagement to Miss Campbell was announced, as Miss Campbell was going to continue living in the house.'

'I understand Sir Bohun's niece was staying here, though.'

'Yes, of course, but she's rather young and inexperienced – not quite one's idea of a chaperone.'

'I see, sir. Very good. Now, sir, just as a formality – can you tell me where you were and what you were doing between three o'clock and five on the afternoon of the eleventh of January?'

Toby Dance pursed up his lips and, to Collins' surprise, obviously hesitated before he answered:

'No, I'm afraid I can't.'

129

'*Can't*, sir?'

'No.'

'Anything you tell me is received on the note of strict confidence, sir, unless it is needed in evidence later on.'

'Oh, it isn't that I *won't* tell you. I simply can't remember.'

'Take it a bit at a time, sir. You would have got up at ... ?'

'Eight-thirty. I never get to the office until ten or half past. My secretary is kept busy opening the morning's correspondence until then.'

'So we can take it you had arrived at your office on the eleventh by half past ten? At what time do you knock off for lunch, sir?'

'A quarter past one. I go to the *Jardin des Gourmets* mostly.'

'And how long do you take over lunch, sir?'

'Depends upon whom I'm with. If it's a client, anything up to a couple of hours if I think it's worth it. Nobody hurries over lunch at that restaurant, anyway. It 'ud be a sin.'

'So we're getting near the time I want to know about, sir. Now, then, you're through with lunch. Whom did you lunch with on the eleventh of January?'

'I can't remember.'

'Were you, perhaps, alone?'

'I must have been. I'd remember if I'd had anybody with me.'

'Very good, sir. You lunched alone. I dare say the waiter would remember you, sir?'

'Yes, of course. I always have the same table, but ... O Lord! Now I come to think, that must have been the day I *didn't* go to the restaurant. Yes, that's right. I – I lunched somewhere else.'

'Where was that, sir?'

'I don't know. One of the Corner Houses, I believe. I don't really remember.'

'Will you give me your business address, sir? Perhaps you've a business card I could have.'

'What the devil for, Superintendent?'

'Well, sir,' said Collins, looking him full in the face, 'when a gentleman who has had some acquaintance with a murdered young woman states first of all that he can't remember how he spent the afternoon on which she died, and then admits that, on that particular afternoon, he changed all his regular habits, and even stalls about the place where he had his lunch, he needn't be surprised if the police think his information can do with a bit of checking.

There's one other thing I'd like to know. What did you know of Miss Campbell before she came here to work for Sir Bohun Chantrey?'

'Oughtn't you to caution me?' asked Dance, suddenly grinning. 'I knew quite a bit about Linda Campbell before she came to do the governessing here. In fact, it might be said that I got her the job.'

'Indeed, sir?' Collins mentally pricked up his ears. Facts relating to Linda Campbell's life before she was employed by Sir Bohun were few, and, with all his suspicions of the house-party, Collins still had in mind the so-far unidentified young man whom Linda had met at the road-house. 'May I ask what was the nature of your acquaintanceship with her, and how you came to meet her in the first place?'

'Certainly. Neither is anything to be ashamed of, I'm relieved to say. Linda was at boarding school with my sister, who is a good deal younger than I am, and Linda used to come to our house for an occasional week-end. After the two girls left school I saw no more of Linda for two or three years. I married, for one thing, and was not living at home. But not many months ago I received a letter from Linda, sent on from my mother's, in which she asked whether I could put her in touch with a job for which she didn't require to train. I hadn't a clue. She said she couldn't even type. Then I heard that Chantrey had had two youngsters wished on him and needed a nursery governess, so I put Linda on to him and washed my hands of her.'

'You have her previous address, then?'

'No. I threw the letter away.'

'What did you think when you heard that Miss Campbell was dead?'

'Nothing in particular. I wasn't tremendously surprised, as a matter of fact.'

'How do you account for that, sir?'

'Well, onlookers see most of the game, and since that Sherlock Holmes party I've felt that Linda was asking for trouble. Apart from anyone from outside – I heard rumours that she met a chap at that road-house on the edge of the heath – she was trying to ring the changes on Sir Bohun, Grimston, and Manoel, with occasional passes at any other blokes in her vicinity. I shouldn't have thought she'd have been such a born fool. Two of 'em aren't really normal, and t'other is a foreigner, and (again according to rumour) Chantrey's bastard.'

'Not normal, sir? How do you mean?'

'Well, everybody knows that Mrs Bradley had Chantrey under her wing for months and months of psychological treatment just before the end of the war, and, as for Grimston, why, the fellow's as mad as a hatter.'

'Indeed, sir?' This confirmation of his own sergeant's opinion was interesting, Collins decided.

'Ought to be certified,' said Dance amiably. 'Mixes laudanum with his port! Nearly had a fit when first I knew of it. It was Bell who tipped me off about that.'

'Laudanum with his port, sir?'

'Oh, yes. He's a suicide type, you know. I'd never put it past him to confess to this murder just to get himself hanged!'

'That's a remarkably interesting suggestion, sir, I must say! You'll be sure to let me have your sister's address, sir, and your business card?'

'Well,' said Dance dubiously; and again suddenly grinned. 'No, I'll come clean. Linda was a pick-up. I met her when I was – when my wife and I weren't on speaking terms. I knew she was a hussy, even then. She was, you know, Superintendent. She obviously had it coming to her. Anyway, I kept her for a short time, but she was a hard-boiled, shrewish little bitch, and I soon got sick of her. However, I couldn't let her down flat, so when I heard that some friends of mine were going to advertise for a nursery governess I sent her along. She'd been trained as a teacher – that emergency scheme they had at the end of the war – so I thought she could do the job all right, and I also thought I'd get her off my neck for good. It was a bit of a jolt, I can tell you, to turn up to that Sherlock Holmes party that Chantrey threw last November and find Linda governessing his small nephew. I had to go into a huddle with her, and, for a financial consideration, she agreed to keep her mouth shut about our little affair. Of course, if I'd realized how things were between her and Chantrey I could have saved my money!'

'Who suggested that she should not give you away, sir?'

'She did, the little harpy! You see, she'd found out – how, I don't know, but for those sort of people the walls seem to have tongues as well as ears! – that I wanted to make up with my wife, so she'd got me cold, and she knew it.'

'Blackmail, sir?'

'Yes, of course it was. But I didn't kill her, for that or any other reason.'

'It's a pity you won't, or can't, tell me about that afternoon, sir, all the same.'

Toby stared down at the palms of his hands and at his interlocking fingers.

'All right, then,' he said. 'I *will* tell you, but it won't do me a ha'porth of good, I assure you. After lunching at the office on sandwiches and a half-bot. I went to call on a chap named Raymond de Philippe. I'd wanted to call on him for some time but he'd been on a business trip abroad.'

'You went to call on him, sir? For any particular reason?'

'Yes, for a very particular reason.' Dance stared down at his hands again. 'I couldn't very well ask him to the office. For one thing, I didn't think he'd come, and, for another, the matter was too private to have even my secretary overhear it. I lunched at the office to save time. I knew, if I wanted to catch him alone, that between two and half past was the best time, so I toddled along to his flat and – and that's where I was at three, and, until about four, I stayed there. Then I went back to *my* flat without returning to the office.'

'Anybody swear to that, sir? This Mr de Philippe can confirm the time of your visit to him, I take it?'

'No, I saw nobody when I went back to my flat. Four o'clockish on an ordinary week-day is a dead sort of hour where I live. All the men are still at work and all the women at bridge-parties or a matinée. As for de Philippe – well, I've no doubt that he *could* give me an alibi, but I'm equally convinced that he *won't*.'

'How's that, sir?'

'Well, you see, Superintendent, I went round there with the intention of putting it to him civilly, quietly, and as one gentleman to another, that I had no intention either of divorcing Brenda or of allowing her to divorce me, and would he, so to speak, kindly lay off her and let me mend a broken romance – my own.'

'Yes, sir?'

'Unhappily, Superintendent, I ended up by punching him on the nose.'

## CHAPTER 13

# THE PURSUIT OF THE
# UNEATABLE CONTINUES

'I must
Not trust
Here to any;
Bereav'd,
Deceiv'd
By so many.'
ROBERT HERRICK – *Anacreontike*

*

'Who next, sir?' enquired the sergeant. Collins grunted and consulted the list on which he was checking off his victims as he interviewed them.

'Better be Sir Bohun Chantrey. I shan't be sorry to get him over and done with,' he said. 'What did you make of that last bird?'

'Honest, sir. Don't you think we could get that chap with the French moniker to cough up that alibi?'

'I'm doubtful,' Collins answered. 'Mr Ready-Fist Dance presumably knows him a lot better than we do. All·the same, I shall try. He may be a better fellow than Dance thinks. Anyway, get Sir Bohun.'

Sir Bohun entered with a great show of affability and declared that the sooner 'this damned mess we're all in' was cleared up, the better.

'Brings one's life to a full stop,' he continued. 'Gets one talked about. Sunday papers, and all that sort of unpleasantness. Photographers lurking in the shrubbery. Glad to do anything I can to help, so fire away, Superintendent, and don't attempt to spare anybody's feelings.'

'Thank you, Sir Bohun,' Collins replied, signing to the sergeant. 'Just one or two questions, then. What can you tell me about the deceased?'

'Nothing much. When I took charge of my brother's two child-

134

ren I engaged a tutor and a nursery governess. Both came with good references and both have proved satisfactory. Miss Campbell was the nursery governess.'

'Yes, sir?'

Sir Bohun looked surprised.

'That's all I know,' he said. Collins studied the walnut markings on the polished table beside which he was seated, and then looked up.

'I had some impression, Sir Bohun, that you had offered marriage to Miss Campbell and that she had accepted your offer.'

'Oh, that!' Sir Bohun waved it aside. 'You asked me what I knew of poor Linda Campbell, and I thought I had answered you sufficiently. As to what you mention . . . yes, I had made her an offer of marriage and she had accepted it. It was a business arrangement. This house needs a châtelaine. The matter could have had nothing to do with her death.'

'Why do *you* think she was killed, Sir Bohun?'

'I? I have no idea at all. She was a vain, harmless sort of girl, a bit of a hussy, I dare say, but nothing that one could take hold of, otherwise I should not have dreamt – couldn't afford it, in my position – J.P. and all that, don't you know.'

'To revert to Miss Campbell's references – I suppose you took them up, sir? – verified them, that is to say?'

'Didn't bother much. Preferred to form my own opinion of the girl. Found her satisfactory. That's as far as it went.'

'Yes, I see, sir. We have a report that she may have left this house at about midnight on the occasion of a party last November. Can you suggest any reason for her doing such a thing?'

'Indeed, no; neither do I attach much importance to the rumour. Of course, she may have gone out that night while the party was still on. Young women take these romantic fancies.'

'To wander about in thick fog, sir?'

Sir Bohun again waved the point aside.

'Fog, hail, rain, midsummer moonlight – it's all one to them,' he declared. 'All women are slightly mad, young women considerably so, and adolescent girls completely so. It's a known fact. Ask any reputable psychologist. Look at *poltergeists*, for example.'

Collins, under his breath, consigned *poltergeists* to the region from which he had no doubt they came, and tried a different tack.

'The tutor, sir, Mr Grimston.'

'Ex-tutor. I sacked him. I don't know why you brought him back here. Lot of nonsense. Apart from his total inability to kill a fly, the fellow's as mad as a coot. You couldn't get any sense out of him, however hard you might try.'

Collins was inclined to agree, but he ignored the statement and asked patiently:

'Can you give me any details as to how you came to engage him, sir? We have to check up, you understand.'

'Came from a scholastic agency – forget their name. Find you their letter, if you like.' He rummaged and soon produced it. Collins pushed it over to the sergeant, who made a note of the address and the date, and returned it to Sir Bohun.

'And you know nothing more about him?' pursued Collins.

'Don't keep a dog and bark myself,' retorted the baronet. 'These scholastic agencies are supposed to vet the chaps on their books, I take it? They sent him, and he brought references, and that's all I knew or cared. Nobody could have supposed that the wretched girl would get herself into this kind of mess, and the wretched boy get himself arrested for it.'

'He *hasn't* been arrested for it, Sir Bohun! We shall not make that sort of move until we are perfectly sure.' Sir Bohun snorted, and Collins went on in gentle tones: 'There are just one or two things we would like to get quite clear. We have received information that Miss Campbell was acquainted with at least one person in this neighbourhood – a youngish man – who was not a member of your household and who did not appear at your party. She met this man at the *Queen of the Circus* near here, and later she disappeared.'

'Yes, so Mrs Bradley told me. I didn't know the girl had any acquaintances in the neighbourhood, if that's what you were going to ask me. I don't know anything about the girl at all.'

'Yet,' said Collins, in inoffensive tones, 'you were proposing to marry her, sir?'

Sir Bohun ignored this.

'Grimston ought to see a psychologist,' he said. 'Why don't you let Mrs B. run a foot-rule over him? He and his dreams! Dreams like that get people into trouble, same as Joseph! Nobody ever learns anything! Dreams, indeed! Silly young fool!'

Collins tapped thoughtfully on the arm of his chair for a moment, and then asked, in a casual, almost uninterested tone:

'Is there anything you yourself can tell us which might help, sir?'

Sir Bohun pulled at his lower lip. To Collins' surprise – for he had expected nothing from this shot in the dark – there was something not only hesitant but furtive in the baronet's manner. The Superintendent waited hopefully.

'Well,' said Sir Bohun at last, 'don't really suppose it has any bearing, but two unexpected things happened on the night of the Sherlock Holmes party, apart from Linda taking that walk in the fog. That is, if it *was* Linda. Mrs B. is not committing herself, you know. But a very odd –'

'We know about the dog, sir.'

'Oh, you do? Well, when the dog arrived I was really expecting something else.'

'Indeed, sir?' Collins sounded only mildly interested. He was anxious not to give any impression of the eagerness which possessed him. One ray of light, however faint, might make all the difference to the enquiry. At the moment there were several suspects, and, except for Grimston and his dream – which might or might not have any bearing on the matter – there seemed no more reason to suspect one rather than another. He had talked matters over with Gavin, who had given him all the information he himself had gleaned, including the affair of the dog at the deserted station and the fact that Celia Godley had fed it under conditions which indicated a desire for secrecy, and he had come to the conclusion that Grimston was not necessarily the most likely criminal. He looked forward to an interview with Miss Godley. 'Something else?' he repeated after Sir Bohun. 'Connected with the dog, do you mean, sir?'

'Not connected with the dog – no. I hadn't thought of the dog. Can't find out who did, either. That's the oddest thing. I know it scared some of the women when we opened the door and saw it there, you see, but it was such a good idea – the *Hound of the Baskervilles*, dash it – that one would have expected somebody to come forward and claim the credit. But I can't get any one of them to own to it. Odd, that. I mean, it was no sort of accident. The dog had been touched up here and there with luminous paint, so it was meant to be part of the evening. You'd think somebody would have owned to bringing it, wouldn't you?'

'What happened to it in the end, sir?'

'I have no idea. Mrs Bradley fed it and turned it out again, and one doesn't go about the grounds on a foggy November night looking for a dog the size of a donkey, even if one *is* an addict of Holmes. I suppose that whoever brought it got rid of it somehow. I suspected that young Miss Laura Menzies, with the connivance of Mrs Bradley's chauffeur, and tackled her on the subject, but she denied any knowledge of it, and she isn't a girl to tell lies. Said she wished she *had* thought of it, and I believe her.'

'So you hadn't planned to introduce the dog, sir, and yet you *had* planned something of a surprise. Would that have had any bearing on what has happened?'

'I don't see how it could, but, for what it's worth, I'll tell you. I'd planned to let a flock of geese into the drawing-room.'

'Geese, sir?'

'Yes, geese. The *Blue Carbuncle*, you know. I was disappointed when they didn't turn up. The idea was to have a sort of competition to see which of the guests selected the one which was supposed to have the blue carbuncle in its crop. I had decided upon the one when I went to see the dealer. I had a nice prize ready, too, a very nice prize.'

Collins mentally dismissed the flock of geese from the case, but enquired, for politeness' sake:

'And what had happened to the geese, sir?'

'Lost in the fog in a van. Driver got hopelessly muddled, and landed up in a ditch on the other side of East Bealing. Never came within miles of my place. I'd paid for the geese, too. Still, I sent them to hospitals for Christmas, which I'd planned to do in any case. Very disappointing not to have had them at the party, though, all the same.'

'Yes, it must have been. You mentioned Miss Laura Menzies, but you had an even younger lady staying here at the time – your niece, I believe.'

'Celia? Yes. She's still here. I *like* to have people in the house. You can see the girl, of course, if you want to, but I don't think you'll get much out of her that will help you.'

'As a matter of routine, sir, I had better see everybody here, including your servants. Sometimes one gets a pointer from a completely innocent person. *He* doesn't realize that what he's telling you may be just the one missing link in a chain of evidence, but time and again it is apt to turn out like that, especially in a case of murder.'

'Oh, well, you go ahead, of course. Celia has nothing to hide.'

From what he had heard, Collins did not share this opinion. He ignored it, and fired in his last and deadliest question, but, so to speak, with a silencer on the gun.

'By the way, sir – a routine point only, of course, so don't answer unless you wish – will you tell me where you were and what you were doing between the hours of three and five on Thursday January eleventh last?'

'Doing? And where? Bless my soul, that would be when it was done, would it? Oh, dear me, now! Let me see. I don't remember doing anything different from usual, so I should have been – yes, yes – in the library, probably looking forward to my tea. I always look forward to my tea.'

'Could anyone confirm this, sir? Just for our records, you know.'

'Ah, now, I wonder! Why, yes, of course! Manoel was with me for most of the time.'

'Er – were you active or passive, sir?'

'Look here, what the devil are you getting at?' demanded Sir Bohun, suddenly red in the face. 'If you must know, we were playing a fool game with his *espada* – the sword bull-fighters use, don't you know. Bell was on short leave, so we had the library to ourselves.'

'I see, sir. Thank you very much.'

'Checking my story against Manoel's, I suppose,' said Sir Bohun, restored to good humour. 'That's the end of the inquisition, then, I take it?'

'Thank you very much, sir,' Collins repeated stolidly. Then, when Sir Bohun had gone, 'Get Miss Godley quickly, before he has time to prompt her,' he said to the sergeant.

Sir Bohun's niece did not give the impression of someone with nothing to hide. Collins saw a slightly-built, fair-haired, insipidly-pretty girl who was patently on the defensive. He wasted no time. He glanced at his sergeant, nodded, asked Celia to sit down, and then said genially:

'Well, Miss Godley, I've come to see a lady about a dog.'

The girl stiffened immediately.

'Yes?' she said. 'The *Hound of the Baskervilles*, you mean, I suppose? But that had nothing to do with me. It was Linda Campbell's idea, I think.'

'Really? She could not have mentioned it to Sir Bohun, I suppose?'

'Oh, no, she wouldn't have done. It was to be a surprise.'

'I gather that it succeeded in its object. She took you into her confidence, then?'

'Yes – well, I mean – well, yes, I suppose she did.'

'And you undertook to look after the dog, and you continued to look after it until her death.'

Celia looked helplessly at him.

'No, of course not. I had nothing to do with it,' she said.

'You were seen to go and feed it more than once, Miss Godley, long after the party was over and done with.'

'I? I feed it? Oh, nonsense! It was an awful great brute! I wouldn't have dared go near it!'

'Indeed? My informant seemed quite certain that you fed it. The evidence was that you cycled along beside the railway track and that the dog was kept at the disused station which has now been superseded by the new halt at Keatsdown.'

Celia moistened her lips.

'Oh, nonsense! I've never been there in my life,' she said, 'except once or twice in the train.'

Collins nodded, and there was a long silence. Celia broke it at last.

'Do you want me any more? May I go now? I have rather a lot to do.'

'Very good, Miss Godley. If you should reconsider what you've just told me I hope you won't hesitate to come along.'

'What do you mean?' demanded the girl. Collins looked at her, and did not reply. She gave him a wild look, began to get up, hesitated, and then sat down again.

'I – I found that there was a dog chained up in that deserted station,' she said in a tone of defiance. 'I couldn't make it out. It didn't seem right, so, as soon as I could, I got on my bicycle and went back to investigate.'

'You had seen it from the train, of course.'

'Yes . . . yes, from the train.'

'And, as soon as you could, you got on to your bicycle and went back to investigate. Where was the dog when you saw it first?'

'On – on the platform.'

'And you took it food and water?'

'Yes. I – I could quite easily manage on my carrier and in my basket.'

'Quite, quite. How did the dog get into the waiting-room, Miss Godley?'

'I have no idea.'

'It was always on the platform when you saw it and fed it?'

'I – I only went once.'

'Only once?'

'Yes. I was afraid I might be trespassing. I didn't like to risk it again.'

'I see. Thank you, Miss Godley. If you should chance to remember something which you have not told me, you won't hesitate to come and find me, will you? I shall be in and out of this house for quite some time, I expect.'

'But there couldn't be anything else! I've told you everything I know!' She sounded hysterical.

'That is not what I have been informed from other sources, Miss.' He nodded, and Celia scurried out like a child glad to escape from a too-inquisitive adult. Collins rang the bell and told the butler to ask Mrs Dance to spare a few minutes for a talk. She could not have been far away, for it was in less than a minute that she sailed in and smiled at the Superintendent. He indicated a chair, and reseated himself in the place he had previously occupied.

Brenda Dance was a *fausse maigre*. Clothed, as she was at the moment, in a dark winter dress, long-sleeved and high at the neck, she gave an impression of slenderness, and such was her charm that the Superintendent, a staid man, had to remind himself hastily of who and what he was, and why she was in his presence. He blushed, and his voice came harshly. Mrs Dance, accustomed to the effect she had on many men, smiled sadly, and extended a shapely foot towards the fire.

'Quite good weather for the time of year,' she remarked.

'Going to snow,' said Collins, recovering, beaming at her, and nodding to the sergeant to take down what she said. 'Now, madam, I'm hoping you can help me over this miserable business. I take it I may anticipate that you will answer a few questions?'

'Certainly.' Mrs Dance smothered a tiny, cat-like yawn, and smiled at the Superintendent. Her dark-brown hair, artlessly dressed by a genius (herself, very likely, thought Collins), was that of a well-cared-for child. It lay on her forehead like silk and curled round about her small ears and the nape of her neck. Her wide-set eyes were as innocent as those of a very young boy, but there was nothing but primitive passion in the flare of her nostrils, her firm, red, quick-tempered mouth, her wilful chin and the curve of the cheek which she turned towards her interlocutor. She was not beautiful, in the literal sense of the word, but Collins had never before been confronted by such a mixture of *gamine* devilment and charm. Moreover (if he summed up Mrs Dance correctly), if Mrs Dance had decided to murder Miss Campbell, nothing, he was convinced, would have come between Miss Campbell and her fate. Incidentally, he reflected, nothing had.

'There is just one thing,' he said. 'What is all this about a dog?'

'A dog? Oh, the *Hound of the Baskervilles!* I know nothing about it, Superintendent. I fled. We all fled except Miss Menzies and Mrs Bradley. It was as good an example of crowd-panic as I've seen since a bull got loose in Crendon High Street on cattle-market day.'

'Do you know how the dog came to be on the premises that night?'

'I've no idea. I knew that Sir Bohun had a surprise for us all, so I imagine he brought the dog here. He is very transparent, and during dinner he hinted, rather childishly, that there were to be two competitions during the course of the evening. We knew we were to be given pencils and paper to record our impressions of the characters or something – I'm no good at all at party games, particularly if it involves writing anything down – I couldn't possibly care less who's who and what's what – but then he indicated something more. I suppose it was the dog he had in mind.'

'But I understood that the appearance of the dog surprised him as much as it did his guests.'

'He ran away. We all did, I tell you, except that terrifying Mrs Bradley and her secretary, but Sir Bohun would do that sort of thing for the fun of it and to keep up the joke. Fly with the rest of us, I mean. He's terribly little-boy, you know.'

'I see. It doesn't seem as though the dog was very important. Did you leave the house that night for any reason, Mrs Dance?'

'Yes.'

'Oh? At what time?'

'At about one o'clock in the morning, I believe – or it may have been rather earlier. I didn't notice.'

'Alone?'

'Well, I was alone when I left the house, but I was joined by Mr Mildren.'

'Where?'

'In the garage.'

'You went for a drive in that fog?'

'No, of course not, but we had to be careful.'

'Indeed? Oh, I see.'

Mrs Dance smiled tolerantly.

'I'm sure you do,' she said. 'It was our own business. We then went to the Dower House, where we'd lighted the fire. It was a previous arrangement, and I can't see that it had anything to do with Linda Campbell.'

'Of course not. No, no. At what time did you return to the house?'

'At three. And, if it's of any help, I can tell you that by that time the fog had lifted.'

'But was not the house locked up?'

'Yes, but a maid let us in. She had her orders.'

'What do you know about the dog that was kept on the station?'

'Nothing. Was there one? I never travel by train if I can help it.'

'Mrs Dance, can you tell me whether Miss Godley is under the influence of anybody here?'

'Little Celia? What a question! I am the last person Celia would confide in. What exactly do you mean?'

'Only what I say, Mrs Dance. Ladies usually get to know one another's little secrets.'

'Yes, but I'm not interested in Celia Godley. I don't care how many little secrets she keeps from me. All I ask is that other people don't interfere in *my* affairs.'

'Thank you, Mrs Dance. Then it is of no use to ask you whether Miss Campbell had any enemies.'

'Enemies?' Mrs Dance looked thoughtful. Collins had a sudden, complete, delightful picture of her at the age of six, innocence, devilment and all. 'I should say she had quite a few. Poor old Manoel hated her, for one. She was trying to hook Sir Bohun, and Manoel couldn't stand that. Manoel, you know, is his son.'

'Illegitimate, though, I believe. I have heard something of the kind from various sources. Sir Bohun does not seem to hide the fact. How do they get on together?'

'Manoel stands a pretty good chance of inheriting the property, if Sir Bohun does not marry again and alter his will. At least, that's what Manoel thinks. He told me so. But – get on together, I don't really think they do.'

'And Miss Campbell, only a very short time before her death, had become engaged to Sir Bohun. Yes, it supplies a motive. Besides, Manoel seems to have asked Mrs Bradley to tell him how to commit murder without being found out!'

'I should call that a point in his favour. Nobody would be such a moron as to ask a thing like that if he really contemplated doing it.'

'It would seem like that, but some criminals are incurably childish, Mrs Dance. I could cite you no end of examples.'

'Some other time,' said the siren, getting up. 'You don't want me any longer, do you?'

'Where were you at the time of Miss Campbell's death?' asked Collins suddenly.

'They said at the inquest that she died at between three and five in the evening, didn't they? Well, I suppose I was resting or waiting for tea, but I can't bring any witnesses to prove it. I hope you don't think *I* killed Linda Campbell?' Her eyes were wide open and unafraid, and her mouth was incredulous and amused.

'I have to keep an open mind, madam.' He went to the door, and opened it with a flourish. Mrs Dance remained where she was.

'Whoever did it was no psychologist,' she said. Collins closed the door quietly and came back to his chair.

'What do you mean, Mrs Dance?' he enquired, nodding to the sergeant again.

'Oh, I don't know,' replied the mistress of the situation coolly. 'As somebody else is almost certain to give it you as a rumour, I might as well give it you as a fact. Sir Bohun did not intend to marry Linda. When she disappeared the last time and did not come back (because she was dead, of course – he knows that now) he was most thankful to make it an excuse to break the engagement.'

'But why? Had he changed his mind so very soon? That was hardly fair treatment for the girl.'

'It wasn't, was it? I don't know to what extent he had changed his mind, but I do know that something had turned up to make him realize that marriage with Linda was an impossibility.'

'Really? What was that?'

'Who, not what, Superintendent.' Her eyes danced, her curved lips were provocative. 'But who turned up is nothing to do with the enquiry.'

'That is for me to judge, madam. Come, now, Mrs Dance, please don't hold out on me. This is a grim business, and, so far, we have very little to go on. A handful of suspects, including, of course, yourself –'

'You will have a long job proving that I killed poor Linda because I wanted Sir Bohun for myself! I wouldn't have dear old Boo if he was the only man left alive!'

'You exaggerate, I am sure,' said Collins. 'Will you answer my question, Mrs Dance?'

'Yes,' said the siren, nodding. 'I think I will. He had reason to suppose – or so he told me – that Linda Campbell was already married – or, if not exactly married, well, that there was very much somebody else!'

'Can you enlarge on that, madam?'

'I'm sorry, but I can't. And how he found it out – supposing it were true – I don't know. He was just a little bit' – she sketched a gesture – 'at the time, so I didn't take very much notice. But there it is, for what it's worth.'

'And when did you learn of this, Mrs Dance?'

'At the Sherlock Holmes party.'

'But he offered her marriage *after* the party – some little time after.'

'I know. I'm only telling you –'

'Quite so, madam. Thank you very much. Is there anything more you can add?'

'Unfortunately not. I wish there were. It has been a most enjoyable conversation.'

'Hm!' said Collins when she had gone. 'What do you make of her, Sergeant?'

'*Femme incomprise*,' said the sergeant. 'The Greeks had a word for it, sir. I wouldn't put anything past her.'

'Oh, *I* would,' retorted Collins. 'I'd put murder past her, for one thing. She can get her own way without anything crude, my dear chap.'

'It depends what you mean by crude,' said the sergeant, who enjoyed a debate. 'And, another thing, sir. I've been routing round among the servants, as you told me to, and there's one bit of her story which isn't true.'

'Eh? Which bit?' Collins sat up.

'The bit about necking with Mr Mildren, sir.'

'We shall have to get in touch with that bird, I suppose. But go on. What about him.'

'Only that it couldn't have been Mildren she went to the car and the Dower House with, sir. According to the servants, he was put to bed dead drunk long before she says she left the house. I've been tipped to get Chief Detective-Inspector Gavin to confirm it. *He* helped to put him to bed!'

'Who was it, then, that she went out with that foggy night?'

'Your guess is as good as mine, sir. It certainly wasn't Mildren.'

'I wonder why she should lie about it? We'll find out later, I expect. I'll ask whether Gavin will confirm that Mildren was put to bed drunk.'

# CHAPTER 14

# THE MYSTERY OF JANE EYRE

> 'Her father he makes cabbage nets,
> And through the streets does cry 'em;
> Her mother she sells laces long
> To such as please to buy 'em.'
> HENRY CAREY – *Sally in Our Alley*

\*

OVER the telephone from his office at New Scotland Yard, Gavin did confirm it. Nobody, he asserted, could have roused Mildren from bed and gone out with him to a car or to the Dower House, or anywhere else, once he had been put to bed at the Sherlock Holmes party.

'He was as clean out as ever I've seen a man,' he told Collins. 'Our charming Mrs Dance is lying.'

'Then that particular lie will bear investigation,' said Collins. 'Thank you very much, Mr Gavin. I'm much obliged. I've a hunch that Mrs Dance had her own reasons for wishing Miss Campbell out of the way, but that's *by* the way, of course. It doesn't mean we suspect her of the murder.'

Gavin laughed. The only reason Mrs Dance could have had for telling that particular lie, he reflected, was that she did not want anybody to know who her partner in the car and in the Dower House had been.

'My guess, for what it's worth, is that she was with Manoel Lupez,' he said.

'Why couldn't she say so, then?' demanded Collins. 'It doesn't matter to *us!*'

'It might matter to Manoel.'

'Oh, I see. Queer his pitch with Sir Bohun, you mean? But Sir Bohun isn't sweet on the lady.'

'How do we know? Besides, she's on the verge of divorce. Sir Bohun may be prudish. After all, Manoel is his son.'

'Where does Sir Bohun get off, querying other people's morals?'

grumbled Collins. 'Still, what these people did on the night of the Sherlock Holmes party doesn't, probably, have any bearing whatever upon Miss Campbell's death. I wish, Mr Gavin, that you'd allow me to ask to have you join us. You've had considerable experience of these cases, and ours is pretty limited. Our first job is to contact any relatives. I thought somebody would be bound to turn up for the inquest, but nobody did. I suppose Sir Bohun has an address of the deceased before she entered his employment? – her private address, I mean.'

'I'll ask him,' said Gavin at once. 'I'd like to be in on this case. It interests me. I've already had a word in private at the Yard. You've only got to phone them. I'd enjoy doing it, and I shouldn't be treading on anybody's corns. I can put you through now, if you like.'

On the following day he came down with his chief's official blessing and made it his first job to see Sir Bohun. Not altogether to his astonishment, Sir Bohun turned extremely obstinate.

'Why should I give away Linda's previous address?' he wanted to know. 'Don't like this idea of ferreting out the poor girl's past. None of us has lived a blameless life; we've all got skeletons in cupboards; besides, an Englishman's home is his castle. You can't go poking your nose into the business of a lot of innocent people just because an unfortunate, very silly girl is murdered.'

'If *I* don't do it, Superintendent Collins will,' Gavin pointed out. 'And, as he says himself, I've had a great deal more experience in these matters than he has. It would help him a great deal if he could fill in the background a bit. Don't you realize, Sir Bohun, that unless suspicion fastens upon some outsider, things may be made very embarrassing – not to say dangerous – for one of your own household? There is Grimston, who dreamt of the murder; there is your niece, Miss Godley, who appears to have been involved in some queer do or other and to have visited the deserted railway station where the body has been found; there is even yourself, who are known to have been in a considerable hurry to terminate your engagement to Miss Campbell – '

Sir Bohun, grimacing wildly, gibbered at him to be quiet. Then he rummaged in a drawer and flung a letter at Gavin. It was headed:

*C/o Mrs Tregidder, Camborne, Cheesebury*, and was signed with Linda Campbell's name.

'Thanks,' said Gavin, pocketing the letter, which was Linda Campbell's acceptance of the post of governess to Timothy. 'I'll get along down there at once.'

Mrs Tregidder's residence turned out to be an old-fashioned house built on to a disused windmill. Gavin's first thought about it was that it must be a paradise for children, and this theory was borne out by the sight of three of them, two girls and a boy, playing in and out of a thick grove of laurel trees which bordered an unkempt lawn. He greeted them cheerfully, and asked whether their mother was in.

'She isn't our mother,' the boy informed him. 'We only play here.'

'We play here because Judith died,' added the older of the girls.

'Judith?'

'Judith Tregidder. She died. Miss Campbell did it, but we mustn't talk about that.'

'I see. She must have died after Miss Campbell left, though, didn't she?'

'Yes, she did, only Miss Campbell let her catch an illness. She took her to a place where someone had it.'

'It was polio,' said the boy. All three children looked at him impatiently. They wanted to get on with their game.

'Is Mrs Tregidder in ?' he asked.

'Oh, yes, she's in, but it isn't tea-time yet. They're still sewing.'

'Who are?'

'The people who come Tuesdays and Thursdays. They make things for bazaars to help polio.'

Gavin groaned inwardly. The last thing he wanted was gossip about himself from a mothers' meeting. However, he had come a long way and he wanted to get back that same evening. He doubted whether Mrs Tregidder would be able to tell him much, and he did not want to waste a day.

'Look here,' he said. 'I wonder whether one of you would do something for me ?' He looked hopefully at the older girl. 'I want to speak to Mrs Tregidder rather particularly. Will you take my card in to her ?'

'We're not allowed in there,' said the boy. 'I'll take it, though, if you like. I'm not afraid of her tempers. She threw a knife at me once, but I didn't care. She was sorry afterwards, and gave me a shilling not to tell anybody.'

'But you've just told *me!*'

'Yes. I've told plenty of people. A shilling isn't enough to shut your mouth for. Nobody buys *me* cheap!'

'I think, after all, I'll go myself, then,' said Gavin, putting back into his pocket the shilling he had just taken out of it. The three children gazed after him and a stone from the unweeded gravel path flicked him between the shoulder-blades. 'All right, my lad. I'll see you when I come out again,' he thought grimly, as he stepped into the porch and rang the bell.

A man answered the door.

'Mr Tregidder?' Gavin enquired; and, when the man had nodded, he went on: 'I am a police officer, and I have called to make a routine enquiry respecting a young woman who was employed here a short time ago, a certain Miss Linda Campbell.'

'Come in,' said Tregidder. 'I hope you won't need to trouble my wife. She took our little girl's death very hard. She's not got over it yet, and won't, I'm afraid, for some time.'

'I'm very sorry.' Gavin followed Tregidder into what was apparently the dining-room. There was no fire, but the master of the house switched on an electric heater and invited the guest to sit down. 'I won't keep you longer than I can help. How long was Miss Campbell employed here?'

'Six or seven months, I believe. She came in the October and left in the following May.'

'Did she give notice, or was she dismissed?'

'Oh, she gave notice. We didn't know, of course, when we parted from her, that she could have given our little girl polio.'

'I don't quite understand, Mr Tregidder.'

'Well, she'd taken her to the pictures several times on their afternoons out. We'd particularly forbidden Judith the pictures, or any other indoor gathering while the polio scare was on. We even took her away from school and put ourselves to the expense of a private governess so that she should not be herded with other children. Miss Campbell had sworn our little daughter to secrecy, and it was not until she was taken ill that we got at the truth. Miss Campbell had gone by that time, of course. In any case, we couldn't have *proved* anything, as I told my wife at the time.'

'No, you couldn't possibly prove that your child caught the

infection at the cinema,' Gavin gravely agreed. 'Well, Mr Tregidder, as you may or may not know, Miss Campbell herself is dead.'

'Dead? Not – ? Did *she* take polio, too? It would serve her right if she did! She betrayed her trust here.'

'Not polio, no. We have reason to think she has been murdered.'

'*Murdered?*' The man's smooth countenance changed as ludicrously as a face seen in a distorting mirror. His cheeks sagged, his jaw dropped, and his eyes grew wide and anxious. 'Oh, but, Superintendent – '

'Chief Inspector.'

'Chief Inspector, that could not possibly have anything to do with us here!'

'Maybe not. I have not come to question you along those lines, Mr Tregidder. All I want to know is Miss Campbell's address before she came to you. She lived in this house, I presume, while she was in your employment?'

'Yes, she lived here, certainly. But where she came from ... Will you excuse me a moment? I've probably got the address in my desk.' He was gone a long time, but eventually he returned with a letter. 'Just pulled my wife out from her sewing meeting to tell her you're here,' he said apologetically. 'She must have heard your knock, and she likes to know all about things. Here's the address Miss Campbell wrote from.'

Gavin copied it down and handed back the letter.

'Did she bring any references?' he asked. Mr Tregidder shook his head.

'She told us she'd trained for school-teaching but couldn't get a job that suited her, so she was filling in time,' he replied. 'We gave her a month's trial, and she seemed satisfactory and said she was perfectly happy, and as we only wanted her until the polio scare was over – '

His face worked suddenly.

'Yes, I see,' said Gavin sympathetically. 'By the way, Mr Tregidder, just for the record, do you mind telling me what your profession is – and your wife's, of course, if she has one.'

'Profession? Oh, I'm not a professional man in the ordinary sense of those words, Chief Inspector.'

'No? You give the impression, if I may say so, of – er – '

'I know. Bank manager, civil servant, business executive – something of that sort, you mean.'

'Well, yes.'

'Nothing like that, I assure you. No.' He hesitated.

'Well, then?' said Gavin encouragingly, wondering whether the man was going to produce the information asked for. 'Something on the shady side?' he wondered. He glanced at Tregidder and added, a trifle sharply, 'Come on, Mr Tregidder, out with it. It's nothing you need be ashamed of, I suppose?'

'I don't think I need be *ashamed* of it, exactly,' said Tregidder. 'I mean, I'm not the sort of chap who appears in the *Police Gazette!*' He laughed uncertainly. Gavin waited. The information, when at last it came, was not at all what he might have expected. 'My wife brought a bit of money with her when we married,' said Tregidder, at length, 'and we've been careful with it. My own living comes what one might call spasmodically, in a sense. I've travelled the world. I've made good money and poor money. I've enjoyed my life, I must say. I wouldn't wish to change my job, which is bound up with an ancient mystery, but –'

'Well, what *is* your job?'

'By profession, I am a sword-swallower, Chief Inspector.'

Gavin returned to Superintendent Collins and told him what he had learned. Collins did not think very much of it.

'It's a motive, though, you know,' said Gavin, reporting to Mrs Bradley at her Kensington house. 'Their only kid, and they blame Miss Campbell for what happened. Added to that, he was very slow to tell me what his job was. It's my opinion he'd have got out of telling me if he could. Doesn't that look like guilty knowledge to you?'

'Not necessarily. A man who looks like a bank manager may not like to confess that he is a sword-swallower. Where does he swallow swords? – and how frequently? Do the neighbours know? Does his wife object?'

'To those questions I have to reply that I haven't the faintest idea.' Mrs Bradley clicked her tongue and looked at him reproachfully. He grinned. 'I can't see that it's at all important, but I suppose I can find out, although I wasn't exactly *persona grata* there, I'm afraid.'

'I will find out for myself. If Mr Tregidder is to be one of our suspects, it is due to him that we learn a little more about his private affairs.'

'Of course, Linda being the little baggage she was, he may have been tempted into something for which she could blackmail him. It's not an unknown thing for a married man to kill the viper that sucks the golden eggs.'

'Lor!' said his fiancée, who was present at the interview. 'How long did it take you to think that one up? Incidentally, not far from the ghost station there's a gipsy encampment – well, they're sort of fair-ground people really. I shouldn't wonder if some of *them* wouldn't be pretty handy with a skiandhu.'

'Gipsies did not kill anybody on that abandoned railway station,' said Mrs Bradley.

'What do you make of Grimston?' demanded Laura of Gavin.

'I don't know,' he replied. 'There's no evidence that he even knew of the deserted station. He hadn't lived in the neighbourhood very long.'

'But neither had Linda Campbell,' protested Laura, 'and yet *she* knew of it, or how could she have been killed there?'

'She must have had an assignment with the murderer,' said Gavin.

'It is the most likely thing,' agreed Laura. 'But that looks as though they couldn't meet in Sir Bohun's house, and *that* doesn't sound like Grimston.'

'Well, I don't know so much,' said Gavin. 'Don't you think it would have been very risky to meet a lover under that roof, as she was already formally engaged to Sir Bohun? Surely that would account for a clandestine meeting, wouldn't it?'

'Yes, of course,' said Laura, looking thoughtful, 'but it would apply to other men besides Grimston, wouldn't it?'

'Well, I'd better have a look at this house where Linda was staying before she went to the Tregidders',' Gavin concluded. He returned that same evening, resigned but sad.

'A blank wall,' he said. 'Linda was brought up in one of those Scattered Homes, or whatever they're called. She got on pretty well at school, won a place at the local grammar school, tried shorthand and typing for a bit, got fed up with it, and went to one of those Emergency Training Colleges which they ran after the war for intending teachers. She doesn't seem to have shown any kind of cloven hoof, either at school or college. At her first job – they give them a probationary year, apparently – she didn't get on too well, though, and before the year was up she threw in the

towel and got a job as governess with some people called Polson.
I went there – a biggish house in the St John's Wood district – but
didn't get any further. The people were cagey at first, but I soon
found out that they were refugees, with a strong anti-police
phobia, who had changed their name. Once they decided that I
wasn't going to run them in, they came across with what they knew
about Linda, and, for what it's worth, here it is, and I can't see
how it helps.'

'How old are the Polsons?' Mrs Bradley enquired.

'He's about fifty-five and she's about forty. There's a son of
eighteen, and two children, both girls, of twelve and ten.'

'These children were Miss Campbell's charges?'

'Yes. She blotted her copy-book by smacking one of them. The
Polsons agreed that the child deserved what she got, but said they
did not approve of that sort of punishment and could not overlook
it. They gave Linda a respectable testimonial and booted her out.'

'No sex?' asked Laura, disappointed with this lame and only too
probable story.

'No sex. Nothing else reared its ugly head at all. The Polsons
both said that they were sorry to get rid of Linda, and had talked
matters over carefully before coming to any decision respecting
her going or staying.'

'That all seems to have petered out, then. We have to rely on
our sword-swallower Tregidder now. I suppose,' Laura added
bluntly, 'she didn't make a pass at the son of eighteen? I can't
imagine Linda being particularly scrupulous where ignorance and
innocence are concerned.'

'A Continental boy of eighteen – or between sixteen and seventeen, as I suppose he would have been when Miss Campbell was
there – might be innocent, but he would scarcely be ignorant,'
Mrs Bradley put in. She looked enquiringly at Gavin.

'I think they would have told me if Linda had been up to that
kind of thing,' said Gavin, 'but, as it happens, the point does not
arise. The boy was at boarding-school while Linda was there. She
was only in the job a couple of months, and she and the son never met.

'How did you find out that she had been brought up in a Home?'
asked Laura.

'Quite easily. The Polsons, being (after their chequered experiences) deeply suspicious of everybody's *bona fides*, had insisted
upon a complete *dossier* and had checked it. From the information

they were able to give me, I checked it, too. It didn't take long. I went to the local authority in whose area the Emergency Training College was situated, and they turned up the dope for me at once.'

'I suppose she didn't fall foul of one of the parents while she was teaching in the school?' suggested Laura.

'It doesn't seem so. Anyway, it would take an unusually irate parent to track her down and stab her to death after all this time. No, she seems to have left the school in a fit of pique because the Inspector in charge of probationary teachers made some fairly telling criticisms of her work. I got the headmistress on the telephone while I was at the Education Office and she agreed that the criticisms were justified, and that she herself had come to the conclusion that Miss Campbell would never make a teacher.'

'Well, it's all very unsatisfactory,' pronounced Laura. 'What will your next move be?'

'I'm afraid I've got to contact Brenda Dance's light of love.'

'Too bad,' commented Laura. But it was not too bad at all. Gavin, next day, went to the flat indicated by Toby Dance as that of de Philippe and found that philanderer at home and very charming.

'Of course I'll alibi the poor b.,' he said cheerfully. 'As a matter of fact, I'll be glad to. After all, what's a sock on the snout? I could have eaten him, if I'd wanted to. I could dashed well see his point of view, so I let him get away with it.'

Armed with the evidence of Toby Dance's alibi, Gavin went back to Mrs Bradley after telephoning to Collins, and received a straight tip.

'I have heard from Sir Bohun Chantrey,' she announced. 'He is aggrieved because Superintendent Collins refuses to take up time in finding out who sent Sir Bohun five orange pips one day and a goose's crop the next, and various other reminders of Sherlock Holmes' cases.'

'The same practical joker as brought the *Hound of the Baskervilles* to the Sherlock Holmes party, I imagine.'

'Oh, that was Mrs Dance, aided and abetted by Mr Mildren in consideration of a lump sum, payable beforehand.'

'Eh?' said Gavin. 'How on earth do you work that out?'

'It was simple. Mr Mildren was the only person who should have been present, but was not, when the dog was admitted to the revels.'

'But the man was completely stinko. I should know. I helped to put him to bed.'

'Mr Mildren is a very fine actor. It would not be the first time that the police have been deceived over a case of drunkenness.'

'Then the girl you saw leaving the house that you thought might be Linda Campbell, must have been that little devil of a Brenda Dance!'

'I was mistaken,' Mrs Bradley blandly confessed.

'You never really committed yourself about the girl,' interpolated Laura quickly.

'I realized very soon afterwards that it could not have been Miss Campbell,' Mrs Bradley continued. 'Linda would never have risked going out of the house in the dark while that dog might be roaming the garden.'

'How do you *know* it was Mildren who put it outside the french windows that night?' asked Gavin.

'I wrote to him. Here is his answer.' She produced a letter from the pocket of her skirt. 'And he has an unshakable alibi. He was playing in a matinée in Leeds at the time of the murder,' she added.

'Really? Then – ?'

'Yes. I think that the *Hound of the Baskervilles* put an idea into the murderer's head. You tackle Mrs Dance, anyhow, when you get back, and I think you will find I am right. Laura and I have both heard how the dog was hired, first, for the night of the Sherlock Holmes party, and, secondly, for about a fortnight prior to the murder. It is incontestable that the person who hired it the second time bore no resemblance whatever to the person who went for it the first time.'

'Right. I'll tackle Brenda Dance. I'd better be getting back. I'm glad about Toby. There's not an awful lot to him, but he seems a decent sort of chap, and this de Philippe I thoroughly liked, too. He's twice the size of Toby, so if Toby did give him a poke in the nose he's got pluck. I don't blame Brenda, but I have a hunch that if the divorce did go through, and she married him, de Philippe could keep her in order. She's an attractive little headache, though – '

Laura gave him a hearty jab in the ribs.

'Less of it,' she said sternly, 'or you'll get the ring back by registered post. We engaged girls have our pride.'

# CHAPTER 15

# MORE CONTRIBUTIONS INVITED

'That were enough to hang us – every mother's son.'
SHAKESPEARE – *A Midsummer Night's Dream*

\*

'AND now,' said Mrs Bradley, 'for another source of evidence.'

She and Laura were alone. Gavin had gone, and the time was after dinner. Henri had made, Celestine had brought in, and Mrs Bradley and Laura had drunk, some very good coffee, and the mistress of the house, Laura noted, was ripe for mischief.

'Another source of evidence? How do you mean?' she asked.

'The written evidence of these competition papers, child.'

'Oh, from the Sherlock Holmes do? But what do you expect to get from those?'

'Who knows? Let us see. They are in the third drawer of my writing-desk.'

Laura went out, found the bundle of papers in a large envelope marked 'Sherlock Holmes Party Competition' and returned to the drawing-room. Mrs Bradley took out the papers and began to read them. As she read she cackled.

'Share the laugh?' Laura suggested.

'Willingly, child. Take your own paper, which, if you remember, won the prize, and check the rest of the papers from it.'

'You're pulling my leg,' said Laura. 'However, here goes.' She took the rest of the competition papers one by one from Mrs Bradley's talons and solemnly checked each one by her own winning list. 'But this is fantastic,' she said. 'People seem to have put down all sorts of objects that don't come into the *Adventures* and the *Memoirs* at all.'

'That is what is so interesting,' said Mrs Bradley serenely. 'Go on.'

'I don't see what's interesting about it. It just shows their ignorance, I should say.'

'Possibly some of them did not devote the same care and preparation to the task as you yourself did. Sir Bohun and his secretary, young Mr Bell, are cunning creatures. A few red herrings were scattered about the house. They must have been.'

'Dirty trick!'

'Not at all. It was perfectly legitimate to include some objects which belong to the *Return, His Last Bow,* and the *Case-Book,* I think. It was done to confuse, and, apparently, it succeeded in its object. But let us have details.'

'Well, here's one paper we can ignore because it's got nothing on it at all, and that's Celia's mamma's. Celia herself has four correct answers, but then she's put down the bicycle of the *Solitary Cyclist* and drawn a little picture of the dancing men. Toby and Brenda Dance don't seem to have troubled at all. They've got the same three answers in a different order, but only the *Blue Carbuncle* goose is correct. They've added the whaling harpoon from *Black Peter* and the bust of Napoleon from the *Six Napoleons.*'

'I think the couple went to ground for a heart-to-heart talk in one of the rooms which was originally open to the hunt,' said Mrs Bradley.

'Oh, yes, that's right,' agreed Laura. 'I remember overhearing a scrap of their conversation. I suppose they shut themselves away to discuss the divorce. Here's Mrs Mildren's paper. Only one thing on it – *paper-chains.* What on earth do you suppose she meant by that?'

'I do not suppose she meant anything by it. I do not imagine that she is a devotee of Sherlock Holmes.'

'Mildren himself has put down two correct answers and added *Slipper with tobacco.* That didn't count because the things had to be connected with the actual cases, not just with Holmes himself. His writing looks all right, though. I suppose he did it before he got sozzled.'

'He was not drunk that night, child. He simply slipped out after he was supposed to be in bed, and procured the dog. A good thing it was not you to go in that terrible fog.'

'Yes, I know about the dog, but – oh, well, if you say so. Here's Gavin's paper – nine correct answers according to my own. I'm glad I beat him. Oh, here's Grimston's. He's got seven right, but he also has put in the bicycle (I didn't see one!) and the harpoon. Then he's put down the dish-cover from the *Naval Treaty.* That would have been all right – it comes in the *Memoirs* – but I suppose it wasn't included.'

'There would be one in the kitchen, no doubt, but that had been placed out of bounds,' said Mrs Bradley. 'Only a person who lived in the house would have thought of it, perhaps. That leaves us only one more list, as Sir Bohun, Mr Bell, and I did not join in.'

'Yes. It's Linda Campbell's. She only got two right, and she's left it at that. I shouldn't think Sir B. was frightfully impressed. Wouldn't she be expected to have studied the book of words? After all, the whole collection is in the house. She'd only to stretch out a hand.'

'Very true. Perhaps she's not a devotee, any more than poor Mrs Godley.'

'I don't suppose she was,' agreed Laura. 'I don't think she was a devotee of Sir B., either. She was simply after his money. You know, if she'd lived, I think he would have slung her out in the end. I don't believe he'd have married her.'

'She was no judge of character,' said Mrs Bradley. 'That fact was her undoing.'

'Where do you suppose she got to when she told that ridiculous yarn about being kidnapped?'

'I am sure she was with a young man.'

'But the one you saw her with at the *Queen* – '

'That was not the one.'

'Well, then, don't you think this man might have been the killer?'

'I am certain of it, child.'

'Yes, I see. But there's no proof, and we don't even know what he looks like. I say!' Laura broke off and gazed with earnest excitement at her employer. 'The disguised man who hired the dog and kept it at the ghost station! That's the man for our money!'

'Yes, of course it is.'

'Then it all adds up! They've been off on this toot together, he's sick of the *liaison* or he's afraid his wife might find out, or Linda was a bit too rapacious, or she had begun to blackmail him, so he gets her to meet him at this lonely station and does for her. How's that for a reconstruction?'

'Almost complete,' said Mrs Bradley. At this moment there came an interruption. Celestine, Mrs Bradley's maid, announced:

'A gentleman, although one asks oneself a question. He is in the consulting-room, *Madame*. Whether *Madame* is at home?'

'His name?'

'He will not give it. He comes in answer to an advertisement in the newspaper and is of a gravity profound, *Madame*. I have removed the silver cigarette case and the picture by Picasso from the room, and have locked all the drawers in the writing-table. I do not trust him. What a type ferocious! One says *un apache*.'

'*Splendid!*' said Mrs Bradley. 'Who knows? You may be entertaining a murderer unawares!'

'*Madame* amuses herself!' Celestine opened the door of the consulting-room. Mrs Bradley walked in to confront, as she had expected, Linda Campbell's companion who had met her at the *Queen of the Circus*.

He stood up, his black Homburg hat in his hands. He was thin-faced, and now looked cadaverous. His eyes were sunk in his head as though he lacked sleep, and his nostrils were pinched as though he had been ill.

'Doctor Bradley?' he asked. She nodded.

'Please sit down, Mr –'

'Wendon. Gally Wendon. I'm Linda Campbell's half-brother. I've been in hospital. Supposed to be in there still, but when I saw your advertisement in the paper I decided I'd better come along.'

'Which hospital?'

'Carnwell Cottage Hospital. How is Linda? Is she all right?'

'I am afraid not, Mr Wendon. Please prepare yourself for a shock.'

'Not *dead*? You don't mean she did it after all? She was always threatening to, but I never believed it would come to anything. I can't really think . . . Are you sure?'

'I am sure she is dead, but she did not take her own life, if that is what you intended to convey.'

'Thank heaven for that! It was an accident, then. That's bad enough, in all conscience. How did it happen?'

'It was no accident, I am afraid. Your half-sister, Mr Wendon, has been murdered. (Laura, dear child, get some brandy.) I have advertised for you in the hope that you can throw some light on what appears to be a very dark business. Please take your time. When you are ready, perhaps you will feel able to answer one or two of my questions.'

Wendon made two mouthfuls of the brandy, and then nodded.

'I would have come forward before this,' he said, 'but the fact is that I had a pretty bad spill, had concussion, and didn't see a paper until yesterday.'

'I saw you at the *Queen of the Circus* road-house with Miss Campbell at the end of November.'

'Yes, I met her there by appointment. She wanted money. We were discussing ways and means.'

'Was she not in receipt of a salary from Sir Bohun Chantrey?'

'Yes, but she was extravagant. I've got her out of more than one mess in my time. As it happened, just before Christmas I'm never very flush – I'm a partner in a small turf commission agency – so it wasn't easy for me to see my way to helping her. Still, it wanted some thinking about. The little idiot had been borrowing off the Sheenies – her note of hand alone; no security required; that sort of thing – and when she couldn't keep up the interest – God knows what she proposed to do about the sum she'd actually borrowed – trouble was threatened. Well, she'd set her cap at Sir Bohun and was all out to hook him, if she was telling the truth (which, all too often, she wasn't), and, once married to him, all her troubles about money would vanish into thin air. That's what she said. Well, I've always been a fool about Linda, so, after we'd talked matters over, I said I could raise enough to keep the sharks at bay, but after that she'd have to fend for herself because I wouldn't be in a position to raise any more.'

'And did she get the money from you?'

'That's the devil of it – no. I rode to the *Queen of the Circus* on my motor-bike, and, on the way back, swerving to avoid a skidding cyclist on the Cordon by-pass, I lost control, hit a tree and collected a knock on the head that laid me out cold. I haven't been allowed a book or a paper, and, as my name is different, nobody connected me with Linda, I suppose. In fact, I don't see how they could.'

'Which hospital did you say you were in, Mr Wendon?'

'Carnwell Cottage. You can check with them there. I take it you are connected with the police. You'll find I was not in a position to be – involved in Linda's death. Do you mind telling me what happened? I can't say I feel a tremendous amount of shock, or of grief, either. I'm pretty soft, I think, but she was always the hell of a nuisance, and rather embarrassing, too. Always after some bloke, and most of 'em couldn't stand her after a bit. She was the gold-digger type, you know. I shouldn't be surprised if, for once, she had picked the wrong sort of mug.'

From what she had seen of Linda Campbell, Mrs Bradley could well believe all that he was saying. She gave the cadaverous half-brother a succinct account of the discovery of Linda's body and of the nature of her death, speaking gently, quietly, and with exact truth, whilst he sipped more brandy which had been brought to him.

'She died instantaneously,' she concluded. 'I am a doctor, and I saw the body. She could have felt nothing. The weapon went right through her heart and came out just clear of the spinal cord.'

'The man was right-handed, then, and must have been powerful beyond the ordinary. I've seen that done by a six-foot Jock with a bayonet. Was it a bayonet he used?'

'The weapon has not been identified yet by the police.'

'Poor Linda! Still, she had it coming to her. Nobody could play the fool as she did and expect to get away with it in the end.'

'You cannot, from your knowledge of her, name anyone of her acquaintance who was likely to have reacted in such a way when he heard of her engagement to Sir Bohun?'

'I haven't a clue. And if I had' – his thin face hardened and his emaciated cheek grew flushed – 'I wouldn't give the chap away.'

'My hat!' said Gavin, when Mrs Bradley reported the interview to him a couple of days later. 'If you hadn't checked that he most certainly *was* in hospital at the time of the murder, I wouldn't put it past him to have done the job himself! Fancy having to act as a bottomless purse to a little such-and-such like her!'

'I have been to see his partner as well,' said Mrs Bradley. 'The last lot of money came out of the firm's account, and the partner, a man named Neville, was becoming tired of helping to subsidize Linda's extravagances.'

'You don't think that *he* – ?'

'No, no. The case is perfectly clear. The only trouble is that at present we can't prove it. How are you getting on at your end?'

'We're not. Some practical joker is still sending Sir Bohun Chantrey some Sherlock Holmes things by post, though. Bell keeps guard all day and waylays the postman. Sir Bohun fools about with the stuff all day long. He's very childish, isn't he?'

'What does the stalwart Manoel think of all this?'

'He scorns it. He keeps asking when we can let him go home, but neither Collins nor I is at all keen to part with him at present.

I think he listens at doors when we're talking or interviewing people, and yesterday he reminded me that he had taken the part of Doctor Watson at the Sherlock Holmes party and would be interested to see me at work. I've promised him that he shall do so to-morrow. I intend to have another go at him. Sir Bohun and he have gone bail for one another. They were fooling about with a bull-fighter's sword at the time of Linda Campbell's death, and that sword could have been the weapon. I'm not at all sure that they weren't in it together, you know.'

'Still, while they both tell the same tale, you can't touch either of them,' said Laura.

'I know. Of course, Manoel is a very tough nut. He's probably frightened Sir Bohun into this alibi business. We know Manoel wanted to get rid of Linda Campbell. Anyway, I shall try to get some sense out of him to-morrow.'

He cautioned Lupez before he questioned him.

'I have to warn you,' he said, 'that what you tell me now will be taken down and may be used in evidence. You are a foreigner, and may not understand the implication of what I say. I am cautioning you that if what I suspect is true, you may be called upon to stand your trial. You have no need to answer my questions unless you wish, but if you decide to do so you're fully entitled to have a lawyer present to look after your interests. Do you understand?'

'Perfectly,' Manoel replied. 'You are very good. I do not think I need a lawyer. Where is your evidence for all this? You cannot even prove that the *espada* was the weapon to kill Linda Campbell. Did you try it in the wound to see whether it fitted?'

He smiled sardonically, as cool and as unafraid as Gavin felt sure he always was in the bull-ring.

'All right,' Gavin said. 'Have it your own way.'

'It is sometimes well,' said Manoel, 'to remember that the great Watson also had his moments. Me, I make a close study of Watson since I play his part. Not a stupid man. Brave, generous-of-heart, alert, of much vigour, a good shot, a good friend – no, I do not call him stupid, nor myself, either.'

'What's all this in aid of?' enquired Gavin. 'If you're trying to tell me something, out with it. Don't beat about the bush.'

'To beat the bush,' retorted Manoel with a slight smile, 'is perhaps to make a little bird fly out of it. May I remind you, also,

163

please, of a saying you have in England that a chain is only as strong as its weakest link?'

'Yes?' said Gavin, his eyes narrowing.

'If I were you, Chief Detective-Inspector, I would put much pressure, such as the police understand well how to apply, upon little Miss Celia Godley. I choose to believe that she has something to hide, but I assure you it is nothing to do with me! You see, if you could cause her to say *why* she fed the dog at the station –'

'How do *you* know she fed the dog at the station?' demanded Gavin.

'One hears much if one takes trouble and exercises caution,' replied the bull-fighter. 'Well, it is my hint to you, Mr Sherlock Holmes, and it is your good friend Watson who speaks.'

Entirely master of the situation, he looked down at the cigar which he had been holding between ringed fingers, smiled as though something amused him and, at the same time, satisfied his vanity, put the cigar between his white teeth and began to walk out of the room.

'Here, half a moment!' cried Gavin. 'Well, Mr Lupez?' he added. The Spaniard, who was now lounging against the sideboard, looked down at the cigar he was holding, and then met Gavin's eyes. He shrugged, took a puff at the cigar, and then smiled slightly.

'*Now*,' he said with unmistakable emphasis, 'I have my hour. *Then* – I think someone else had his. It is true that the sword you speak of is an *espada* – the sword we use in the bull-fight. It is *not* true that the sword belongs to me or that I killed Linda, either with it or in some other manner. My father also has such a sword, and the police must believe, please, that he has used it when we imitate the bull-fight together.'

'So you accuse Sir Bohun of murder, do you?'

Manoel glanced out of the window. As suddenly as a January freeze-up had begun, so, just as suddenly, a thaw had set in. What was more, a heavy rain had fallen. Water was streaming down every drainpipe, the terrace's uneven flagstones held pools three inches deep, and the countryside for miles was a morass.

'Love,' said Manoel softly, 'must be a powerful swimmer.'

'Eh?' said Gavin. 'Oh, I see! I didn't know Spaniards could quote from the Song of Songs.'

'If the song is of love, why not?' asked Manoel, in the same quiet, friendly tone. 'But why do you question *me* ?' And, with a good-humoured air, Manoel seated himself in an armchair, and went on, 'You should talk to Bell. He knows all that goes on in this house. And the parcels, he knows what comes in them.'

'No, no. I should talk to you,' responded Gavin. 'Look, I'll tell you the whole story, and you can correct me if I'm wrong. This is what I think happened. I think you came here with the intention of killing Sir Bohun Chantrey. How you proposed to do it I don't know. You ended up by killing Linda Campbell, and your motive was pure greed. On your father's death you thought you would gain a good deal of money. When you realized that if he married Linda Campbell and had children by her – legitimate children – your chance of inheriting anything from him might be gone, you decided that Linda must be eliminated.

'The practical joke staged by some of the party on the Sherlock Holmes night gave you the chance you needed, particularly as, on that night, the dog they introduced as the *Hound of the Baskervilles* frightened everybody, and, as it turned out, Linda Campbell most of all, because, on her own admission, she was terrified of dogs.

'Your plan was simple. You let Celia – the other possible bene-ficiary under Sir Bohun's will – into the secret. It was to persuade Linda Campbell to visit the deserted railway station where the dog, which was still on daily hire to you, was kept, and, at a given signal, while you were holding Linda in conversation, to get Celia to unchain the dog. Then, on some pretext, you got Linda to walk into the waiting-room, knowing that as soon as she saw the dog and realized that he was loose, she would rush out again.

'You shouted to her and she ran to you for protection, probably glancing over her shoulder to see whether the dog was following. The dog, of course, *was* following. You called, probably, "To me! Here!" But this was a signal to the dog, and not to Linda. Sword in hand, you waited. She, poor girl, thought that the sword was to protect her, but, instead, you spitted her on it as you intended. You made no mistake. A professional bull-fighter makes no mistake when it comes to "the moment of truth". Now, what do you say to all that? – and, before you say anything, remember that I have cautioned you.'

Manoel studied the lighted end of his cigar.

'I have nothing to say,' he replied. 'I cannot help it if the police are stupid.'

Gavin let him go, and sent for Mrs Dance.

'Now, look here, Brenda – ' began Gavin sternly. Mrs Dance ogled him shamelessly. He was compelled to laugh.

'All right,' she said. 'It's all lies. I can't give poor Toby an alibi, and I haven't one for myself. Just as a matter of interest, I suppose you *don't* suspect Toby?'

'No, we don't. Your friend Mr de Philippe has seen to that. Toby is definitely out, if it's any comfort to you to know it.'

'I did know it. I only wanted to see your face,' explained Brenda sunnily. 'You're so handsome when you look stern, and I adore men who can frighten me.'

'I'd do more than frighten you, if I had my way!' retorted Gavin. Brenda Dance smiled sweetly.

'Well, why don't you?' she enquired.

'Laura wouldn't like it,' said Gavin, grinning. 'Now, let's get one thing clear.'

'Laura might not like that, either.'

'Shut up and listen. Did you, or did you not, think up that *Hound of the Baskervilles* stunt at Chantrey's party?'

'Yes, of course I did.'

'Did you get Charles Mildren, the actor, to help you?'

'Certainly – for a small consideration.'

'Hard cash?'

'Yes. Ten pounds.'

'Did he fetch the dog while he was supposed to have been laid out cold on his bed?'

'He did.'

'My God! The man really *is* an actor. He deceived me *in toto*.'

'I shouldn't think that was such a terribly difficult thing to do,' said Brenda, half-closing her eyes. 'Why don't you go and worry Toby? You say he's out of it all, so it's much fairer to go and badger *him*. I can see you think the dog had something to do with the murder, and as I'm still on your list of nasty suspects you ought not to question me unless you caution me first.'

'As Toby's far more likely to tell the truth than *you* are,' said Gavin, 'I'll away to him at once. Behave yourself, if you can, until I return.'

'To clap the handcuffs on me? I'm not one of those who come quietly!'

Gavin did go to see Toby, and obtained a story which not only bore the stamp of truth but fitted the known facts.

'Yes,' said Toby, 'it can't do any harm to tell you the tale, since Brenda has admitted to introducing the dog into the party, so, here goes, for what it's worth, although I can't see what the devil it's got to do with the murder. The dog was Brenda's own idea, but, naturally, she didn't want that to appear for fear Chantrey should take it amiss and get annoyed. I was to approach young Celia Godley to find out whether she knew of a likely animal whose owners lived in the neighbourhood and would be prepared to join in the joke. I said I didn't see how the stunt was to work – '

'But how did Mildren come into it?' asked Gavin, although he believed Brenda's answer to this question.

'To do the character of a drunk, you know. Brenda felt that if it was obvious that she'd left the revels directly the dog had been seen it would look pretty fishy, and she didn't want to upset Chantrey by appearing to guy his party. So the only thing was to provide a stooge who wouldn't be *expected* to be among the revellers, and, Mildren being a character actor, he was the obvious choice. She found he was not at all averse to being "sweetened" – personally I thought ten quid was a bit steep, but it wasn't *my* money – so there it was. He slipped out at the appointed hour and fetched the dog. Apparently amused himself by putting on a thick German accent to disguise his own voice. He's been on the radio, you see. He got the large hound, took him into the summer-house, which is electrically lighted, dabbed a bit of luminous paint on him, and introduced him on to the terrace at the proper time. The fog had Brenda worried, though.'

'Afraid Mildren might get lost?'

'No, afraid the dog wouldn't get to the house in time. You see, it would never have done for Mildren to have appeared to be plastered *too* early in the evening, so what with the fog and so on, he probably had to cut it rather fine. I suppose you noticed it was Brenda who went to the french windows that night, although I believe Grimston actually let the dog in.'

'Right. Thanks,' said Gavin, and rang the bell to ask whether Celia Godley could spare him a few minutes.

'Look,' he said when she appeared, 'I don't suspect you of the murder, but tell me all about the dog.'

'What dog?' the girl enquired. Gavin smiled at her.

'Look, Miss Godley,' he said, 'I want you to answer my questions without hedging. Will you?'

'Why, of course!' said Celia, putting on a baby-face.

'Right. I know you told the Dances about that dog which turned up at the Sherlock Holmes party, but how did you come to know that it had been put in that waiting-room? I am speaking of about a fortnight before Miss Campbell was killed.'

Celia's face changed. She looked scared.

'If you think I know anything at all about Linda's death – ' she began. Gavin interrupted her.

'Never mind about protesting your innocence,' he said curtly. 'Just answer the question. Truthfully, if you don't mind.'

'But the dog had nothing to do with what happened to Linda!'

'That is *my* business. Now, will you answer, or shall I take you along to the station and question you there?'

'You can't do that!' wailed Celia, near to tears. 'You're just bullying me, Robert. You know you are.'

'Be a sensible girl,' said Gavin briskly. 'Quite frankly, I don't suspect you, but you must expect me to take a very dim view if you're going to stall the minute I ask you a perfectly simple question, especially as you've already lied to us. Come on, now, be reasonable, do.'

'All right, then. It was Brenda's idea to have the dog at the party, but I don't know whose idea it was to put it in the station waiting-room.'

'How come that you went along and fed it there? The truth, please, this time. You *didn't* see it from the train.'

'I had a note.'

'Yes?'

'Somebody put a typed notice under my bedroom door, telling me that the dog would be in the waiting-room and giving me directions how to get there in a roundabout sort of way because, it said, the joke would be spoilt if anybody else found out the dog was there.'

'That sounds like somebody who knew the countryside pretty well. Who was the note from? Did you recognize the writing?'

'No, because it was typed and there wasn't a signature.'

'Didn't you think it might be a practical joke to send you on a fool's errand?'

'No.'

'Why not?'

'Well, the joke about the *Hound of the Baskervilles* had gone off rather well, and I just thought this was another one.'

'By the same people? – or, rather, by the same person?'

'No, I didn't think Brenda would think it funny to use the dog again. She isn't like that. I thought she had put an idea into somebody else's head.'

'Whose?'

'I thought it might be Manoel's,' said Celia, unwillingly and after a pause.

'Why?'

'The note being typewritten. Foreigners don't form their writing like English people, and I thought he'd typed it because his writing would give him away.'

'And you were prepared to assist Mr Lupez by feeding the dog if he wanted you to?'

'Yes, of course. We're going to be married, I think.'

'Really? I had no idea!'

'He hasn't, either, yet, but I admire him and I want to go to Spain and Mexico, and it would be a sensible plan if we could put our two legacies together when Boo dies, wouldn't it?'

'And that's all you can tell me?'

'Really and truly it is!'

'Where's the note?'

'I burnt it. It said so.'

'That's helpful! Never mind. You couldn't possibly have realized that it would ever be as important as this. Where can I find Sir Bohun? Have you any idea?'

'I expect he's in the library, and Manoel is with him, I think. They've become awfully thick lately. Manoel is taking such an interest in Sherlock Holmes, and in all those things that somebody keeps sending Boo, that he's quite won Boo's heart. I am more keen to marry him than ever. If I don't, I may never get anything from Boo at all!'

Gavin grunted, and let her go.

## CHAPTER 16

## NO SURFEIT OF ALIBIS

'O where hae ye been, Lord Rendal, my son?
O where hae ye been, my sweet pretty one?'
Old Ballad – *Lord Rendal*

\*

COLLINS was a determined but not an obstinate man. He realized that, so far as discovering the identity of Linda Campbell's murderer was concerned, he had come to a dead end. He found himself hoping that he might soon be taken off the case.

'Nobody's got an alibi,' he confided to Mrs Bradley, 'except Mr Dance and the servants. They can all alibi one another, and I've never, in any case, suspected any of them. Of course, there's Sir Bohun Chantrey and Mr Lupez – but – *I* don't know!'

'Well,' said Mrs Bradley, who, because she liked Collins and because she did not want the killer to remain undetected, had thrown out some strong hints, 'you know what *I* think, and, in your own mind, I believe you agree that there is more than a possibility that I may be right. Why don't you push your enquiries hard in that direction and see what happens?'

'Because, as you said yourself, there's no proof, ma'am, and there *is* such a thing as Judges' Rules. Besides, with three suspects like Mr Lupez, Mr Grimston, and Sir Bohun himself still in the picture, there's no picking out one more than another, so far as I can see. No, ma'am, I've talked matters over and I've thought matters over, and I only hope I can leave it to Mr Gavin. The job is much more in his line than it is in mine, and I dare say he'd like a free hand. As for me, there's been some funny work in connexion with switching some lorries over at a place called Ponteston which I'd rather like to look into, and I can't while I'm on this case. I'd much rather leave this job to Mr Gavin, and I dare say he'd like to be on his own to break it down.'

'Well, the first thing, as I see it,' said Gavin to Mrs Bradley when Collins had left, 'is to break down a few more of these non-alibis.

170

Dash it all, the rest of these people can't *all* have lived only to themselves between three and five that afternoon! What's the matter with them? Guilty little secrets or what? I'm going to tackle Brenda Dance again. I'm certain she didn't do it, and I'm going to clear her once and for all, and send her home.'

'But I can't tell you any more, Robert darling,' said Mrs Dance. 'I expect I was just simply lying down in my room, as I said before.'

'With whom?' asked Gavin, masking, to some extent, this crudity with a confident, boyish grin. 'Come clean. It doesn't matter to us. All I want is for you to clear out and leave me with the people I *really* suspect. Be good, now, Brenda. Who was it?'

Mrs Dance looked demure.

'If you *must* know,' she said, 'it was with Toby.'

'Toby? But I thought –'

'You thought quite right, darling. But it was just one of those things that *do* happen in an ill-regulated world.'

'But why didn't you tell Collins right at the beginning?' demanded Gavin, affecting to believe her.

'Two reasons. First, he hasn't your priceless nerve in asking really rude questions, and, secondly, I can trust *you* not to make use of the information in the wrong way. You see, we still want that divorce.'

'Then you're a fathead,' said Gavin. 'Toby is worth ten of anybody else you'd get.'

'But he's not worth ten times as much money.'

Gavin laughed. Then he composed his face again and said severely:

'Stop lying, Brenda! Who *was* with you? We know it wasn't Toby. He was at Mr de Philippe's flat that afternoon. They had a row. de Philippe confirms this.'

'I know. I just like to annoy you. Honestly, Robert, dear, I would like to provide myself with an alibi, but I can't. I really was alone and I don't see who else can possibly tell you so.'

'Hm!' said Gavin. At this moment there came a violent crash against the door. Gavin stepped across to open it. Sir Bohun stood there. He appeared to be both angry and agitated.

'Just had to get the doctor to Grimston,' he explained. 'Bell went up to talk to him for a bit, and found that the silly fellow had tried to poison himself. Bottle of laudanum and a half-glass of port on the table. Port doped with the stuff! Doctor has pulled him round, though, so you needn't take official notice, I hope?'

'Laudanum?' said Gavin. 'He tried it on the night of your Sherlock Holmes party. Miss Menzies spotted the bottle on a bathroom shelf while the competition was on. She did not realize its significance immediately. She thought it was one of the Holmes series of objects – to wit, the laudanum in the *Silver Blaze* case. It was only when she discovered the curry that she decided the laudanum was nothing to do with the competition.'

'Um!' commented Sir Bohun. He tapped the table with the nail of his right-hand index-finger. 'In a bathroom? Could have been put there for medicinal purposes, couldn't it? How did you connect it with Grimston?'

'For one reason at the time; for another shortly afterwards; and for a third, of course, now. I suppose you have established that he administered the laudanum to himself? It wasn't an accident or somebody else's attempt to do away with him?'

'He says he did it himself, and there's no reason to disbelieve the silly fellow. He's always been unbalanced, and, of course, Linda's death hasn't done him any good. I gather that you don't suspect him of having committed the murder. I can't understand it. I simply can't. I should have thought the whole thing hung together. He was in love with the girl, and he did for her in a fit of jealousy when he heard she was engaged to me. He's quite capable of any crazy action. Look at that rubbish he told about his dream!'

'Quite,' Gavin agreed. 'Superintendent Collins had him for questioning, as you know. He thought him unbalanced, as you say, but he also formed the opinion that he didn't kill the girl. Grimston was much too anxious to convince us that he did. He certainly has offered no alibi for the time of the murder. In fact, he confessed, but he got one or two details wrong.'

'Sheer cunning, my dear Gavin. Grimston's got plenty of brains – of a kind!' said Sir Bohun, hastily and eagerly.

'The police,' Gavin replied, 'have plenty of experience in sifting the stories of would-be newspaper head-liners. No, the fact – the obvious fact now – is that Grimston is a suicide type. He couldn't find the nerve to do the job the way he'd planned it, so he thought that, by confessing to the murder, he'd get the public hangman to muck in.'

'The way he'd planned it?'

'Brings us back to the night of your party. He put the laudanum in a bathroom which was originally one of the rooms left within bounds for the purposes of the competition, and then put a notice on the door to keep people out. As it chanced, Miss Menzies and I both noticed what had happened, and she took the notice down and opened the door because she thought that one of the guests was playing unfairly, and had discovered a Holmes object in that bathroom which he did not intend that anyone else should see.'

'Who did a dirty thing like that?' Sir Bohun spoke excitedly.

'Nobody. That's what I'm explaining. That was only what Laura thought. It supplies her reason for removing the notice and opening the bathroom door. As she did so, she nearly cannoned into Grimston, who seemed unduly affected by the encounter and at seeing that the bottle of laudanum was in full view of anyone who happened to be passing.'

'But, from what Linda told me during our brief engagement, the fellow waited until near the end of the evening, and then proposed to her,' protested Sir Bohun. 'That doesn't sound as though he'd planned to commit suicide at the party.'

'Mrs Bradley told us about the bit of argument she overheard on her way to her room, and Grimston agreed, when the Superintendent had him under observation, that he had decided to take another pop at pressing his claim because he regarded Laura's discovery of the laudanum as a direct intervention of Providence and a sign that there was some hope for him after all. Unfortunately for both himself and Linda, it didn't work out like that.'

'For both of them?'

'Certainly. If Linda Campbell had accepted Grimston, it is possible, don't you think, that she would have been alive to-day?'

'Why, then, you *do* mean the mad fellow killed her!'

Gavin shook his head hopelessly and said:

'I'll see him when he's quite recovered. Meanwhile, I'd better interview Mr Bell, although I don't suppose it will help. Is the doctor still with Mr Grimston?'

'No. He says the fellow will be all right now. Just thought I'd better let you know. Hope no action necessary on your part?'

'Where is Grimston? Up in his room still?'

'Yes. Second landing, third door along.'

'Right. I'll go along a bit later. Would you mind sending me Mr Bell?'

Bell, his red hair standing up stiffly, had nothing to add.

'He'd taken it, apparently, just before I got there,' he said. 'I saw the laudanum bottle, of course, and, knowing he's a queer sort of stick, I challenged him and he admitted what he'd done, so I bunked off to the phone and called the doctor. Luckily he could come at once, so not much harm has been done. Will you need to take official action?'

'I don't know. It seems he'd done it before – put laudanum in his glass of port. Mr Dance seemed to know about that.'

'Horrible taste, I should think! Of course, there isn't a gas oven in this house!'

'By the way,' said Gavin, 'to change the subject for a minute, can you tell me where you were and what you were doing between three o'clock and five on the eleventh of January?'

'The eleventh of – ? Oh, I see! I should suppose I was in the library. I'm re-cataloguing it when I get any spare time. No, wait a minute, though! I wasn't in the house at all that day, come to think of it. I had leave of absence from Sir Bohun and went to see some friends at Easthill, and then went on to London.'

'Your friends' telephone number? I am most anxious to get this business cleared up, and I'm nowhere near it at present.'

'Easthill X7. Shall I get through for you? It's a trunk call.'

'No, no, I'll get it myself, thanks.' He smiled. 'Can't be too careful, you know!'

'Of course not. Is there anything else I can do?'

'Yes. Tell me, how do these parcels of Sherlock Holmes stuff come to the house?'

'By post.'

'Invariably?'

'Oh, yes. I have instructions to take each parcel straight to Sir Bohun. The butler doesn't touch them. Sir Bohun's tickled pink by the presents. Plays about with them all day.'

'Childishly so, it appears.'

'Well,' said Bell, smiling, 'it is hardly for me to agree. I'm a bit of a Holmes maniac myself.' He went out, and, after staring thoughtfully at the closed door for a moment, Gavin went out after him to the telephone in the hall. He rang the number and waited to be connected. When connexion was established, a woman's voice answered.

'Who's that speaking?' she enquired.

'A police officer, madam. Mr Bell, who has given us your number, visited you on the afternoon of the eleventh of January last, I am informed.'

'Oh, dear! I *knew* there would be trouble with that motor-cycle!' the woman exclaimed. 'Was anybody hurt?'

'Yes. A young woman was killed, madam.'

'Oh, dear! How dreadful! Did he do it on his way home?'

'Possibly. At what time did he arrive at your house?'

'I don't really remember. He wasn't there to lunch, but he was with us for tea.'

'Tea? At what time?'

'We have it at four.'

'This may be very important. You are certain that Mr Bell was with you at four o'clock?'

'Oh, yes, of course.'

'Forgive me for pressing the point, but can you give me any contributory evidence? Was Mr Bell with you more than the one afternoon and evening?'

'No, just the one.'

'Did he stay the night?'

'Oh, no. I suppose that accounts for the accident. It was a very nasty night. Very dark.'

Gavin allowed that to pass. He thought it better not to disabuse her mind of the notion that Bell had run over somebody. Any mention of the murder might give her a shock and dry up what looked like being a promising alibi for Bell.

'Let me get it quite clear, if you please. You are certain of the date?'

'Oh, yes. He had tea and supper with us, and then went off on his motor-cycle. I assure you we gave him nothing but tea and coffee to drink all the time he was with us, so it could not be his fault if he ran into somebody in the dark.'

'That's as may be,' said Gavin. 'But I do want to know about the date. Are you *sure* it was January eleventh?'

'That was – yes, I'll just – excuse me – I'll just pop in and have another look at the calendar. Hold the line a minute, please.' She returned in an instant. 'Yes, that's right,' she said. 'It was a Thursday. I remember we had the sound radio going, instead of TV, and heard *Archie's the Boy*. Most amusing.'

'That seems to clinch it,' said Gavin. 'You need not worry any more about Mr Bell. That lets him out nicely.' (Damn! he thought,

175

as he put the receiver down. In some ways Bell would have fitted a few facts nicely! Still, it lessens the number of possibles, and that's a help in a way.)

He turned round to find Bell within distance.

'I'm awfully sorry,' said the secretary, smoothing down his hair with an apologetic sort of gesture, 'but I'm afraid it won't do for a let-out, Chief Inspector.'

'Eh?' said Gavin, staring.

'No. You see, I wasn't with them on the Thursday. She's talking about the Wednesday. I was in London on the Thursday seeing my sister off on the boat train at Victoria. Sorry! I'd mixed up the dates.'

'I can't see why your friend declared that you were with her, then.'

'That's easy, I imagine. You simply called me Mr Bell, I expect. You should have said *Tony* Bell, then she would have told you, of course, that it was my brother Walter who was there on the eleventh.'

'Oh, I see,' said Gavin. 'No, I never thought of that possibility. Your brother – was he with them on the Wednesday as well as on the Thursday?'

'No. He and I don't mix much. Fell out, a year or two back, and have never fallen in again, so to speak, so each counts himself out when he knows the other will be present.'

'I see. Well, you've very neatly busted your own alibi!'

'I had to,' said Bell simply. 'You see, I don't possess a motor-bike, whereas Walter does, and I know the police are thorough in these matters.'

Gavin, who had been working out how comparatively simple a matter it would be to get from the deserted railway station to Easthill in time for tea if the murder had been committed close on the stroke of three, grinned amiably in defeat, and said:

'Nice to find somebody intelligent enough to forestall criticism, anyway.'

Grimston made rapid recovery – so rapid, indeed, that Gavin came to the conclusion that, far from attempting suicide, he had simply made a gesture in order to bring himself into the limelight. Gavin put this view before Mrs Bradley, who shrugged and said:

'He isn't the murderer, anyhow. If I were you, as I told you before, I should keep an open mind about Mr Bell.'

'But, hang it, I produced a beautiful alibi for the man and he chucked it away! I wasn't dreaming of doing anything further about it except to check times and distances on that motor-cycle which he was supposed to own. Still, I'm never too proud to take a tip, and if our chaps in London can discover that a red-haired man saw a girl off on the boat-train at Victoria that Thursday afternoon –' He stopped and shook his head. 'It's daft,' he said. 'Why should he bust his own alibi if he's guilty? It doesn't make sense!'

'What *does* make sense,' said Laura, 'is that red hair runs in families, so I'm jolly glad that you and I haven't any, because I'd hate to have red-haired children!'

## CHAPTER 17

# THE WEAPON?

'Water, water everywhere – nor any drop to drink.'
COLERIDGE – *The Ancient Mariner*

*

MRS BRADLEY, leering affectionately at Laura and Gavin, who had just come back from the theatre, decided to put into practice a plan she had formed some time previously. She went to stay at Alice's farm, a base from which operations (as Laura expressed it) could be conducted with the minimum of interference from any of the suspectedly interested persons.

As though (also according to Laura) the climate itself was for once on the side of the angels, with almost no warning the mild weather which had succeeded the first cold snap of January gave way to an old-fashioned winter, and an iron frost clamped down upon the most of the country.

To the great excitement and delight of the little boys, even the river froze over, the most picturesque and impressive feature of this being the arrested flow of a small lasher which precipitated water past the mill-wheel which was distant less than forty yards from the road to the *Queen of the Circus*.

Alice, who had a firm faith in the ability of little boys to preserve their lives (which, in her opinion, were at least as numerous as those of cats), allowed the two children to go out in all weathers as long as they ate well and did not catch colds. She believed, probably with some justification, that frost had a tonic effect upon the healthy human frame, so she encouraged the boys, wrapped up warmly, to go off whenever it pleased them.

One day they set off, as usual, and upon foot, for she had forbidden the use of bicycles because she was afraid that these might skid on icy patches on the roads. The children had discovered a new interest, that of watching the sand-pit ponds becoming frozen over.

After eight successive days of hard frost, when cart-ruts turned to iron and breath was like smoke upon the air, the ice thickened and the boys rejoiced in the knowledge that a long-cherished dream was coming true – they could, at last, walk over to the island.

This magic Tir-nan-Og was some fifty yards long and fifteen yards broad, and it lay in the middle of the largest sheet of water near the farm. The island itself was an ugly hunk of gravel, sand, and clay, and offered, to the adult mind, no romantic possibilities at all, for it boasted no vegetation of any kind except the sparse, coarse grass which grew everywhere on the sand heaps round the gravel pits. It was also extremely ugly, for it had never even formed part of the heath but had been the centrepiece of some rough pasture before a built-up area had commandeered the gravel under the grass.

The children, however, were delighted with it. John's contention was that the island formed the stronghold of robbers; Philip spoke excitedly of buried treasure. They reached the edge of the broad sheet of ice which had enclosed the island, after having scrambled through a stiff hedge and crossed a piece of waste ground which led to the gravel pit. Work at the gravel pit was at a standstill. There was nobody about. The boys, torn and sooty, stepped confidently on to the ice, and half-walked, half-slid their way across it.

To less determined idealists the island must have proved a disappointment, but the little boys were enchanted with it. They explored it a dozen times, quartering it from every direction. The bitter cold of the late-January day did not affect them, for they took no heed of it, and for a time they kept themselves warm by searching for flat stones and skating them across the ice towards the mainland shore.

At last John looked at his wrist-watch.

'Time to be moving,' he said. 'There's hot roast pork for dinner.'

Philip, whose appetite for food was still not as keen as the motherly Alice would have wished, demurred, and a compromise was reached. They would each take an end of the island and meet in the middle; then they would make tracks for home. But before this plan could be carried out, Philip had a better idea.

'Let's walk on the ice round the island, opposite ways, and keep crouched down so that we can't see one another,' he said. 'That would be much more exciting.'

John agreed.

'Let's make it a race,' he suggested. Philip adopted this plan with great enthusiasm. John had more stamina than he had, but it had been proved more than once that over short distances he was the fleeter of foot.

Each child cascaded down the almost vertical four-foot-high bank to the ice, and John gave the signal to start. Almost as soon as they had both rounded opposite ends of the island and were within sight of one another again, a large pebble dropped between them on the ice, having soared over the top of the island to land on the frozen pond on the opposite side to the road along which they had come from the farm.

John signalled violently, and crouched immobile where he was. Philip accepted the hint, and remained in position like a statue. Two more large stones came hurtling over the top, and others landed on the island itself.

The boys remained where they were. They had once been chased and stoned by a gang of louts, and were not anxious to repeat the experience. Nothing more followed, however, and at last John, signing to Philip to remain where he was, crawled cautiously up the bank and lay flat on the stiff, frozen grasses to spy out the lie of the land.

There was not a soul in sight. Whoever had flung the pebbles had vanished from the scene. Greatly relieved, John crawled along on hands and knees until he reached his companion.

'It's all right. They've gone,' he said. 'Let's begin again. Over the top, and back to the start.'

Unknown to the boys (or, indeed, to anyone except the men who had been in charge of a small dredger before the frost came), there was a deep hole about twelve feet across, just under the bank and on the northern end of the island. Philip reached this first, but John was almost as quick, so that both were on a danger spot at the same instant. The ice split and spread in a cracked and crooked grin, for over the ten-foot depth it was too thin to bear the combined weight and elephantine tactics of the boys.

John flung himself sideways, clutched at some grass on the bank and held on, kicking away with one boot to make foothold on the gravel bank. Philip, less experienced in rapid physical movement, went through into ten feet of water, icy cold in the dangerous and narrow hole. He yelled in terror and anguish as he felt his foothold go, and then disappeared below the surface. He came up threshing and choking, John, unperturbed, shouted:

'Spread out your arms on the ice!'

Philip, however, flung himself slightly sideways towards some long grass on the bank. More ice cracked and gave way, but this time his head was not submerged. He had got one plunging foot on the edge of a spit of gravel where the excavating dredger had not yet been at work. The bank sloped here. The quick-witted John, on his stomach, leaned over and gave him a hand. With his other hand Philip clutched at a particularly large but insecure pebble, and dragged it into the water. The sturdy John hung on. Philip flung himself at the bank, and, suddenly, everything was over. Soaked, coughing up water, and very cold, he was lying on the bank beside John.

'Better run about a bit,' said John, thumping him well-meaningly between the shoulder-blades. 'Might catch a cold this weather. I say, you might have been drowned. What did you want to whang through the ice like that for? I say, that was a whopping big stone that went into the water. I say, are you all right now? If you are, you ought to run about a bit.'

Philip got to his feet. Together the little boys did their best to squeeze, press, and wring the water out of his clothes, but, with all their efforts, his garments remained too heavily weighted with water to allow him to do more than jog-trot miserably about the tiny island, cold, sodden, and in desperate discomfort.

It was John who stumbled upon the harpoon. He stopped and picked it up.

'*This* wasn't here before,' he said. 'Those people throwing stones must have thrown it over here. Fancy leaving it, though! I don't know quite what it is, but it's something rather good.'

Philip said, jerking his head, 'They couldn't come after it. The ice wouldn't bear them. Anybody who could throw that, and those big pebbles, would be a lot bigger than we are. Let's take it home. I wonder why they didn't want it, though? My uncle's got one of these.'

Alice was horrified at the state in which they arrived. She bathed both, put them to bed in hot blankets, gave them huge basins of thick soup, and generally made what Laura called 'an old-hen fuss' of them. At sight of the harpoon, however, Laura whistled.

181

'You didn't see who threw it?' she demanded. Regretfully the boys were obliged to say that they had not.

'You see, it must have come over after the big stones, when Philip was in the water,' explained John.

'What do you make of it?' Laura enquired of Mrs Bradley at supper.

'It looks like the one Sir Bohun had, but why, as it has been in full view of everybody since (as well as before) the death of Miss Campbell, somebody decided to get rid of it is a minor mystery,' Mrs Bradley replied. 'However, it is one which may tie up with that other minor mystery which I suggested our dear Robert might investigate – the minor mystery of the Sherlock Holmes *insignia*, so to speak, which continue to be showered upon Sir Bohun by some unknown and, I fear, unfriendly hand. He telephoned while you were out for your afternoon walk. He has now received a parcel containing a photograph of two young people in late nineteenth-century costume bearing the caption: Irene Adler and the Hereditary King of Bohemia. What do you think of that?'

'A cinch for Gavin,' replied Gavin's fiancée. 'If he can't find out where *that* came from, he must be a chump.'

'I agree. By the same post, Sir Bohun received a short, block-printed communication to this effect: "What about the *Crooked Man?* See Samuel ii, 11 and 12." '

'Good heavens! Sir Bohun must have quite a museum of the things by now, counting what he and Bell got ready for the Sherlock Holmes party. We ought to push over and see him. Didn't he ask you to go?'

'Indeed he did, and I have promised to join him to-morrow.'

'What do you think is the point of sending him all these things?'

'To compass his death, child.'

'Are you serious? That *does* mean Manoel, then. He's been quite open about wanting to do for Sir Bohun ever since he's been over here. Gavin ought to pinch him before he can do any damage. I know Gavin thinks he's the murderer.'

'I want to see the island on which the boys found the harpoon,' said Mrs Bradley, taking no notice of these statements and opinions.

'Whoever it was – and Manoel is still my guess – he couldn't have known the kids were there. It's quite a thought that he might have hit one of them,' went on Laura, in no way abashed by her employer's lack of interest in her remarks. 'What was the idea, do you suppose?'

'There is nothing to show. There was no advantage to the murderer in getting rid of the harpoon, since it has been on view both before and since the murder, and no doubt has been tested for fingerprints.'

'I wonder what the idea was, then?' said Laura. Mrs Bradley made no reply.

Immediately after lunch the next day, leaving a disappointed and disgruntled Laura to amuse the little boys, whom Alice, as a precautionary measure, was, to their mingled resentment and alarm, keeping in bed for the day, Mrs Bradley drove to Sir Bohun's house from the farm and was welcomed effusively by the baronet.

'Oh, so *you've* got my harpoon!' he exclaimed, looking at the implement which Mrs Bradley was using as a walking-stick. 'I couldn't think where it had got to!'

'It got to the Lake Isle of Innisfree,' she responded. 'I want to speak to Mr Lupez.'

'Manoel? I believe he went out. Bell would know, perhaps.' He rang for the red-haired secretary.

'Ah, Mr Bell,' said Mrs Bradley, lunging at him in a playful manner with the harpoon. 'I have come to return Sir Bohun's property and to ask after the health of Mr Lupez.'

'Lupez?' said Bell, flinching away from the harpoon. 'I think he went out to the post-office. I'll go and find out.'

'Obliging sort of fellow,' said Sir Bohun in a discontented tone. Mrs Bradley waited for what was to follow, but it did not come immediately, for Sir Bohun was staring out of the window at the secretary who was walking up the drive. 'Some more of these damned Sherlock Holmes things,' he commented. 'You know, Beatrice, the joke's gone stale on me. In fact' – he lowered his voice – 'I find myself dreading the sight of the beastly things.'

'Where are they posted from?' Mrs Bradley demanded.

'I've no idea. Bell unwraps the things, as he does all my parcels and correspondence, and I've never bothered to ask him. I'll tell him to bring this one in, and we'll have a look.'

He rang again, but Mrs Bradley slipped out into the hall to take a parcel from the hands of the secretary whom the butler had just admitted.

'It's very heavy for you to hold, Doctor Bradley,' said Bell, yielding it into her outstretched hands. Mrs Bradley grinned in her terrifying fashion, and observed:

'It is indeed heavy. I take it that this is one of the Six Napoleons.'

'I couldn't say.' He stood aside, smiling, and added, 'Our own bust of Napoleon is in the hall, but this is another little present for Sir Bohun, I imagine, anyway.'

Mrs Bradley handed the parcel back to him with the remark that it *was* heavy, and preceded him into the room. Bell placed the package on the table and began to undo the string.

'Not another of those Sherlock gadgets?' said Sir Bohun, obviously reluctant to have the parcel opened.

'It looks like it, Sir Bohun,' said Bell. 'This is like all the other labels I've seen, and, now I come to look, the postmark's the same.'

'Is it? What *is* the postmark?' demanded Sir Bohun. He took the wrapping-paper and studied it carefully. 'Blest if *I* can make it out. What do you say it is, Beatrice?'

Mrs Bradley took out her small magnifying glass.

'Difficult to say,' she replied, studying the label and then the wrapping-paper. 'What do *you* make of it, Mr Bell?'

'Wapping,' said Bell. 'You can't see it at all clearly on this parcel but it is just the same as all the others. Shall I open the box, Sir Bohun, or, as you have it here, do you prefer to de-box it yourself?'

'No, no, go ahead,' replied Sir Bohun, who was still puzzling over the postmark and had borrowed Mrs Bradley's magnifying glass as an aid to further study.

'Good Lord! The fellow's becoming ambitious!' said Bell, withdrawing a bust of Napoleon Bonaparte from the box. 'Plaster, but not a bad copy! I wonder how Doctor Bradley guessed!'

He placed the bust on the table. Mrs Bradley picked it up and said casually:

'You'll have to break it, you know. That's what Holmes did.'

'Eh?' said Sir Bohun. 'Oh, yes, of course! Might hit on the black pearl of the Borgias, eh? Go on, Bell. Might as well get some amusement out of the thing. Go and ask in the kitchen for a tablecloth – one of those large ones the servants use themselves. And bring back a hunting-crop with you from the harness-room.'

Bell hesitated.

'I trust you're not going to destroy the bust, Sir Bohun,' he said. 'It looks quite a good piece to me.'

'It's Sir Bohun's property and he must do as he likes with it,' said Mrs Bradley. 'But perhaps it will make rather a mess if we break it up in here, you know,' she added. 'Why not let Mr Bell take it into the kitchen garden and toss it lightly against a wall?' As she said this she turned to Sir Bohun. Sir Bohun looked at her enquiringly. She grinned in a fiendish manner and without mirth, and nodded vigorously.

'All right,' said Sir Bohun, whose rubicund face had gone grey. 'There you are, Bell. Go out and break it. Be careful.'

The secretary picked up the bust, looked wildly from one to the other of them, and then dashed out of the room.

'After him!' cried Mrs Bradley. Sir Bohun caught her by the sleeve.

'What is it?' he said. 'What's the matter with that bust?'

'Come along and see,' said Mrs Bradley, jerking herself free with some impatience. 'Look! There he goes!'

Bell had shot past the french windows. He was holding the bust in both hands like a Rugby football three-quarter about to lob back a pass. Mrs Bradley darted to the french windows and opened them. Immediately she pursued Bell, but he had a fair start and was running well. She lost sight of him as he darted into a shrubbery. It was quite certain that he was not making for the kitchen garden, but for the road. She dropped into a saunter. Sir Bohun came up with her.

'What's come over the fellow?' he panted. 'Why doesn't he go and chuck the damn thing at a wall?'

'For a very good reason, I should say,' Mrs Bradley replied. 'What would you have done with the bust if I had not interfered?'

'Same as the great detective did with his,' Sir Bohun replied, stepping out smartly because of the freezing cold. 'Tablecloth, hunting-crop, and all. Why?'

'I wondered. You have a truly remarkable knowledge of the Sherlock Holmes stories, have you not?'

'There would hardly be my equal,' replied Sir Bohun with self-satisfaction. 'The only person whose knowledge is perhaps as great as my own is this silly fellow we're chasing now. What the devil does he think he's going to do with the bust, confound him? Has he gone mad?'

'It would be too much of a coincidence for two young men in

your employment to render themselves suspect in such a way, surely?'

'Well, what is Bell up to, then?'

'I think he is getting rid of the bust.'

'Getting rid of it? But why?'

'Because it contains something which he knows would not please you.'

'Stop talking in riddles, Beatrice! Anyone would think the bally thing contained a bomb!'

'Well, it does,' said Mrs Bradley quietly.

# CHAPTER 18

# THE EVIDENCE OF A WIG

'Well, I will undertake it. What beard were
I best to play it in?'
SHAKESPEARE – *A Midsummer Night's Dream*

\*

'THE object, madam,' said George, Mrs Bradley's irreproachable chauffeur, 'is at present in the river under the little stone bridge as you go towards the heath. It is easily recoverable, I think, should you require it.'

'Mr Gavin shall recover it,' Mrs Bradley observed. 'It will be needed in evidence. And young Mr Bell?'

'Mr Gavin should have picked him up by now, madam. Yes, here comes Mr Gavin's car.'

A white-faced Bell was between Gavin and a plain-clothes detective on the back seat of a police car. Gavin's sergeant was driving. Sir Bohun, who was looking haunted, opened the french windows and let them all in. He offered chairs to everybody. The wretched Bell sank into his without a word, and buried his face in his hands.

'*Mr John Turner!*' said Sir Bohun dryly. 'It's too late to be sorry for your sins, my boy. Lucky for you you didn't get your own way with *me*, that's all.'

'And very *un*lucky for him that he did get his own way with Linda Campbell,' said Mrs Bradley.

'He didn't kill Linda?'

'Indeed he did, and in the manner that I foreshadowed.'

'That's enough, you old hag!' shouted Bell, suddenly lifting his head. 'But for you, it would all have come off!'

'Yes,' said Mrs Bradley, eyeing him with a glint of pity. 'But for me, it would all have come off. I will not recapitulate in front of you, because that would add insult to injury.'

She glanced at Gavin, who nodded. He cautioned Bell in an impersonal, not unfriendly manner, and placed him under arrest. Bell made no reply in response to the charge, and Gavin took him away.

Mrs Bradley asked Sir Bohun for the use of the telephone, and rang up Laura.

'You may like to know all the details now,' she said. Laura came over directly.

'There was really no evidence until the bust of Napoleon turned up,' said Mrs Bradley. 'After that, it was all plain sailing.'

'But how did you jump to the conclusion that the bust contained a bomb?' demanded Laura.

'Well, when all these mysterious Sherlock Holmes gifts continued to arrive, it seemed to me that, sooner or later, one of them would be lethal.'

'I don't see why. I should have thought it was someone's idea of a joke, that's all.'

'Yes, but who was the joker? That was what interested me. There were various possibilities. First, Mrs Dance, who had set the ball rolling, so to speak, by producing the *Hound of the Baskervilles;* second, the unknown person (clearly neither Mrs Dance nor Mr Mildren, since the description was of a *young man*) who had introduced the *Hound* into the waiting-room of the disused railway station and who, by doing so, had encompassed the death of Linda Campbell; third, Sir Bohun himself.'

Sir Bohun swelled.

'Whatever next? Really!' he protested. 'Why should *I* think of such a thing?'

'To make a mystery. You have a great deal of time on your hands and don't do very much with it,' said Mrs Bradley rudely. 'If you had thought at all, you would have realized, when you feared for your life, that Bell was dangerous. At any rate, he was suspect, and, of course, so was Mr Grimston. It was at the last two that I looked the hardest. At first there seemed little to choose between them. Both were young, both might have had good reason first to love Linda Campbell and then to hate her –'

'Both? But we've never known of any connexion between Bell and Linda!' protested Laura.

'True, but it was noticeable that on the day of the murder they were both out of the house; also it was an established fact that

Linda could not leave any man alone. It is therefore axiomatic that she did not leave Bell alone. Besides, Bell has red hair.'

'Well?' asked Laura, puzzled. 'Temper, do you mean?'

'The young man who called to hire the dog from Miss Galbraith was wearing a wig,' Mrs Bradley explained.

'Oh?-oh, yes, I see!'

'Yes. Once I heard about the wig from an ex-actress who would be certain to distinguish between a wig and natural hair, I realized that Bell had come into the picture. Therefore I began to think about Bell. His knowledge of the Sherlock Holmes stories equalled, if it did not excel, the knowledge of Sir Bohun himself. Together they had worked out the characters for the Sherlock Holmes party. For both of them Linda Campbell was *The Woman*. Sir Bohun went in fear of his life. He suspected Grimston, but Bell, who had known him and worked for him very much longer, was, to my mind, a more likely enemy. Sir Bohun' – she looked at him indulgently – 'is not popular.'

'Yes, it would be Bell who thought of using the harpoon to murder Linda,' said Laura. 'I can see that. But why did he draw attention to it by throwing it away? And what a coincidence that it happened when the boys were exploring the island!'

'Oh, *Bell* didn't throw away the harpoon. That was done by Manoel Lupez,' said Mrs Bradley.

'Manoel? Oh, but why?'

'Manoel is a very intelligent man. He realized, very early on, that his plan to murder his father was doomed to be stillborn.'

'But – ?'

'Manoel worked out as quickly as I did that Sir Bohun's fears for his life were only too well-founded. He realized, too, that it was not himself of whom his father was afraid. He summed up Linda – accurately, as Latins are wont to sum up women – and then he waited and watched and used his efficient brains. When he was sure, he acted. He took down the harpoon, trailed the little boys, and made certain that the harpoon would be found. He knew it would be taken to the farm. He knew that, from there, it would come into my hands, and he was extremely interested, I expect, to see how I should react, for upon my reactions, he calculated, the murderer's next move would depend. That move was to produce the bust containing the bomb, and that before he had intended to – that is, days before I left the neighbourhood. The result we know.'

'Well, I'm glad it's all over,' said Laura, 'and I think Linda deserved what she got. I suppose she was with Bell those nights she didn't come home.'

'Yes. Nobody appeared to notice that Bell also was absent from the house except, of course, the watchful, logical Lupez, although Robert also recognized the fact when he questioned Mr Bell. Robert, however, thought little of it at the time, for Bell himself pointed it out.'

'Gavin is losing his grip. I'd better hurry up and marry him and goad him into action. What made Bell decide to kill Sir B., though?' demanded Laura.

'He had intended to kill him as soon as he knew that Linda proposed to become engaged to him. Red-haired people are naturally impulsive, but Bell's training as a secretary, especially as secretary to such a trying person as Sir Bohun, acted as a brake. Damped-down fires can be dangerous, however, and Bell was particularly dangerous both to Linda and to Sir Bohun because he had studied them carefully and knew them well. He had no difficulty, I feel sure, in enticing Linda to that railway station. She was sufficiently a nymph to betray any man with another for the sheer naughtiness of it. As for the Sherlock Holmes presents Bell sent to Sir Bohun, there he overreached himself.'

'It was quite cunning, though, to send all those harmless things first. And, of course, he'd know that, left to himself, Sir Bohun wouldn't have been able to resist smashing that Napoleon just to see if there was anything inside it. And again, of course, it didn't come by post, I suppose,' said Laura.

'None of the things came by post, child. It was a most significant thing that Bell was the only person who had ever declared that they did!'

'There's only one thing that I don't follow,' said Laura thoughtfully. 'Why did you say a minute ago that Manoel realized that his plan to kill his father was doomed to be stillborn?'

'Oh, because he realized, before he had been in Sir Bohun's house a week, that they loved one another. It is not an uncommon relationship between father and son, whatever the Oedipus enthusiasts may say.'

penguin.co.uk/vintage